PROTOCOL

A James Acton Thriller

Also by J. Robert Kennedy

James Acton Thrillers

The Protocol	*Wages of Sin*
Brass Monkey	*Wrath of the Gods*
Broken Dove	*The Templar's Revenge*
The Templar's Relic	*The Nazi's Engineer*
Flags of Sin	*Atlantis Lost*
The Arab Fall	*The Cylon Curse*
The Circle of Eight	*The Viking Deception*
The Venice Code	*Keepers of the Lost Ark*
Pompeii's Ghosts	*The Tomb of Genghis Khan*
Amazon Burning	*The Manila Deception*
The Riddle	*The Fourth Bible*
Blood Relics	*Embassy of the Empire*
Sins of the Titanic	*Armageddon*
Saint Peter's Soldiers	*No Good Deed*
The Thirteenth Legion	*The Last Soviet*
Raging Sun	*Lake of Bones*

Special Agent Dylan Kane Thrillers

Rogue Operator	*The Agenda*
Containment Failure	*Retribution*
Cold Warriors	*State Sanctioned*
Death to America	*Extraordinary Rendition*
Black Widow	*Red Eagle*

The Messenger

Kriminalinspektor Wolfgang Vogel Mysteries

The Colonel's Wife	*Sins of the Child*

Templar Detective Thrillers

The Templar Detective *The Unholy Exorcist*
The Parisian Adulteress *The Code Breaker*
The Sergeant's Secret *The Black Scourge*
The Lost Children

Delta Force Unleashed Thrillers

Payback *Forgotten*
Infidels *The Cuban Incident*
The Lazarus Moment *Rampage*
Kill Chain *Inside the Wire*

Detective Shakespeare Mysteries

Depraved Difference *Tick Tock* *The Redeemer*

Zander Varga, Vampire Detective

The Turned

THE
PROTOCOL

A James Acton Thriller

J. ROBERT KENNEDY

Copyright ©2011-2022 J. Robert Kennedy

ISBN: 9781990418327

For Espie, Niskha, Mom, and Dad.

THE
PROTOCOL

A James Acton Thriller

THE
PROTOCOL

AUTHOR'S NOTE

The crystal skulls referred to herein have been confirmed to be of unknown origin and unknown method of manufacture by top scientists at Hewlett-Packard.

"And he bearing his cross went forth into a place called the place of a skull, which is called in the Hebrew Golgotha: Where they crucified him, and two other with him, on either side one, and Jesus in the midst."

John 19:17-18 King James Version

"All men dream: but not equally. Those who dream by night in the dusty recesses of their minds wake in the day to find that it was vanity: but the dreamers of the day are dangerous men, for they may act out their dream with open eyes, to make it possible."

Seven Pillars of Wisdom, Lawrence of Arabia

PREFACE

On October 23rd, 2012, the Washington Post began a series of articles about President Obama's Disposition Matrix, informally known as the Kill List. It was a formalization of the previous Bush administration's own equivalent, and is believed to still be in place as of this writing.

Those on the Kill List have been deemed enemies of the United States, and authorization to terminate them has been granted by the president. As of this writing, thousands have been targeted by United States forces, their deaths authorized by the president, including American citizens on foreign soil.

When this novel was originally written, the existence of this list was only rumor, and is referred to herein as the President's Termination List.

What follows is an illustration of what can happen when soldiers are given orders they believe are lawful, by a chain of command that has been coopted by someone with their own agenda, turning innocent service members into unwitting pawns.

London, England
AD 1212

"Papa! Help me, please help me!"

Lord Richard Baxter picked himself up from the ground, his knee torn open, the wound demanding attention, its sting ignored. Consuming all his thoughts were his daughter's desperate cries as they tore at the night like a dagger, slicing through the tortured wailing surrounding him, while fire engulfed home after home. With the smoke choking him, the heat searing his lungs, he held the sleeve of his tunic over his mouth and raced toward the pleas of his precious daughter. Tears streaked the soot on his face, his eyes irritated by the smoke and the overwhelming mental image of his daughter's plight.

As he pushed through the carnage and destruction, he wondered what could possibly remain of his family home, a home paid for in blood six years earlier while saving King John's mistress from brigands. His heroics had earned him the King's thanks, and a lordship over a small plot of land. As a member of the council, he kept a modest home in London with his beloved wife and daughter, the taxes he now collected from his new territory affording him the luxury of improving their lot.

He stumbled forward, the pain in his knee now too much to ignore. He couldn't help but conjure images of his wife and daughter, any happy thought of them shoved aside with horrid imaginings of them burning alive, his name on their lips, asking why he hadn't been there to save them.

It crushed his heart, the thought of not being there with them in their hour of need. His work had run late, very late, and if it weren't for the unexpected happenings at the council, he would have been home with them, able perhaps to save them from the plight they now suffered.

They're dying because of you!

He had been in the council chambers, meeting with the elders to discuss the latest discovery, when a terrific explosion had leveled the once mighty walls. One of only a handful to survive, he was in the process of attempting to rescue those still trapped in the chamber when word had reached him of what was happening outside.

THE PROTOCOL

Then his only thought was to get home to his family.

What he had found had rendered him speechless. As far as the eye could see, almost every structure had been flattened. Twisted bodies lay strewn about, fires springing up all around him, spreading fast, lighting the thatched roofs of the houses left standing.

He rounded the smoldering embers of what was once a proud stand of trees, to see flames devouring the last remaining section of his home not knocked over by the blast. His servants were desperately dousing the flames with water from the nearby well, but it was of no use. The house was a loss, the hellish flames consuming every surface as if possessed by an unquenchable thirst.

His daughter's screams reached him from inside.

"Lord Baxter!" cried his valet. "Thank the good Lord you are all right. I had feared the worst."

"My daughter—"

"She is trapped inside, milord, and we are unable to reach her. I'm afraid your wife was killed in the initial conflagration."

Richard's chest ached at the news of his dear wife's death, his eyes filling with tears as his heart silently broke, but another cry from his daughter had him cautiously approaching the roaring fire as he pushed his grief aside, knowing if he didn't act quickly, he would lose all that remained of his wife. Shielding himself from the intense heat with his cloak, he retreated, the flames licking the night air as if searching for another taste of the blood it had already claimed.

"Papa!" The pain and desperation in her voice tore at his heart as he imagined his wife, crying from Heaven for him to save their daughter. He ran toward the entrance of the home, determined to salvage what remained of a once happy family, but was grabbed by two of his servants.

"Milord, 'tis suicide to enter!" one cried. "You will surely die!"

Wresting free, he rushed for the door when the front wall collapsed inward, silencing the terrified voice. He fell to his knees and sobbed, his fists slamming into the ground as all hope, all dreams of the future, died in that moment, as his will to live left him.

The servants pulled him to safety, and to the body of his

cherished wife. He stared upon her still form, her lower body charred from the flames, and wept as he imagined the agonizing death she must have endured. He gazed upon her face and noticed her neck, twisted and broken, and prayed it happened before the burning, this small comfort lessening his anguish only slightly as his chest heaved with sobs, his family wiped from existence with one swing of an unforgiving and unknown broadsword of evil. He raised his hands to the heavens and prayed for God to care for their souls, and to reunite them all.

Soon.

A throat cleared behind him, causing a momentary flash of anger to rush through his body as he reached for his sword, rage consuming him as his tortured soul demanded retribution, demanded that all things die so there was no possibility he could experience joy or happiness again, his entire being overwhelmed in grief and self-pity.

Control yourself.

He sucked in a deep breath, holding it as he again stared to the heavens, silently praying for easy entrance into the celestial paradise for his loved ones. Rising to his feet, he wiped the tears from his face before turning to see who had interrupted him.

It was his manservant. "Yes, what is it?"

"I am so sorry to intrude in your hour of grief, milord," his trusted man murmured, his head bowed, "but the council page has said that your presence is required immediately. I told him that you were unavailable, but he was most insistent."

Richard raised his hand, cutting him off. "Tell him I will be along in a moment." He turned back to his wife, kneeled, and placed one last tender kiss upon her forehead, before rising to fulfill his greater duty, a duty handed down for over a thousand years.

THE PROTOCOL

The British Museum
London, England
Present Day

Clive Obrock sat at the central security station of the British Museum with his black Nike-shod feet crossed at the ankles, perched on a corner of his desk, with his chair tilted precariously back, his long ponytail suspended in the air. His bony hands were clasped behind his head, revealing the beginnings of yellow sweat stains under the armpits of his threadbare shirt. His mother had told him to replace it, but he hadn't seen the need—when he had his jacket on, which was all of the time when outside of this room, nobody could see his armpits anyway. He had told her to mind her own business, then wondered why he'd ever agreed to move back into the old family home.

The room hummed with the fans of the computers, almost drowning out the annoying buzz of the overhead fluorescent lighting. Banks of monitors surrounded him, each alternating between different areas of the museum. Various entrances and exhibits flashed by, revealing security guards on patrol, empty corridors, and lonely displays. Clive had worked here so long, the priceless works of art, and artifacts of mostly forgotten ancient civilizations, had lost their allure and fascination.

The only screen that interested him now was the one showing the Man-U football game.

So engrossed was he, that he didn't notice the car pull up to the Montague Place entrance, or its lone occupant dash to the maintenance door, sheltered from an incessant English rain by the jacket pulled over his head. He rang the buzzer.

Clive nearly fell out of his seat. He killed the game and turned to the monitor demanding his attention. The jacket protected the hunkered over figure from both the rain and the camera. Clive punched the intercom button.

"The museum is closed, sir."

"Clive, it's me, Rodney! Let me in, I'm freezing my bollocks off!"

Clive laughed and tapped in the code to open the maintenance entrance. A buzzer sounded and the door opened as Rodney Underwood pushed against it. A moment later his friend appeared on the inner corridor camera, shaking the rain from his jacket and running his hands through his hair, the water puddling around his discount-store Oxfords. Rodney flashed a grin then mouthed something at the camera, prompting Clive to punch up the audio.

"—E-R-P! Double O-L, Liverpool FC!"

Clive pressed the intercom button. "United's goin' to kick yer arses!"

Rodney flipped him the bird then continued toward the security station. Clive laughed and turned the game back on, propping his feet on the desk corner again. A few minutes later, there was a knock at the station door. He reached under the desk and pressed the entry buzzer. The door opened behind him.

"Hey, Rodney, United's up by one."

He kicked off the desk, spinning his chair to face the door, keeping his eyes on the game as long as he could. As his chair completed its spin, he turned his head around to see the barrel of a gun pointed at him. The gun fired and a stinging pain radiated from the center of this chest as he was hit. He slid from the chair into a heap on the floor, and the last thing he saw before the world blackened around him was his friend of five years standing over him.

On the monitor, Liverpool tied the game.

THE PROTOCOL

Andes Mountains, Peru
One Week Earlier

Garcia swung the pickaxe against the cave wall. The clumped dirt and rock sprayed back at him, mixing with the sweat glistening on his head and soaking through his shirt. "Este trabajo de Puta me lleva al Diablo," he muttered under his breath.

I feel like a mule. I don't see the Americanos getting dirty.

He swung again, and another shower of dirt flew back from the wall. It was slow, hard work, but the professor had said there might be a secret room on the other side. Garcia respected the professor.

He gets dirty.

At first, he had agreed to be a guide, his deeply ingrained superstitions too strong to participate in disturbing the ancient home of the ancestors. But the professor had a way of making him feel at ease, so he had agreed to help with the heavy labor. Now he was regretting it. Another swing, and this time the axe almost came out of his hands as he broke through.

Excited, he cleared away more dirt, exposing the other side. After a few minutes of digging with his hands, he stuck his head through the hole. The pungent smell of centuries of rot and decay threatened to overwhelm him, yet he persevered, pushing his head in further. He couldn't see anything. Then he remembered the flashlight on his belt. He fumbled for it, his fingers numb from swinging the axe, his heart drumming with excitement. Finally grasping it, he shone the light through the hole as he stuck his head back in. At first, he saw only more dirt, then as he played the light around, it struck something shiny. He focused the light and gasped as two disembodied eyes glared at him.

He jerked back, tripping over his axe. As he hit the cave floor, his flashlight flew from his hand, smacking the ground and going dark. "El Diablo!" he muttered as he stared at the hole in horror. He scrambled to his feet. "El Diablo!" he screamed as he ran down the narrow passage back to the surface. "El Diablo!"

Archaeology Professor James Acton was on his knees,

7

carefully brushing dirt away from what appeared to be an intact clay pot. One of his students, working in the same grid, carefully sifted the soil for any small shards. Students in other grids, each cordoned off with twine staked at the corners, were painstakingly removing over five hundred years of earth, burying what Acton was now confident was an ancient Incan city.

This was the part of the job he loved—getting his hands dirty. Teaching in front of a class full of students was a close second, but taking those same students out of the environment they were familiar with, and sticking them in the middle of what was now nowhere, but where once an ancient civilization thrived, was indescribable.

The excitement on the young faces when they discovered something even as simple as a clay pot, brought joy to his heart each time, something he prayed would never grow old. His hunch the city was actually here had been proven several years ago when he and a single grad student had received funding to confirm if an ancient Spanish map was accurate.

And it had been.

Precisely.

He had wanted to stay, to tell the university to forward his mail here, to the middle of nowhere, but of course returned to begin the long fight for funding a real, long-term dig. And now they were here, half a dozen of his best students, funded by the university, various endowments, and some well-off parents of the lucky ones.

It was a shoestring budget, yet he didn't care. What they were learning was invaluable, much of it routine, though some of it puzzling with no explanation as of yet. And that was what he lived for.

The unexplained.

He sat back on his haunches, his grid forgotten as he gazed at their most puzzling find yet, not twenty feet away.

It makes no sense.

He leaned back and stretched when screams erupted from a nearby cave at the top of the embankment bordering the southern side of the site. He leaped to his feet, rushing toward the hillside. Garcia, one of their local hires, burst from the entrance and tumbled down the hill to the camp below, striking his head on a small rock.

"Señor Professor! El Diablo esta en la cueva! El Diablo is

in the cave!"

Acton reached him as the terrified man's eyes fluttered then shut, a nasty gash on his forehead oozing blood. "Get some water and a med kit over here, now." Acton kneeled beside the unconscious man, examining Garcia's body for broken bones, and finding none. One of his students, Robbie Andrews, arrived with a canteen of water and the medical kit. Acton opened it as he eyed the now moaning Garcia.

He soaked a cloth in water, then began cleaning the wound. Garcia moaned louder as the cool liquid revived him, and gradually he came to, trying to sit up. Acton held him down.

"Drink," he ordered, holding a canteen to Garcia's lips. The still weak man drank gratefully, and when he had his fill, he pulled away. Acton handed the canteen to Robbie, then waved the rest of the gathered students away. "Let's give Garcia some space, shall we?" The students moved off, disappointed, but his primary concern was for the health of their hired help, a man who had impressed Acton repeatedly over the past few weeks as he had taken on more duties, despite his grave reservations of disturbing "the ancestors." Acton sat beside him and placed a hand on the man's shoulder, giving it a gentle squeeze. "Now, tell me what you saw. And remember," he said, looking down at Garcia with a reassuring smile, "you're safe now."

Garcia sighed deeply, trying unsuccessfully to control his breathing, his chest still heaving. "Señor Professor, I see the Devil in the cave," he said in his thick Peruvian accent, the fear still tingeing his voice despite Acton's assurances of safety. It was clear the man's superstitions had got the better of him, and it was something Acton had dealt with across the world. Superstitions were pervasive in all cultures, including Western, and especially so outside of the "First World." It made hiring local help difficult at times, though the almighty dollar would usually win out.

Until one day something was stumbled upon that would send them into a panic, and the camp would suddenly find itself devoid of workers.

He feared if he couldn't calm Garcia down, they might lose the limited help they managed to attract up to this remote location, which at the moment included only Garcia, two guards, and one driver who brought their supplies.

"Tell me exactly what happened." Acton continued to smile as he pressed slightly harder on the gash, stemming the flow of blood.

"I was digging at the wall like you ask me to, and I finally get through—"

"You got through?" Acton and Robbie exchanged excited smiles. "What did you see?"

"El Diablo, I see El Diablo! I look through the hole, and I first could see nothing so I get my light and then I can see. I see two red eyes staring at me. It was the Devil, Señor. I swear! I run outta there."

Acton was skeptical, to say the least, knowing Garcia's superstitious nature. Whatever he had seen, however, was enough to send this poor man into a panic. And two red, glowing eyes, had to be something, perhaps a reflection off of some jewels. The thought of what Garcia might have found had his own heart racing, but for now he had to calm the man whose breathing had quickened its pace.

"Two eyes?"

"Yes. Come, I show you if you not believe me!" pleaded Garcia.

The best way to calm him was to humor him—expressing any doubt in what he had seen would insult the man's honor. Besides, regardless of what Garcia *thought* he had seen, Acton had no doubt he had seen *something*, and was as eager to find out what that might be as Garcia was to prove he wasn't lying.

"No, you rest here. I'll go and look myself." Acton rose and started up the path leading to the cave entrance. He motioned for a couple of students to watch Garcia and for Robbie to follow him. "Grab some gear." They soon arrived at the entrance and crawled through the narrow opening of the cave discovered by a couple of amorous students the day before, behind a thick growth of bushes. Once inside, the narrow passageway opened up, allowing them to walk upright, though single file, deeper into the damp, dripping cave. Two hundred feet in, they found the hole Garcia had been laboring at all day. Acton shone his flashlight through, coughing at the overwhelming stench. At first, he too saw nothing.

Then he gasped.

National Security Agency Headquarters
Fort George G. Meade, Maryland

Echelon chewed through every phone call, e-mail, fax, and telex message sent either by land or satellite from its laboratory in the National Security Agency building. Its Dictionary watchlist was programmed to listen and search for certain hot words such as "bomb" or "anthrax." Any such messages or calls were flagged for review, and depending on the priority of the words and number of hits in a particular conversation or sequence of communications, meant either immediately reviewed, or put on file to be analyzed possibly months later. The call from Peru at 17:52 Eastern Standard Time was immediately escalated:

```
[CLASSIFICATION TOP SECRET UMBRA GAMMA
PRIME]
[DICTIONARY HITS: CRYSTAL, SKULL, NEW YORK]
[SOURCE ILC INTERNATIONAL LEASE CARRIER
INTSAT-ALPHA]
[CALL ORIGIN: LIMA, PERU, ROAMING CELLULAR
PHONE 212-555-7723]
[CALL DESTINATION: NEW YORK, NY, USA, LAND
LINE 212-555-8838]
[# OF SUBJECTS = 2]
[SUBJECT IDENT: CALLER1 = ANDREWS, ROBERT
IDENT SRC = TELCO]
[SUBJECT IDENT: CALLER2 = ANDREWS, JOHN
IDENT SRC = TELCO]

[START OF TRANSCRIPT]

[CALLER1] "John, it's me, Robbie. Can you
hear me?"

[CALLER2] "Barely, man. Where are you?"

[CALLER1] "I'm still in Peru, on the dig
with Professor Acton."

[CALLER2] "Oh yeah? I didn't think I'd hear
```

from you until you got back. What's up?"

[CALLER1] "The professor shut down the dig and sent us all to Lima for the night, so I thought I'd call and see how you and Dad are doing."

[CALLER2] "We're fine. Dad's starting to recover from the stroke. I really wish you could be here, but he understands how important getting to work for Professor Acton is. How're things going there? Why the shutdown?"

[CALLER1] "He found something. Something pretty cool, but we're not allowed to talk about it. Only two of us have seen it."

[CALLER2] "What is it?"

[CALLER1] "I'm not supposed to tell, John. If the professor found out, I'd be kicked off the dig."

[CALLER2] "How would he find out? I'm your big brother, man, come on!"

[CALLER1] "Okay, okay. We found a CRYSTAL SKULL, perfectly preserved in a hidden chamber. It's incredible, John, I've never seen anything like it before."

[CALLER2] "A CRYSTAL SKULL? What the hell is that?"

[CALLER1] "According to the professor, a few of them have been found around the world, but nobody knows who made them. He was extremely excited when he first found it, but then he seemed to get scared."

[CALLER2] "Scared?"

[CALLER1] "Yeah, I don't know why. Maybe he doesn't want to attract attention, what with the problems down here. Anyway, my cellphone is starting to die, so I'll say goodbye. Tell Dad I love him and I'll see him as soon as I'm back in NEW YORK."

[CALLER2] "Okay, you be careful down there."

[CALLER1] "I will, bye."

[END OF TRANSCRIPT]

Washington, DC

What a day.

Steve Masters swirled his glass containing three fingers of an eighteen-year-old Ardmore single malt, the distinct aroma of smoke bringing back memories of his stay several years ago with his wife in Speyside, Scotland. He raised the glass, toasting the empty rear of his limo, and took a long drag of the harsh liquid. He loosened his tie and undid the top button of his shirt as his reward began its job, his entire body enjoying the effects. He leaned back into the plush leather and closed his eyes as he let a long sigh escape.

His phone rang.

Shit!

He left his eyes closed, debating whether to take the call, but he had to—his job was too important to let them go unanswered. Though at the end of a long day like today, he yearned for what it must have been like decades ago when cellphones and car phones didn't exist.

Downtime!

That's what he needed, desperately. Downtime.

A second ring.

When he had agreed to take on this job for President Jackson, a longtime friend, he hadn't realized how much work there'd be. And neither had his wife. She was tolerating it better than he had feared, and he took her with him on business trips whenever he could, scheduling an extra day or two of "alone time" when possible. Unfortunately, intelligence conferences, especially surrounding black ops as he was involved with, weren't always held in the most hospitable of conditions.

Three rings.

He sighed and put the leaded Steuben crystal glass on the drink tray, and retrieved his phone from the breast pocket of his jacket that lay tossed on the seat beside him.

I can't wait until Jackson's administration is over and I can get fired.

No matter what he did while Jackson was president, his job was safe, for he was there for one specific task, one the American public could never know about, one even his own wife knew nothing of.

One handed down to him by his own father.

He pressed the talk button. "Masters."

"Sir, we have an Umbra Gamma Prime document here for immediate review."

"I'll be right there." He hung up the phone and pressed the button to lower the glass partition separating him from the driver. "Jerry, turn us around, I need to get back to the office, fast." His chauffeur of many years radioed the escort vehicles as Masters raised the partition, picked up his glass, and gripped the overhead handhold.

The mini-motorcade's lead Lincoln Navigator cut left, jumped the median, and blocked oncoming traffic. The Town Car limo locked up its brakes and followed, jostling its well-prepared VIP as the trailing Navigator cut across, assuming the role of lead vehicle. All three turned on their lights and sirens, leaving a trail of burnt rubber, smoke, and a dozen confused drivers in their wake.

Umbra Gamma Prime.

It was one of the highest classifications of Top Secret there was in his business. In fact, he had never had one cross his desk since he had taken the job, despite dealing with countless terrorist threats—both foreign and domestic—and having deployed teams around the world in secret.

Yet tonight, on a night when nothing was going on in the world he could think of that would warrant such a high classification, he was called back to read a file that couldn't even leave his office due to the high level of security.

There was only one thing that might have triggered this precaution, and it had his pulse racing the entire fifteen minutes it took to arrive.

"Sir, here's the communiqué." His aide took his jacket, then handed him the dossier, sealed and tied with a red and white ribbon reading "TOP SECRET UMBRA GAMMA PRIME—DIR SPC OPS EYES ONLY."

"No interruptions." His aide closed the door as Masters entered and headed for his desk. He sat, his leather-backed chair exhaling under him as he glanced around the large office to make sure he was alone. He removed a device resembling a small tape recorder from his top desk drawer. He pressed a button to activate the Radio Frequency Interference Generator, disrupting any bug in his office, which, despite the device's effectiveness, was swept three times a day, and after any visitor. The Umbra Gamma Prime document in his hands, however, demanded every possible precaution against someone eavesdropping.

Breaking the seal, he opened the dossier and scanned the identified keywords. His eyes shot wide as his suspicions were confirmed. He skimmed the conversation, then read it again carefully, making sure he hadn't misinterpreted it. His heart slammed against his ribcage as he hit the intercom button on his phone. Static. Cursing, he turned off the jamming device then jabbed the button again. His aide answered.

"Yes, sir?"

"Get me Darbinger."

White House Chief of Staff Lesley Darbinger jogged down the corridor leading to the Oval Office. He stopped before the door and took several gasping breaths.

This is ridiculous. I need to get back into shape.

He used to jog five miles a day, though not anymore. No more time.

But winded at 200 feet?

These days, he did more running *in*side the office than out.

And it clearly isn't enough.

"Is he in?" he panted as he stepped into the outer office.

The fifty-something woman behind the desk looked up and stuck a pencil in the tight bun on top of her head. "Yes, sir." She picked up the phone. "Mr. Darbinger to see you, Mr. President." She hung up and motioned toward the door. "Go on in, Mr. Darbinger." A Secret Service agent opened the door to the Oval Office, and Darbinger stepped through.

President Stewart Alfred Jackson sat behind his desk, reading a briefing paper. He tossed the folder on the oak desktop and laid his glasses down as Darbinger entered. They had met at Yale over thirty years ago, and had been close since. Darbinger had worked on Jackson's gubernatorial, senate, and presidential campaigns, and with everything they had been through together over the years, he knew Jackson trusted him implicitly. He was his friend, his confidant, and his sounding board. He was the man he told all his secrets to. He was the man Jackson trusted more than his own wife.

And today, both of their lives were about to change,

forever.

Jackson circled the desk and motioned to one of the leather couches. "What's on your mind, Les?"

Darbinger sat and glanced around the office, making sure they were alone, and taking in the history represented by every object that adorned it at the same time. He leaned forward and lowered his voice, as he was about to add to that history. "Mr. President, I just had a conversation with the Director of Special Operations."

Jackson sat on the opposite couch. "Steve Masters?"

"Yes, Mr. President." Darbinger lowered his voice further. "He thinks they found it."

Jackson leaned forward. "Found what?"

Darbinger steadied his breathing as his heart shoved blood through his system at too quick a pace, the excitement and terror of the moment overwhelming. He inhaled deeply and stared into his friend's eyes.

"The final missing skull."

17ᵗʰ Street, Washington, DC

Billy Guthrie sat up in bed and rubbed the sleep out of his eyes as he looked around to see what had woken him. Nothing appeared out of the ordinary, though sunlight poured through the window. Too much sunlight for 6:00 a.m. A glance at his alarm clock showed a flashing *12:01*.

"Shit!" He leaped out of bed as he realized he had been awoken by the beeping of nearly every electronic device in the apartment when the power came back on. Running to the dresser, he grabbed his Tag Heuer watch. *8:15.* "Shit!"

He rushed to the bathroom and splashed some water on his face, then ran his wet fingers through his sandy-brown hair, trying to make it not too obvious he had skipped the shower. Swishing some mouthwash, he found a clean pair of slacks on the floor and thrust his legs in. Running back to the bathroom, he spat into the sink, grinned at the mirror to check his teeth for last night's dinner, then pulled on a pair of socks from the floor. He grabbed the dress-shirt hanging on the back of the bathroom door he had planned to iron the night before—but had put off—and willed the wrinkles out with his hands. Tossing a tie around his neck and a blazer over his shoulder, he bolted from his apartment with his electric razor, shaving a weekend's worth of growth off before his first day on the job.

This is all I need, to be late on my first damned day! Dad will kill me!

He hailed a cab and climbed in.

"Where to, buddy?" asked the cabbie in a thick Middle Eastern accent.

"The White House. Employee entrance."

The cabbie glanced in his rearview mirror, eyes narrowing. "Aren't you a little young to be working there?" He cranked the wheel, pulled a U-turn, and surged them toward the hallowed residence.

Billy shrugged, gripping the "Oh Jesus" bar, debating if he should put his seatbelt on. "Intern."

"Ahh, that explains it." The cabbie floored it, blasting through the red light. Billy's eyes bulged as he yanked on the seatbelt too hard, the tensioner halting him in his haste. Easing back on the belt, he eventually got himself secured, though only minutes before they arrived. He shoved a few bills through to the driver and jumped out, rushing through security and toward the rally point for the new interns.

He skidded to a halt, gaping at a line zigzagging like an international arrivals area, threatening to spill out into the hallway if any more showed up. Surrounded by the excited buzz of dozens of young interns getting to know each other, he soon realized he needn't have worried about being late his first day. Everyone was being fingerprinted, photographed, swabbed for DNA, and retinal scanned. Even a voice sample was taken.

Man, what's next, a semen sample?

His watch beeped noon as he arrived at the front of the line.

"Name?" asked the bored clerk.

"William Augustus Guthrie."

"Guthrie?" The clerk snapped his gaze up. "As in the former Speaker of the House?"

Billy nodded and lowered his voice. "Look, I'd kind of like to keep that quiet."

The clerk grunted. "Yeah, good luck with that." He waved him on. "Next!"

Billy moved down the line and placed his hand on an electronic palm scanner. Giggles from behind him drew his attention. Two girls in the line ogled him. They giggled again. He blushed. One of them pointed at his feet. Glancing down, he found his left pant leg partially tucked into his sock. A sock that didn't match the other.

Shit!

He quickly fixed his pants, resigned to going through the rest of the day with mismatched socks and a pair of coworkers aware of his predicament. He put some people between him and the girls as the last couple of interns who had been even later than him finished processing.

Then a tour he had been looking forward to for years, finally began.

He studied every room and corridor in awe, his chest pounding in excitement as the White House intern tour wound through the building. He had been here years before with his father, though had been too young to appreciate it. When the administration changed, his father didn't take him back to the White House again. "When they're voted out, and our people are in, then you can go back," he recalled his father saying. That had taken eight years. Now he was back, but to work.

Eighteen years old, working in the White House. Shit yeah!

A voice from behind startled him out of his reverie. "Rough morning?"

He spun on his heel to see one of the girls who had been laughing at him earlier. Blushing again, he nodded. "Yeah, my power went out, so…you know?"

She extended her hand. "My name is Rachel."

"Billy." He shook her hand nervously, realizing he was as crimson as a lobster.

"Next time you do the laundry, Billy, you should match your socks after they dry. That way that doesn't happen." She pointed at his feet and laughed again, walking back to her friend who covered her own cackle with a hand.

Bitches.

They giggled some more, then Rachel said, "But he *is* kinda cute." The other one agreed then laughed again as she tugged her friend toward the group that had moved on.

Very hot bitches.

THE PROTOCOL

1st Special Forces Operational Detachment-Delta
Fort Bragg, North Carolina
A.k.a. "The Unit"

Command Sergeant Major Burt "Big Dog" Dawson expertly flipped each of the several dozen burgers on the charcoal grill, while sweat glistened off his chiseled chest, partially revealed by a half-buttoned Hawaiian shirt. The aroma of grilled meat filled his nostrils, and his stomach growled.

I love barbecue.

It was a perfect summer day. The sun shone down out of a crystal clear sky, the light breeze taking the edge off the heat. As he flipped the final burger, something smacked him in the back of the head.

He swung around, ready to defend himself.

"Sorry, Mr. Dog, I didn't mean to hit you." The small boy grabbed the stray beachball and ran back to the group of waiting kids.

"No problem, Bryson," he called after him.

Mr. Dog. Now that's funny.

His buddies in boot camp, well over a decade ago, had filled out his initials to "Big Dog." At first, he couldn't stand it, though eventually it grew on him, especially once it had been shortened to BD. And it was better than some of the other nicknames he'd heard over the years.

He now led Bravo Team, a group of the most highly trained black ops specialists the U.S. Military had to offer. The 1st Special Forces Operational Detachment—Delta, known to the public as the Delta Force, had been created in the 1970s as an answer to the growing problem of international terrorism. Since the Iran Hostage Crisis debacle—which if you asked insiders had more to do with political interference than poor training—they had served with distinction in many operations the American public knew nothing about. This was their lot in life—to do spectacular things, under the radar, for no credit, and the promise of complete deniability if something went wrong.

Dawson had served with Bravo Team for over seven years, and had been on missions in Iraq, Afghanistan, Kosovo, Serbia, the Sudan, Syria, Iran, and others. All had been successes in two ways. One, the mission was

21

accomplished, and two, nobody knew they had been there. His men were fiercely loyal to him, and he to them, having been through hell together too many times to remember. All were NCOs, Non-Commissioned Officers—sergeants of various stripes—command structure fairly loose among each team, though ultimately there was always one man in charge, and for now, it was him. The officers at their HQ planned the missions, the Non-Coms executed them.

Today was one of many family barbecues the team hosted behind the Unit in the secluded complex on Fort Bragg, where they could train away from the prying eyes of the public or regular forces. Normally, they weren't all able to be there, but today was a rare day. A roar of laughter erupted from one of the picnic tables, a reaction to a joke that likely couldn't be repeated in polite company, a.k.a. the wives and girlfriends, who sat at another table talking among themselves. Dawson had only ever been married to the Unit, and the way his life was going, he expected it to remain that way.

He checked the burgers again.

Almost ready.

He laid the buns out on the grill to toast them. More laughter from the table. He glanced over and saw the comedian was one of the two new guys, Sergeant Trip "Mickey" McDonald.

Speaking of bad nicknames.

Mickey's huge ears stuck out of his head like Prince Charles'. One comparison to Mickey Mouse during training had saddled him with "Mickey" since.

What's so funny?

He loved manning the grill, though sometimes he missed just sitting at that table with his men, laughing and telling one of his blue jokes from his extensive repertoire.

Shit! The cheese!

He hastily peeled off slices from the stack next to the grill as Mickey laughed hard.

"So, what did BD do?"

Sergeant Clive "Smitty" Cameron, a long-time member of the team, gestured toward Dawson. "Well, you'd never believe it, but BD is a very chivalrous man." This elicited several guffaws from the men, even a raised eyebrow from Dawson. "So anyway, this hostage just wouldn't stop screaming. He kept telling her to shut-up, that he was there to rescue her, but she wouldn't believe him."

"Yeah, and she had taken one of those self-defense courses," chimed in Master Sergeant Mike "Red" Belme, his second-in-command and best friend. "You can see where this is going, right?"

"Don't tell me—"

"Yup, as soon as he cut her bindings, she hoofed him in the balls, kneed him in the nose, then ran out of the building screaming at the top of her lungs," finished Smitty.

Dawson winced.

"Luckily, I'd already taken out the hostiles, so she was safe, but the local Yemenis had no clue what she was saying," explained Sergeant Carl "Niner" Sung, the Unit's best sniper. Korean-American, he had earned his nickname in a bar fight years ago, a redneck calling him "slant-eyed." Niner embarrassed him by slinging back a few of his own, including "Nine Iron." With the bar laughing, the irate man took a swing. The ensuing brawl had resulted in several arrests— after the team had left. From then on, he had insisted his nickname be "Nine Iron," which had been shortened to Niner over the years.

"She was half-naked in the middle of a bunch of burqa-clad women! The locals—" Red's face now matched his nickname as he struggled to stifle his laughter. Losing the battle, he motioned to Smitty to continue.

"Yeah, the locals were about to start stoning her when BD comes stumbling out of the building she'd been held in, cupping his boys."

"So he grabs her, throws her into this piece of shit Toyota truck we'd commandeered, and drives away," said Red. "But the chick starts screaming again and tries to get out."

"Yeah, but this time BD's not havin' any of it. He backhands her in the face and knocks her out cold!"

"No shit?"

"No shit!" laughed Niner. "I'm tellin' ya, Mickey, I saw it through my scope. Out cold."

Smitty nodded hard, his sunglasses falling off their perch on top of his head. "Yeah, so after we get picked up at the rendezvous, she's nursing a bloody nose, and BD is nursing a set of sore balls. And you know what he said?"

"What?"

Everyone at the table said in unison, "From now on, I don't go anywhere without a cup!"

Dawson smiled as his men exploded in laughter.

And his boys twinged at the memory.

"Burgers are up!" he announced. Cheers from the kids preceded their stampede to the grill as he rationed the burgers onto Styrofoam plates. He was about to fill one up for Bryson when his cellphone rang.

Shit.

He flipped it open. "Speak."

"Mr. White, you're needed." The monotone voice signaled the imminent end of the afternoon's festivities.

"Five minutes." He snapped the phone shut and motioned to Red, his friend and comrade of over ten years. "I have to go, you take over."

"No problem, BD." Red took the lifter from Dawson's hand and smiled at his boy Bryson as he held out his plate. "I'll hold down the fort 'til you get back."

"Thanks. Have the boys watch the beers, I have a funny feeling we're going to be busy soon."

Red nodded. "Will do."

Dawson crossed the field to the parking lot and climbed in his prized 1964½ Mustang convertible in original Poppy Red. The engine roared to life with a turn of the key, and minutes later he was pulling into the HQ parking lot, wondering what the presumed mission would be and where.

Anywhere would be fantastic.

As he covered the short distance to the Colonel's office, he hoped for one thing. That it was interesting. He wasn't a big fan of surveillance missions—too much ass sitting. He preferred the adrenaline-fueled infiltration type missions, ones where hands got dirty, weapons got fired, and C4 was put to its intended use.

At the end of the day, he wanted to have done something useful for his country, something that would make a difference, even if the general public never realized it had happened.

He passed through the outer office, Maggie, the Colonel's secretary, not there.

Odd.

He knocked on the inner office door.

"Enter!"

THE PROTOCOL

Dawson pulled the door open and stepped inside. "What's up, sir?" he asked as he closed the door behind him.

Colonel Thomas Clancy, the head of Dawson's unit, sat behind his desk, fishing a cigar out of an antique humidor occupying a prominent position on his workspace, exposing his one last vice. An impressive array of medals and awards decorated the walls, revealing a career that only recently involved a chair.

Never one for formality when within the confines of his office, Clancy grunted an acknowledgment as he ran the cigar under his nose, inhaling the intoxicating smell. "I don't know." He motioned to the chair in front of his desk. "Have a seat."

"Thank you, sir." Dawson sat. "You don't know?"

"Your team was specifically requested." Clancy snipped the tip off his cigar. "Beyond that, I have no idea. I'm out of the loop on this one, Sergeant Major."

Dawson didn't like the sound of that. Clancy was a commanding officer Dawson respected—not the rank and position, but the man. Whenever he was on a mission, Clancy had his back, but with the Colonel out of the loop—which was rare—he couldn't trust he and his men wouldn't be left hung out to dry should something go wrong.

He had asked for interesting, and it seemed like he might get it, the old Chinese curse, "May you live in interesting times," coming to mind.

"When do I get briefed?"

"Now." Clancy flicked his butane lighter and carefully lit the cigar, rapidly puffing until he was satisfied. Placing the lighter back on his desk, he took a long drag and exhaled, letting the smoke waft over his face, allowing him to enjoy the fragrance one more time. His ritual finished, he turned back to Dawson. "Report to the comms center and don't report back to me until Control says to. Understood?"

Dawson rose and snapped to attention. "Yes, sir!"

Darbinger Residence
Washington, DC

"What's on your mind, dear?"

Lesley Darbinger glanced up at his wife of over twenty-five years, recognizing her concerned look. Nora knew him well enough to know something was wrong, and despite his best efforts, he was unable to hide this afternoon's news.

"Anything you can talk about?"

Darbinger swirled the cognac in his glass, watching the viscous fluid stick to the edges.

Good legs.

He looked up and smiled. "Oh, nothing wrong," he reassured her. "Just finishing up some old business." He knew damned well she would read right through the lie. Besides, cognac this early in the day was always a dead giveaway to something being wrong. Jackson had sent him home shortly after the news had been delivered, the president himself canceling all of his appointments for the rest of the day. Her joy at seeing him home early—something rare these past few years—had been short-lived, his gloom obvious.

Old business.

He was tired of this business. It wasn't his, it was never meant to be. He had merely joined in something his best friend had thought important. He would be lying to say what he had become involved with for friendship's sake hadn't become important to him as well—very important—but it had never been all-consuming as it was for Jackson.

For Jackson, it was an obsession.

"Old business?" She frowned and sat beside him. "You don't mean—"

He cut her off with his finger. "Remember, we don't say their name. *Ever.*"

He could see the color drain from her face as she nodded, a fear clouding her eyes he hadn't seen in years, a fear that was one of his few true regrets in life. He should have never told her all those years ago why he had been troubled, yet he had. After all, she was his wife, and she deserved to know what was bothering her husband. She had understood, never truly believing, though when the rift had come between

Jackson and his former masters, and Jackson's actions had put their collective lives at risk, she had been shaken to her core.

And he didn't blame her.

"Are we going to be okay?"

His heart ached at the fear, her bottom lip trembling slightly as she asked the question. He smiled, trying to convey confidence, strength—neither of which he had at the moment. "They can't touch us now." He patted her hand. "But a thirty-year journey may finally be about to end."

"You promised me it was over before, Lesley." Her tone was firm. "After that Smithsonian incident, you promised me. I don't want to go through that again."

It was one of the few lies he had ever told her, telling her it was over, that he had left that part of his life behind. Yet he knew deep down she didn't believe him, though like a good partner, had indulged the lie, realizing it was told for her benefit to mollify her fears.

But it was still a lie.

"Like I said," he repeated, "they can't touch us now."

She rose and left him alone, the fear and anger in her posture evident as his thoughts drifted to the Smithsonian incident that had changed their lives almost ten years ago.

He sighed, draining his glass.

Ten years of lies and deceit might finally be coming to an end.

The Unit
Fort Bragg, North Carolina

Burt Dawson didn't have much time to pull his thoughts together. His briefing from Control was true to the word— brief. This was often the case in his business, so it didn't raise any red flags. He would still rather be reporting to Colonel Clancy, though apparently the secrecy of this op was so tight, even their regular Ops Center wouldn't be used, the mission instead controlled from elsewhere. Where, he wasn't privy too. All he needed to know was that his team's comms would all be patched through to this secret location.

That meant they would be cut off from those he trusted at the Unit.

Again, unusual, though not unheard of.

What Control had told him could be seen as justification for all the secrecy. Apparently, a homegrown terror cell had stolen a highly classified DARPA project during transport, killing four military guards in the process. The perpetrators had fled the country to a training camp they had set up in Peru, and intercepted chatter suggested they were planning multiple attacks on American targets around the world and at home.

Their orders: infiltrate the training camp, recover the stolen item, interrogate the prisoners if necessary, upload video of them, and once identified, eliminate them if they were on the President's Termination List.

A straightforward mission he had done dozens of times, if not more. The difference this time were the terrorists. All young apple pie eating American men and women who had fallen under the spell of a madman named James Acton.

Dawson's orders for Acton were different. Once the item was retrieved, Acton was to be executed immediately—he was already confirmed on the Termination List.

Dawson wasn't sure how he felt about the mission—he had even asked if Control would rather the targets be captured and returned to the United States for prosecution. The suggestion had been angrily shot down, the orders reiterated. The only explanation Dawson had for the reaction was that what they had stolen was too secret for them to remain alive now that they had seen it. His only problem with the orders was the age of the targets.

Remember 9/11 and how young those hijackers were.

He sometimes had to remind himself the bad guys weren't always men who had experienced enough of life to know they didn't like it. Too often today, it was young people still battling acne that were pulled into extremist activities.

Normally it was foreign nationals they targeted, but with the president now having executive power to target and eliminate Americans on foreign soil, this would be a first for him and his team.

It was sickening.

As he pulled up to the Unit and watched the young kids running around playing, he couldn't help wondering if some bastard in their future, like this James Acton, would corrupt their young, innocent minds, and have them hating the very country their fathers were fighting to protect.

Acton is mine.

He parked, not looking forward to what he was about to do. He strode up to the party and noticed a couple of burgers still warming on the grill. Red walked up to him.

"Hey, BD, burger?"

Dawson nodded, and Red put one together. Nicknamed for the red hair he shaved off with a bowie knife whenever a hint of it showed, Red was the second highest ranking member of Bravo Team, Dawson's second-in-command, and his best friend of almost a decade. Dawson had been named godfather to Red's son Bryson, and spent many a holiday dinner at the Belme household as part of their family.

Which meant Red knew him too well. Red's eyebrows narrowed as he handed over the burger. "What's up?"

Dawson took a monster bite, realizing how hungry he was. "We've got a mission," he finally managed after swallowing enough to talk without revealing the ongoing mastication process.

Red turned toward the group, now in the third inning of a softball game. "When do we leave?"

"Now."

"Okay, I'll break the news."

Dawson stopped his friend. "No, I'll do it. Let the kids blame me and not Bryson's dad." Red smiled gratefully, but stayed by Dawson's side as he walked into the group of operators, better halves, and children.

"Hate to break up the party, folks, but we've been called up." A string of "aws" came from the kids, this not the first time they had been disappointed. He hated it whenever this happened, which in today's insane world was too often. His men gave hugs to their families and loved ones, then headed into the Unit to be briefed.

THE PROTOCOL

Somewhere Over the Pacific Coast

The Chinook MH-47E helicopter raced toward the Peruvian coastline, its two Textron Lycoming engines pumping out four thousand shaft-horsepower, and propelling it at over 180 miles per hour as Command Sergeant Major Burt "Big Dog" Dawson, mission-designate Bravo One, took a knee amidst his men. He inhaled deeply through his nose, drawing in the intoxicating smell of the fumes, a smell he would never tire of. His men leaned in, each cocking an ear for their final briefing.

"This is the primary target," Dawson bellowed over the thunder of the rotors and the rattling of the hold. He held out a photo labeled 'James Acton.' "He must be captured alive so we can recover the item. Eliminate the guards and any other resistance."

"What's the item?" asked Mickey.

"Need to know."

"Got ya."

Dawson glanced at Mickey for a brief second. Mickey had hesitated to carry out an order on the last mission, and an enemy combatant had got the drop on Red, his friend taking a round in the vest. He survived, though three inches higher and he would have been dead. It hadn't been necessary to chew Mickey out, he had learned his lesson. He'd never hesitate or question orders again.

"The primary objective is to capture the target alive and recover the item. Video will be sent to Control, and they'll determine if the remaining targets are on the Termination List. Intel has them as members of a domestic terrorist cell. This James Acton guy is their leader. Apparently, he's convinced these people to join him in his cause. Remember, just because the hostiles are young, doesn't mean they're innocent. They've already killed four of our own. The only difference from any other mission is this time they're American, but no less a risk than any other Islamic fundamentalist cell we've taken out before. These people hate their country and our way of life. They mean to destroy it from within, and we're here to stop that. If they're on the Termination List, they'll be eliminated. According to UAV overflights, the camp is lightly guarded." He glanced at

31

Niner. "Overseer, you'll be dropped one mile from the camp. You'll eliminate the guards, then we'll move in." He looked at his men. "Understood?"

"Yes, Sergeant Major!" they answered in unison.

"Five minutes to Overseer drop," the pilot announced over the comms.

Dawson activated his tactical throat microphone. "Acknowledged." Checking his watch, he rose, ending the briefing. "Five minutes to the drop. Check your gear."

THE PROTOCOL

Andes Mountains, Peru

Professor James Acton entered his cabin, followed by Robbie Andrews. Though austere, this cabin was the only bit of semi-luxury in the camp, despite its plywood walls with narrow gaps between each board that let the cold Andes wind whistle through during the night, his kerosene heater merely taking the edge off. Acton walked over to the only cabinet with a lock in the entire camp, his pulse already racing. What they had found was remarkable. He had, of course, heard of the crystal skulls, the most famous of which, the Mitchell-Hedges skull, was on display at the Smithsonian.

And as far as he knew, they were all fake.

Testing had shown they were carved by nineteenth-century European craftsmen, then sold off as Aztec, Incan, or Mayan relics to unsuspecting collectors. There were rumors of testing at Hewlett-Packard that had confirmed at least one to be of unknown method of manufacture, though he had never taken the time to determine whether that story was true.

Frankly, he never cared. They were sculptures made by modern man.

Yet their discovery here turned everything on its head.

This carving was found in a temple dug out of the side of a mountain, trapped for a minimum of five hundred years, centuries before any European craftsman could have fathomed to create it.

If it weren't for the original discovery that had made this entire dig unique, protected under a tarp nearby until they could arrange for its return to the university, he might jump to the conclusion this crystal sculpture was indeed carved by the ancient Incans. Which had him wondering if the Hewlett-Packard story was true, and how many of the skulls discovered over the years were genuine relics.

Taking out the key, he unlocked the cabinet and carefully pulled out a case from the bottom shelf. Placing it on the lone table, he sat in the only chair and opened the case. Inside was a package, carefully wrapped in cloth. He gently unwrapped it, revealing the translucent life-sized crystal skull. Holding it up to the light, he gently caressed the smooth cranium.

"It's beautiful," gushed Robbie. He had returned earlier in the day, and this was the first chance he had had to see the skull since its discovery. Acton had sworn him to secrecy, so he wasn't even allowed to talk about it with the other students on the dig. After the evening campfire had broken up, where they ritually collected together and discussed the day's discoveries, Robbie had pretended to need to talk to him about something, so as not to raise suspicions. Acton saw through his intentions, but indulged his young protégé.

"Yes, it is." Acton rotated the skull, the light from the gas lantern reflecting off the crystal, casting a breathtaking display of ever changing colors and iridescent shapes on the plywood walls.

"Can I hold it?"

Acton handed it to him, and Robbie carefully took it with both hands, holding it up to the light. Brilliant shades of red, orange, and yellow, resembling a stunning sunset, collected in the eyes, the design of the crystal making it appear as if it were staring directly at him. Robbie shuddered. He handed it back to his professor, slightly shaken.

"Are you okay?"

Robbie nodded unconvincingly. "Yeah, just a little creeped out, that's all. I can see why Garcia flipped out when he first saw it."

Acton agreed. "Yes, it can be very unsettling in the right light. It was probably used by ancient priests to instill fear in their subjects." He carefully placed it back in the case then locked it in his cabinet.

"I have no doubt it worked." Robbie rose. "I'm going to go relieve Paul at the cave."

"Okay, if Sandy doesn't relieve you in two hours, go get him. You know he's got a habit of sleeping through his alarm."

Robbie smiled. "After seeing that thing, I don't think I'll be able to sleep for a while." He opened the door and stepped outside. "Good night, Professor."

"Good night, Robbie." Acton closed the door behind him, then lay down on his cot. He didn't think he'd get any sleep, either. As he tossed and turned, trying to get comfortable, he became increasingly frustrated as he sought to settle his jumbled mind. He couldn't stop thinking about their two discoveries and what they meant. The first turned modern thinking of ancient Incan contact on its ear, the other was an interesting curiosity, which would set the conspiracy theorists aflutter.

This is why I became an archaeologist!

He sat up, realizing there was no way he was getting to sleep while his mind refused to relax. He reached over to his Coleman lamp and turned up the gas. The cabin flooded with light, his belongings casting eerie shadows on the plywood walls. He climbed out of his sleeping bag, shook out his boots to rid them of unwanted visitors that might have crawled in, then put them on. He unlocked the cabinet, removing the case. He lifted the lid when a noise outside made him pause. Carefully closing the case, he turned down the light and approached the door.

Niner, designated Overseer for the mission, quickly set up his weapon while his spotter checked the camp below and completed his range card. The Chinook had dropped them off about a mile from here, and they had double-timed it into position, a grueling run with the heavy Ghillie suits they wore, designed to make them nearly undetectable to the enemy. Each was customized by the operator to their own liking, since there was the potential of spending hours or days in these outfits—someone else's idea of a one-size-fits-all suit didn't cut it. When they had neared the top of the hill, they had hit the ground and crawled the rest of the way, the extra canvas in the front of the suits protecting them from the hard rock and dried brush underneath, and now, less than a minute after arriving, the Unit's best sniper team was ready.

Niner glanced at his spotter, Sergeant Gerry "Jimmy Olsen" Hudson. "You set?"

"Yup." Jimmy had earned his nickname when the team found out he had been editor of his school newspaper. Red started calling him Jimmy Olsen, and the name stuck. Niner knew he wished they could have chosen another Superman character, though when Spaz joined the Unit, Jimmy had thanked his lucky stars.

Niner activated his comms. "Overseer in position, over." He surveyed the camp through the scope on his rifle, Jimmy doing the same through his finder. They were far enough from the camp that any shot would reverberate through the valley below, making them almost impossible to locate.

Several cabins were clumped together not far from a ring of tents. A dig site, cordoned off about three hundred feet south, had Niner confused as to its purpose.

Are they searching for something?

Jimmy filled the details in on his range card when a burst of static through the comms was followed by the go-ahead from Dawson. "Overseer, Zero-One, proceed, over."

"Roger that, Zero-One, Overseer beginning to oversee!" Niner flashed a grin at Jimmy then they both peered through their scopes, readying for the first target.

"Two targets, Target One, Sector A from TRP I right fifty add forty," said Jimmy rapidly in a harsh whisper as he looked through his finder.

Niner shifted slightly. "Roger, Sector A, from TRP I right fifty add forty."

"Single target, dark fatigues, smoking cigarette, carrying AK."

"Roger, single target, dark fatigues, smoking cigarette, carrying AK," repeated Niner as he searched for the target through the scope of his M24A2 SWS Sniper Weapon System. He located the target as the man stamped out the cigarette. "Target One identified. I have two mils crotch to head, confirm."

"Roger, two mils crotch to head, dial five-hundred on the gun."

Niner adjusted his weapon. "Roger, five-hundred on the gun, indexed."

"Wind left to right, three miles-per-hour, hold one-eighth mil left."

"Roger, wind left to right, three miles-per-hour, hold one-eighth mil left." Niner dialed the final setting. He gently squeezed the trigger, the recoil hammering into his shoulder, the ground vibrating from the shot.

I love that feeling!

The target collapsed in a heap and Niner smiled. "Broke one-eighth mil left."

"Center hit, stand by."

"Roger, center hit, standing by," acknowledged Niner as he waited for the next target from his spotter.

"Target two, Sector B, from TRP I left sixty add twenty."

Acton peered out the door to see what it was that had drawn

his attention. He scanned the camp and didn't see anything out of order except one of the damned guards asleep on the job. Giggling emanated from one of the tents, apparently some extra-curricular activity going on in the shadow of the Andes. Several fires from earlier in the evening were now smoldering embers, wisps of smoke rising into the night sky. He turned to the other end of the camp where a guard should be stationed. At first, he didn't see him, but a moment later spotted him walking along the perimeter, smoking a cigarette. Acton breathed a sigh of relief and was about to go wake up the other guard when the one he was watching dropped to the ground in a heap.

Then he heard the rotors of a chopper.

Staring at the night sky, he spotted the silhouette of a helicopter clear the rise to the south, obviously coming in for a landing. He opened his mouth to shout a warning to his students, but stopped, realizing all he would do is create a panic. His National Guard training and Gulf War I experience told him the guards had been eliminated by a sniper, which meant they were under observation right now. Screaming kids running around the camp were likely to get shot, but if they were rounded up peacefully from their tents, they might survive the night.

And there was one last hope.

If he could draw their attackers after *him*, his students might be ignored.

There was only one reason they had come—the skull. Between the corrupt police and the various rebel factions little more than gangs, plenty would stop at nothing, including killing, to get their hands on something of value. That was why he had given strict orders to tell no one about their discovery.

Someone had obviously not followed them.

So he ran, skull in hand, hoping the sniper might spot his escape and direct their comrades after him. He couldn't care less what happened to him, all he cared about were the students who had come with him, who had trusted him to keep them safe. If these criminals followed him, he might be able to buy their freedom with the crystal skull, but he needed to hide it first, otherwise they would just take it and kill them all.

As he sprinted away from his cabin, he figured the best

place to lead them was the cave where the skull had been found. Behind the hole Garcia had dug, had been a small chamber that led into a much larger one. If he led them in there, they might have a chance. He took the long way to the entrance, a winding path unfortunately shielded by brush and scattered trees. Peering down at the camp, he spotted the attackers setting up a perimeter as four of them raced to his cabin.

They didn't see you leave!

He prepared to yell, to draw their attention as he approached the cave, when he saw Robbie and cursed, having forgotten he had sent the boy to guard the entrance. He was sitting on the ground, leaning against a rock, sound asleep.

Won't be able to sleep for a while, huh?

Acton had wanted one of his own he could trust to make sure no one else, especially one of the hired guards, sneaked into the cave searching for more valuables. Now he wished the boy was asleep in his tent below, but it was too late. He bent over and shook Robbie's shoulder, his presence forcing Acton to reevaluate his hastily laid plans.

Robbie nearly jumped out of his skin. He removed his iPod ear buds, his eyes wide. "Professor, what's wrong? I didn't hear you coming."

Acton helped Robbie to his feet. "I thought you were asleep."

Robbie shook his head. "You know me, Professor, I can't live without my tunes!"

Acton cut him off. "Listen, the guards are dead, and a chopper just landed in the camp. I think they're here for the skull. Come with me."

They ran inside the cave, and once far enough in that he felt safe the flashlights wouldn't be seen from outside, he turned his on, and Robbie did as well.

"A chopper? Do you mean military? Whose?" asked Robbie as he ran behind Acton, his flashlight bouncing off the walls.

"I don't know. Rebels, Peruvian police. Definitely professional and well-equipped." Acton stepped through the hole and into the first chamber. It was cubic, about ten by ten by ten. The walls, as well as the floor and ceiling, were made of uniform tiles. Some of the ceiling tiles that had fallen centuries before, lay broken on the floor. In the center was a tall, narrow altar atop which the skull had been discovered.

"Why don't we just hide the skull and go back out? They'll never think to look in here."

"Because if they don't get what they want, they'll probably kill us. They've already killed the guards, and we've seen before where camps have been wiped out just so there are no witnesses." Acton grabbed Robbie by the shirt to get him moving again. "That's why I gave strict orders to tell no one about this. It's too dangerous." Acton noticed Robbie's face turn gray as if he were about to vomit. "What's wrong?"

Robbie hesitated. "It's my fault. I told my brother, John. He must have told someone."

Acton shook his head. "I doubt it, not unless he knows some Peruvian police or paramilitaries."

"Wh-what are we going to do?"

Acton frowned as his mind raced, realizing that a return to the original plan was in order, the skull still the best leverage they had. He would prefer it if Robbie weren't here, but he was, and it was too late to change that. Sending him back outside could lead him straight into the hands of their attackers. "We need to have them focus on us, and the skull is the only leverage we've got."

Robbie stopped. "Focus on us? Are you nuts?"

"I'm hoping they spotted us coming in here. If they did, they might ignore the others, then we can use the skull to negotiate for our freedom."

Acton moved to what had once been a hidden cache in the floor, and placed the case inside. "Give me a hand. We need to hide this." Together, he and Robbie moved a large tile, pried away earlier in the day, back over a hole in the floor discovered accidentally when he dropped a canteen, the hollow sound underneath demanding further exploration.

In place, Acton stood, shining the flashlight over the tile, making sure there was no evidence of their hiding spot. Satisfied, he turned to Robbie. "Stay here."

"Wh-where are you going?"

"I'm going to go talk to them."

Dawson and Mickey searched the cabin while two of the team stood watch outside. Dawson flipped over the cot as

Mickey tipped the cabinet over to see if anything was underneath. A complete search for Acton and the package yielded nothing. Dawson radioed his other men. "Bravo Team, Zero-One. Does anyone have eyes on the target, over?" A string of "negatives" replied. "Start rounding everyone up for interrogation, and send video to Control. Zero-One, out."

He switched his comms channel. "Control, Zero-One. Come in, over."

"Zero-One, Control. Go ahead, over."

"Control, package and target not located. Do you have anything from the UAV, over?"

"Negative, Zero-One. UAV malfunctioned as op began, replacement has just arrived. All vehicles still accounted for, and infrared shows nothing outside the camp. Your target is still on site, over."

Dawson kicked the cot again in frustration. "Copy that, Control. Beginning interrogations, over."

A different voice replied, the words sending shivers up and down his spine. "Zero-One, Control Actual. Targets are confirmed on the Termination List. Eliminate when interrogations complete, over."

Shit. This isn't going to be pretty.

"Roger that, Control Actual. Zero-One, out." Dawson stepped out of the cabin to begin the grim task ahead of him.

THE PROTOCOL

London, England

In a dimly lit, underground room on Fleet Street in downtown Old London, twelve people sat at a long, oval-shaped marble table facing a series of integrated displays mounted on the wall. Six high back leather chairs lined either side of the table with a thirteenth at the head. Behind that chair, a large symbol had been carved into a slate wall—two thin horizontal lines on top of each other with a third, thicker and heavier line below, curved slightly upward.

In the chair at the end of the table sat a tall, lean man with silver hair. He calmly puffed on his 1937 Cuban La Carona cigar as the operation unfolded in front of him. The unique aroma of the tobacco from Cuba's Veulta Abajo, a district that is to cigars what Bordeaux and Burgundy are to fine wines, filled the air. Eleven of the twelve other chairs were occupied with people in various levels of excitement.

"If they do recover it, what do we do?" one of them asked.

"You know what we do. We implement The Protocol once again," answered another.

"The Protocol, isn't that a little bit of an overreaction?"

"Maybe, but we've kept the plans current."

"But we don't know their intent."

"What the hell are you talking about? Of course we know their intent. Remember who we're dealing with. This is the same tosser—"

The Proconsul leaned forward. "We are the Triarii!" his booming voice grabbing everyone's attention, spinning them from the monitors. "Just as our forefathers did for generations, we swore an oath to do whatever it takes to prevent what may happen if they do successfully recover it. The Protocol may not have been executed in our memory, but if it is to be, then it shall be. No matter what the cost to us, or to those who get in our way!"

On the screen, one of those being interrogated fell to the ground, a green pool of infrared blood forming beside the body.

41

Andes Mountains, Peru

Mickey glanced at the crumpled body at his feet, his face revealing no emotion.

My God, he's young!

He looked away, turning his attention to the other prisoners. The rest of the team were redeployed to hold the perimeter, leaving Red, Spaz, and himself, to stand guard as Dawson interrogated the prisoners behind one of the cabins. Mickey had been on dozens of missions, killed at least as many terrorists during his short time with Delta, and many had been even younger than these.

But this was the first time they were Americans.

It shouldn't make a difference, yet it did. These were the very people they were supposed to be protecting, not killing. But domestic terrorism was a growing problem, mostly with Muslim converts, though Timothy McVeigh was American and Christian—and he hated his country enough to take 168 innocent souls.

He glanced at Spaz and could see he was troubled too. They all were, even Dawson. He could tell by the way he was talking, that he hated what he was doing, and Mickey knew him well enough already to know Dawson was doing the dirty work so none of them would have to live with it afterward.

He'll suffer the nightmares.

Though Dawson might suffer the most, the rest of them witnessing this massacre wouldn't rest easily either. When they had taken the pictures of the prisoners and transmitted them to Control, he had been surprised by how quickly the orders had come back to eliminate them, as if they had already known who was there.

Or they didn't care who was here, they just wanted them dead.

It had him wondering what the hell the item was that these terrorists had stolen, and how important it must be. Dawson was right to not tell him when he had asked what it was—it was none of his business. And if it were hush-hush enough to kill all these American terrorists without a trial, it was best he didn't know.

Dawson barked at another of the prisoners. "Where's James Acton?" he shouted at the next one, crying and staring at her fallen friend. "Where is he?" He pressed his gun against her forehead.

"I don't know! I don't know!" she cried. "Please God, don't let them kill me!" She fell to her knees and tried to hug Dawson's legs. "Please! I have a child!"

Dawson kicked her onto her back and straddled her. "And so did some of the guards you killed." He placed a bullet between her eyes.

Mickey turned away again, noticing Red and Spaz both had their backs to the proceedings, their eyes scanning the surrounding area. He wondered if their prisoners knew they were dead regardless of whether they talked. He had to admire their dedication. To watch your friends die beside you, and still not answer the simple question of where their leader was hiding, showed a loyalty he had rarely seen. Loyalty to one's God or country wasn't unusual, but to a leader? It was rare. Even Osama's men spilled pretty quickly for the most part.

"If someone doesn't start talking, you're all dead," said Dawson calmly. Mickey turned back, and Dawson pointed to the injured Peruvian. Mickey pulled him out of the group and shoved him to the ground at Dawson's feet. "Where is Acton?"

"I-I do not know!"

Dawson kneeled in front of the trembling man and put his hand on his shoulder. "What's your name?"

"G-Garcia."

"Tell me, Garcia, where *could* he be hiding?"

"I do not know, I swear to God I do not know! Dios mio salvame!"

"Kill him." Dawson rose to his feet, motioning to Mickey. Mickey had learned the hard way what could happen if he hesitated to carry out orders. When an order was given, there was no time to think it over, no debate in whether you should carry it out. An order should be followed immediately in combat situations where moments could mean the difference between life and death. If you trusted your commander, you had to trust the orders were legal, and they were in the best interest of the mission.

And he trusted Dawson implicitly.

He walked over to Garcia and raised his weapon, catching the look from Dawson indicating he wasn't to shoot until ordered to.

"The cave!"

Dawson spun back toward Garcia and motioned for Mickey to stop. "What cave?"

Garcia pointed up the hill, stammering. "He could be in the cave!"

Mickey looked up to where he was pointing and could barely make out the entrance. Dawson gestured at him and Spaz. "Check it out."

Acton watched in horror as his students were murdered, one by one. He fought the urge to vomit, as well as the urge to race down into the camp and try to save them. It was no use. These people were here to kill them all. Even if he tried to negotiate for their lives with the crystal skull, they would still kill them, for it was too late. Unspeakable crimes had already been committed, and witnesses couldn't be left.

He closed his eyes, saying a silent prayer, when he heard Garcia's voice cry out. He looked and saw their attackers turn toward the cave entrance. He ducked back inside, then sprinted as fast as he could toward where he had left Robbie.

"What's going on? I thought I heard gunfire."

Acton debated telling the young man what had just happened, and decided he deserved the truth. "They're killing everyone. We need to hide."

Robbie's eyes shot wide as Acton hauled him into the second chamber where they had hidden the skull. He pointed behind the altar that stood in the middle, the only structure in the room. "Turn off your flashlight and just stay quiet. They might not know we're here."

It was a lie, but Robbie's breaths were coming faster and faster as panic set in, and he had to somehow calm him, the boy continually muttering, "It's my fault, it's my fault."

Acton picked up the pickaxe and turned off his flashlight, joining Robbie behind the altar.

Something echoed through the chamber, his heart joining the race Robbie's was already in.

Footsteps.

"Quiet!" he said in a harsh whisper. "They're coming."

Acton heard Robbie slap his hands over his mouth to quiet himself, Acton's own heart pounding so hard he was sure anyone listening carefully would hear it. He peered around the altar and spotted a shaft of light from a rifle-mounted tactical flashlight, as it shone into the room. The attacker entered the chamber cautiously, aiming his weapon as he searched for them.

Suddenly Robbie jumped out from behind the altar before Acton could stop him.

"I surrender!"

The man aimed his weapon at him, training the light on his face. "Where's Acton?"

Robbie gulped. "H-he's not here. He left for Lima when he heard you coming."

"Bullshit!" was the barked reply. "All of the vehicles are accounted for. Where is he?"

Robbie held his hands up in front of him, shielding his eyes from the light as Acton desperately thought of some way to rescue his foolish but brave pupil.

"He didn't take a Jeep, he took one of the horses!" cried Robbie as the gun was pointed at his head.

There was a pause, then the cold reply. "You don't have any horses." A sharp report of a single shot roared through the confined space. Robbie crumpled to the floor, his head hitting the ground, facing Acton, the tactical light shining on his face revealing his still open eyes as they stared at his professor, his protector, blood trickling from the head wound.

Rage surged through Acton. Knowing he was going to die, he gripped the pickaxe tightly and came out from behind the altar with a roar. He swung the axe high around as he did, and before his target could react, the axe had buried deep in his thigh. The man screamed out in pain and collapsed. Acton used his foot to push him away from the blade so he could remove it for another swing. He swung again, this time at the man's head, but as he did, his opponent turned to avoid the blow, the axe instead broadsiding him, knocking him out cold, and leaving a panting Acton straddling his opponent's body.

"Mickey!"

Acton jerked his head toward the voice. Someone else was running toward the chamber. Grabbing the now prone man's weapon, he ran to the entrance of the room. As soon as he spotted the man's partner, he opened fire, hitting him in the stomach. He went down.

There'll be more.

Death awaited him if he left the cave, so he made a split-second decision.

He snatched two grenades off the belt of the unconscious man and ran to the entrance of the chamber. Lights were moving at the mouth of the cave now. Pulling the pins, he threw them toward the entrance, then ran back behind the altar and waited.

The resulting explosion rocked the room. Acton had covered his ears, yet hadn't been prepared for the volume resulting from the confined space. He was disoriented momentarily, then slowly regained his bearings, struggling to his feet. He stumbled back to the entrance and stared down the shaft. It was blocked, the cave collapsed.

He was safe.

Until the oxygen runs out.

Dawson heard the gunfire then explosion, turning in time to see a puff of debris spew from the cave entrance. If he had any doubts a moment ago, they were gone. Innocent people didn't have guns and grenades to fight back with.

Using hand signals, he directed the rest of his team to the cave as he stood guard over the terrorists, tensing when Red reported. "Zero-One, Zero-Two. The cave has collapsed. No sign of our people. We're going to need some equipment to get through."

Dawson frowned. "Copy that. Stand by." He switched channels. "Control, Zero-One, come in, over."

"Zero-One, Control here, go ahead, over."

"Control, we believe the subject is either terminated or trapped inside a cave. It will take some time to clear the debris to confirm. We have two men missing, presumed on the other side. Request permission to begin rescue operation, over."

"Negative, Zero-One. A supply truck is due at the camp in an hour, and we can't risk you being seen by the locals. The package will be safe in the cave if Acton has it with him. Once the area is clear again, we will send you back with the proper equipment, over."

Dawson was about to object when another voice cut in over the comms.

"To hell with the locals!"

Dawson recognized it as Control Actual, the real man behind the mission, the other voice merely somebody in an ops center. This was the man who had ordered the deaths of the terrorists now at his feet, several more awaiting their fate. The calmer voice responded.

"Sir, with all due respect, if our guys are caught there, it could create an international incident. Right now, they will execute their orders and make it look like a rebel raid. Nothing will point back to us."

There was a pause as Dawson kept his expression free of the shock he was feeling. To hear this type of argument over the comms was unheard of. It was clear to him Control Actual was not in the same room as the Ops people, and also had no experience in proper comms procedure.

"Zero-One, Control Actual. Execute the terrorists then return to base, over."

"Roger that, Control, Zero-One, out."

As he turned to fulfill his final orders, Control Actual's voice erupted from his earpiece, as if the man were whispering heavily into the mic. "All these years of searching, we're closer than we've ever been, and now we're stopped by a supply truck?"

Dawson turned his back to the prisoners, his eyes narrowing. "Control, Zero-One. I didn't copy that, over?"

"Shit!" was the response. "Disregard that, just follow your orders. Control, out."

There's definitely something I'm not being told.

He turned back to the prisoners, their eyes staring up at him, pleading. He shoved the emotions aside, his heart shouting at him to not follow through, but his disciplined mind was winning out. As it should. The orders were legal, the Termination List valid, the targets on it. These innocent looking prisoners were actually domestic terrorists training to kill his—and their—fellow Americans, and had shown no mercy when they executed the four Armed Forces members guarding the DARPA package.

This is for you.

He quickly placed a single bullet in the heads of the remaining prisoners, then radioed his men to rendezvous at the rally point for pick up. Red ran up to him and came to a stop, eying the crumpled bodies. Dawson stared his old friend in the eyes. "Control gave the orders. They were all on the list."

Red nodded, saying nothing, the look on his face mirroring the confusion swirling through his own mind.

These kids didn't act like enemy combatants.

The team, less Niner and Jimmy still on station, and Mickey and Spaz still trapped in the cave, boarded the chopper in silence. Minutes later, the sniper team was retrieved, and they were racing toward the coast and their ship sitting in international waters. Nobody was speaking, nobody was making eye contact with anyone else. They were all disturbed by what had happened, and about leaving their comrades behind.

"There's a civilian supply truck arriving in less than an hour, so we were ordered out," he said to the group, none privy to his conversation with Control. "We'll be heading back with the proper equipment as soon as the area is clear. We'll dig them out and get them home in no time."

His words were meant to be reassuring, but Mickey and Spaz were only part of what was troubling the men. It was the same thing troubling him. The kids? Terrorists? He didn't know what to call them. All he knew was they hadn't acted like terrorists—they had acted like scared, innocent young men and women.

Then again, so had countless terrorists he had encountered over the years when they knew they were going to die for their crimes.

Control had said they were on the Termination List, and that was reserved for the worst of the worst, so he had followed his orders. There was no reason not to, and with the gunfire and explosion in the cave, and loss of communication with two of his men, somebody was willing to fight back.

Perhaps Acton was the only real terrorist?

It pissed him off that the bastard responsible for all these young deaths was probably the only one to survive their assault.

If I ever get my hands on you, you're dead.

Andes Mountains, Peru

Acton aimed the tactical light of the liberated weapon around the chamber, settling on one of the portable battery-powered floodlights used earlier when exploring. Flipping the power switch, the chamber flooded with light, momentarily blinding him. Blinking rapidly, his eyes slowly adjusted, then he checked to see if the soldier was still unconscious before stripping him of his weapons and communications gear. He bound the man's hands and feet with plastic ties he found on the soldier's utility belt, then inspected the leg wound, treating it with the man's med kit.

As he tore open the man's pants to gain access to the wound, he had mixed feelings. He had watched as several of his students were murdered, and he was certain the rest were now dead. And this man had killed Robbie in cold blood—unarmed, surrendering.

Why? All because of that stupid skull?

But the man, clearly a soldier, had asked for *him*.

"Where's Acton?"

If they were truly after the crystal skull, wouldn't he have asked, "Where's the skull?" or "Where is it?"

No, for some reason they were after *him*. And that made no sense. He wasn't special, wasn't worth any money to ransom, and had been here for weeks. It was no coincidence these soldiers had arrived after the skull had been found.

But why? Why kill kids over a crystal sculpture?

He poured iodine over the wound, causing his patient to come to with a gasp. The man struggled against his bonds and Acton pushed his chest into the floor. "Take it easy, you've got quite the hole in your leg, and a nasty gash on your head as well."

"What happened?" asked the man, still confused as to the situation.

"I sealed the cave. Your friends are going to take a long time to get to you. Mickey, is it?" He eyed the man's ears.

Must be.

"Who are you and why are you here?" He was answered by a glare. "Not going to talk, huh? So be it." He applied a pressure bandage to the leg wound then poured more iodine on the head wound. Dressing it, he decided against giving the man painkillers.

Let him suffer.

Finished, he searched for markings on the uniform. Nothing. He picked up the sidearm and removed the magazine. Fully loaded, save the bullet that had killed Robbie. Reinserting the mag, he cocked the weapon and pointed it at Mickey's head. "Ready to talk now?"

Mickey remained silent.

"I'm not afraid to use this, and, yes, I know *how*. I was in the National Guard when I was younger, learned how to fire all kinds of neat toys." He stared down at his prisoner. "No, you black ops boys don't talk. Too bad." He raised the gun and brought the butt down on Mickey's head hard enough to knock him out cold again.

Now to find a way out of here.

He returned to the cave entrance and inspected the debris. It would take him hours to dig through, and he didn't know what was on the other side.

Time to Indiana Jones it.

He picked the axe up from the floor and tore the sleeve off his shirt, wrapping it around the pick. Next, he took a lighter from the soldier's utility belt, lit the shirt, and held it out in front of him.

No fuel, so it won't last long.

He approached the far end of the chamber and held the torch up to the wall. Carefully watching the flame for any movements from wind, he slowly made his way across the wall. Nothing. He came back along the bottom of the wall, and halfway across, the flame whipped and crackled as it changed direction. He smiled, air blowing from somewhere under the floor the only thing that could cause that.

He moved the torch along farther, and it returned to normal. Sweeping the flame slowly around the stone seams, he didn't see anything. Examining the floor, he spotted a crack. He moved the flame over it, and the torch sputtered again. Then it went out.

Dammit!

He reached into his belt and pulled out his flashlight. Turning it on, he shone it down at the crack.

It must be another hollowed out floor section!

He ran back into the other chamber and grabbed the prybar used to remove the stone tile earlier in the day.

Jamming it into the groove in the floor, he leaned on top of it. It took all of his weight to get it to lift, though once it did, he worked the prybar further under the stone. He then kneeled on the bar, and the stone rose up, allowing him to swing it out of place with his hands. Sweating, he collapsed backward on the floor and panted for several minutes before shining the flashlight into the hole and sticking his head in.

Definitely not a hiding place. This is a tunnel!

He took the prybar, retrieved the case containing the skull, and checked one last time on his prisoner.

He'll survive. Bastard.

He lowered into the tunnel, then struggled to pull the cover stone back in place and conceal his means of escape. The tunnel was dank, dark, and grown over with centuries of roots. Lined with the same tiles as the chambers, some had collapsed in, forcing him to dig and tear his way through, pushing forward with the flashlight shoved out in front of him several feet at a time. After what felt like well over an hour, he came to a collapsed section and paused.

What the hell do I do now?

He glanced back and could see nothing, his entrance sealed, blocking any light, then looked forward again. If the tunnel continued past the collapsed portion, then the tiles might continue only a foot or two beyond the blockage. And if the tunnel were to end, then it should end in another chamber, or perhaps even outside.

He shoved the prybar through the damp soil and heard a noise that had him freeze. Cocking his ear, he tried to place the sound, yet couldn't. He pulled the prybar out, and for a split-second, he could have sworn he saw a shaft of light. He turned off his flashlight, drowning him in the pitch black of his potential tomb, then thrust the prybar through again. He quickly pulled it out, his eye near the hole, and a grin spread as indeed sunlight was momentarily visible until the soil collapsed in again.

He turned the flashlight back on and dug at the dirt, pushing it to his sides as he inched forward, pulling the case with the skull on one side, the flashlight and prybar on the other. Reaching forward with his hands, he pulled fistfuls of dirt and roots, there no evidence of tiles here to support the narrow passage. Finally, he broke through with his right hand, the immediate sensation of fresh, crisp mountain air on

51

his damp, dirt covered hand, instantly recognizable.

With his heart thumping from excitement and exhaustion, he rapidly clawed the final two feet, shoving the case out the hole, then pushing his head out into the sunlight. His ears filled with the sounds of nature absent in his confined space, the only other sounds that of the rocks and dirt tumbling down the side of the hill toward the camp below. He froze, realizing their attackers might still be nearby. Scanning the area, he saw no movement, so pulled forward the final few feet. The slope was loose, and with a yelp, he spilled down the steep grade, head over heels, finally sliding the last dozen feet on his back, feet first.

He froze, knowing full well anyone within several hundred feet would have heard his descent. A slight breeze swept across the camp, gently swaying the low brush, the only sounds the chirping of the birds and the flapping of the canvas on the tents. If their attackers were here, they were hidden and quiet.

Dusting off, he made his way into the eerily silent camp. The bodies of five of his grad students lay in the center, along with Garcia. Each had a bullet in the head. His chest tightened, and the muscles in his body slackened, his hands dropping the forgotten case and prybar.

My God, what have I done?

He collapsed to his knees and sobbed, covering his face, then grabbing the back of his head as he doubled over, fighting the urge to vomit. This was his fault, of that there was no doubt. His dean and best friend, Gregory Milton, had told him it was too dangerous an area, but Acton had convinced him he was wrong, that the area was too remote for there to be trouble. Milton had given in as he usually did, not out of weakness, but out of trust in his friend.

This time Milton had been right.

I was too pigheaded to listen. I should never have brought them here.

The gnashing of gears and the roar of a diesel engine caused Acton to leap to his feet and bolt for cover. He stared at the far end of the camp and watched the supply truck lumber around the bend of the only road that led to civilization. When the driver came into sight, he honked his horn several times and waved out of the window as he did twice a week.

Acton emerged from behind the cabin and ran to the

body of his oldest grad student, Jason. He pulled his wallet out of his pants, grabbed the case with the skull, then ran to the truck as it stuttered to a stop.

"Good morning, Professor," hailed the driver, opening his door. "Sorry I am late."

Acton sprinted toward the truck. "Don't get out!" The driver stopped halfway out of the cab as Acton rounded the truck and jumped in the other side. "Let's go, now!"

"Si, señor." The confused driver returned to his seat and closed the door, putting the still running truck back into gear. "What is wrong, Professor?"

"They're all dead," muttered Acton. "They killed them all."

"Who?" The driver's face clouded in fear as his gaze darted to his mirrors to see if they were being followed.

"I don't know. Rebels probably," lied Acton. He knew damned well who had done it.

But why would my own government kill for an ancient artifact?

Mickey sat propped against the altar, watching as the batteries powering the floodlights failed, the light gradually dimming as the hours passed. The sharp pain in his leg had eased to a dull throb, and now he had no feeling at all. The bleeding appeared to have stopped, thanks to Acton. Every fifteen minutes he tried his radio again, to no avail. The hole in the floor Acton had used to escape was only ten feet away, the tile slightly out of alignment, but he was too weak to make the attempt. His team wouldn't leave him behind, and it was only a matter of time before they came for him.

In the meantime, he had plenty of opportunity to think. At first, it had been spent evaluating his surroundings, figuring out if he could go out the same way Acton had appeared to. The fact he hadn't returned, suggested he had escaped successfully. He was of mixed feelings on the matter. If it weren't for Acton having attacked him, he wouldn't be where he was. However, if it weren't for him, he'd be dead now. He had treated his wound expertly, and stopped the bleeding.

The guys will pick him up outside.

For the first few hours, he had stared at the corpse of Acton's partner. The eyes were still opened, and from his position against the altar, they seemed like they were staring at him. He had finally tired of this at one point, and struggled over to where the body lay, and closed the eyes. This effort had exhausted him, and he had been forced to lie beside the body for some time while he caught his breath.

This was just a kid.

Yet that didn't mean much nowadays. Kids were as likely to be terrorists as anyone else, and this kid wasn't much younger than he was. But if Acton was such a bad guy, why had he bothered with saving the life of his enemy? Something wasn't ringing true here. When he was in the camp, the only weapons were on the two guards Niner had taken out, and they appeared to be local hires. Shouldn't the terrorists have been armed? Shouldn't they have at least had weapons in their tents? And why, when they left the helicopter, had they been jumping through what appeared to be an archaeological dig site?

If this was a terrorist training camp, it was the worst equipped one he had seen.

But if these weren't terrorists, then why were they on the Termination List? That list was one of the most carefully vetted the country had. It was one of the few that legally authorized agents of the government to kill on sight, no questions asked.

And he had been on missions where they had indeed done just that.

And they had all left him with a feeling of satisfaction.

Though not this time.

This time something wasn't right, and during the hours of waiting, a pit formed in his stomach as he became convinced they had made a terrible mistake.

His comms crackled. He squawked three times and waited. Three squawks came back at him.

They're close!

About ten minutes later, he heard the scraping of shovels at the cave entrance.

"Anybody in there?"

"Just me!" he tried to yell, only now realizing how parched he was.

"Identify yourself!" commanded the voice.

He tried to reply, but couldn't. A few minutes later, somebody broke through and entered the chamber. He didn't have his weapon. Acton had taken it or hidden it somewhere. A flashlight shone in his face, and he squinted to see who was behind it. A moment later, Red grabbed his shoulder.

"Good to see you, man. We thought you were a goner." He held a canteen up to Mickey's lips. He drank as much as he could without coughing. When he had enough, he pushed it away.

"Spaz?"

Red shook his head. "Dead. We found his body under the rubble. He was shot." Red cut his bindings then helped him up, slinging Mickey's arm over his shoulders. "The target?"

"Not here, he escaped through there hours ago." Mickey pointed to the shifted tile. "You didn't get him?"

"No. But we will."

Mickey nodded, his previous doubts forgotten as he thought of his friend Spaz, dead.

You will be avenged, my friend.

St. Paul's University
St. Paul, Maryland

Gregory Milton's pen tapped on his desk rapidly as his mind raced. He had been Dean of St. Paul's University for four years, and though he loved his job, what he was working on now was one of the lesser enjoyable aspects of it. As he sat in his high back chair, his head against the sumptuous leather, he stared at the oak beam casings in the ceiling, his mind sifting through endless permutations on how to start yet another speech at an alumni dinner without it sounding like all the others.

I hate speeches.

It wasn't that he was scared to talk to a group of people, it was simply that he found it a waste of time. Any information he could convey could also be done in an email, saving untold dollars hosting people just to get even more dollars out of their wallets.

But alumni, with checkbooks, expected to be wined and dined, and made to feel important. Which, unfortunately, they were. Without the alumni, their small university would be far humbler than it already was.

So he soldiered on, trying to pick a clean joke from his head, his preferred crude ones coming out instead.

They'll kick me out of the state for some of those.

He pulled at his thinning hair in frustration when he flinched at the buzzing of the intercom.

"Yes, Rita?"

"Two men here to see you, sir."

"Send them in."

More damned alumni. Time to kiss some ass.

He rose to his feet as his two guests entered. He covered his surprise with a smile. Both were clearly government. Dark suits, ties, shoes, and glasses.

Suits and shoes too cheap to be alumni.

He offered his hand.

"Hello, gentlemen, I'm Dean Milton. Call me Greg." The first agent shook his hand, the other hung back at the door.

"Dean Milton, I'm Special Agent Jasper, and this is Agent Lambert," said the first agent. "We're from the State Department."

"State Department?" Milton motioned toward the chairs in front of his desk as he tensed. State Department meant something foreign. Which meant something must have happened to one of his students while out of the country.

Jim?

His mind was racing to conclusions without any facts.

Stay calm!

"To what do I owe this honor?" he managed, keeping his voice steady.

"It's about the archaeological team you have in Peru." Jasper sat. "I'm afraid there's been an incident."

"Incident?" Milton froze behind his desk, hovering over his chair, his fingers spread across the blotting pad, there more for decoration or the occasional scratch pad for numbers, rather than its original purpose.

Incident. Not accident.

His stomach churned and his mouth filled with bile. He swallowed. "Are they okay?"

Jasper drew a long breath. "I'm afraid not, sir, they're all dead."

"They're dead?" Milton collapsed into his chair, his mind reeling at the news as flashes of his best friend and their years together consumed him, as well as the few but recent memories of the eager students taken on the expedition—an expedition he had said was too dangerous.

Oh, Jim! Why did I let you convince me!

He squeezed the bridge of his nose with his fingers. "All of them? How? How did it happen? When? Who did it?"

"It appears that there was a rebel attack on the camp. There were no survivors. However, Professor James Acton is missing. Have you heard from him?"

"They're all dead?" Milton shook his head, struggling to come to grips with what he had heard. "All of them?"

"Except the professor, sir. Have you heard from him?"

Milton took a moment to compose himself as the agent's words echoed through his head. His students were dead. His best friend was missing, and probably dead as well. No, the agent hadn't said that last part, but that interpretation of events was all he could think of.

Jim!

His eyes glassed over and he removed a handkerchief from his pocket, dabbing them dry. He drew a deep breath and nodded. "Yes, just last week. There was no service where their dig was, so he drove into the city once a week. The expedition was on a shoestring budget, so there was no money for a satellite phone. He would send me a text message each time he was in Lima. It was cheaper than a phone call."

"Did he mention anything unusual in his last message?"

"No, he said the dig was going well, and that there were some interesting finds, ancient Incan I believe."

"Anything in particular?"

"No, nothing." Milton's blood pressure was rising as his frustration level reached critical.

What's with all the damned questions?

"What does any of this have to do with their deaths? I thought you said rebels did this?"

"Just routine questions, sir. If the rebels had thought something of value had been found, it might explain why they raided the camp. As it is, they took all the supplies and vehicles, but not before killing everyone."

Milton placed his forehead in the palm of his hand and massaged his temples. "The families. Have they been notified?"

"Not yet, sir. We can take care of the notifications for you."

Milton shook his head, a lump unlike anything he had felt before, pushing up his throat at the thought of what was to come over the ensuing hours. "No. They were all students here, it should fall on me. The bodies?"

"They'll be arriving in Houston this afternoon. We'll coordinate with the families to have them sent to the appropriate locations." Jasper rose from his seat, retrieving a business card from an inner pocket of his jacket. "Here's my card, sir. If you hear from Professor Acton, please contact us immediately."

"Yes, yes I will." Milton shook his head in disbelief. Jasper placed the card on his desk, then he and his partner left. Milton pushed the button on the intercom.

"Yes, sir?"

"No calls, and cancel all my appointments for the rest of the day."

"Yes, sir. What reason shall I give?"

"J-just do it, Rita!" cried Milton as he turned off the

intercom, his head hitting the blotter as tears flowed, creating tiny puddles on the paper while his shoulders heaved. He pushed his head up from the desk and stared at the two photos he kept on the corner. One, he with his wife and daughter, the second, with his best friend of over twenty years, arms around each other's shoulders as they crossed the finish line of the New York Marathon years ago. As the memories of that day flooded out today's nightmare, he half cried, half laughed, as he recalled having grossly overestimated his own fitness level, forcing Acton to come back and help him the last few miles.

He reached out and pulled the photo closer as the tears poured down his cheeks, his ragged breaths now easing as he forced himself back under control.

He pressed the button for the intercom. "Rita, please bring me the files on the students in Peru."

"Yes, sir," came the voice, subdued from his outburst earlier.

He turned his chair to face the window, clouds filling the sky as rain seemed to be on the horizon.

Please, God, take care of my friend.

Special Agent Jasper climbed into the back of their surveillance van, preparing for a long, uncomfortable wait. While many agents enjoyed stakeouts, he despised them. They were tedious, boring, and after enough hours stuck inside a poorly ventilated van, someone was bound to start launching surreptitious air biscuits then plead ignorance. Yet it was part of the job, and he loved his job, though he hoped one day soon, he'd be promoted out of the field.

He looked at his partner as he closed the doors. "Is it done?"

"Yeah, while you were talking to him. We now have complete audio, video, and electronic surveillance of his office. Any phone call, email, anything, and we'll know it."

"Excellent. Now we wait." Jasper dropped into his seat and put his feet up on the console, closing his eyes and interlocking his fingers over his stomach as Lambert mimicked him.

"You really think he's going to be dumb enough to call?"

Jasper opened his eyes. "Why wouldn't he? This is his school, his best friend from all accounts, and if he's innocent, he's got nothing to hide."

"*If* he's innocent," emphasized Lambert. "Are we sure of that?"

"I hardly think a university professor is going to kill his entire team with automatic weapons, leave dozens of different footprints, and steal his own vehicles."

"Maybe he was in on it, though?"

His underling desperately wanted Acton to be involved in some way, and this conversation would never end unless he threw him a bone. "Perhaps."

Lambert smiled smugly and clasped his hands behind his head. "I thought so."

Jasper sighed and closed his eyes again.

Rookies!

THE PROTOCOL

Lima, Peru

Acton peered around the corner of the dilapidated warehouse. The dock bustled with cranes loading massive containers onto even more massive ships, forklifts and transport trucks moved around in organized chaos, and crew chiefs yelled at their teams in their quest to keep the docked ships in port no longer than necessary. It had taken him hours to get here, his Peruvian driver having abandoned him on the road out of fear of the rebels Acton said had committed the massacre.

On every dig, he placed his passport, credit cards, and a stash of cash, in a local safety deposit box for safekeeping. This time had been no different, and he had retrieved his belongings minutes ago from a local bank. He was now flush with cash and identification, though fewer supplies than he'd like. There had been no time to shop around after he found the ship he now stared at was the only one going in the direction he needed for the rest of the day.

Despite hundreds of people in sight, he figured none would notice him if he acted with purpose. He strode briskly toward the gangplank of the massive container ship he had confirmed was heading to Mexico, and with one final look around, he raced up the stairs. He cringed with each step as the entire structure swayed and scraped against the hull, making a noise that, if it hadn't been for the incredible din coming from the loading docks, would have been heard by everyone. Once at the top, he again scanned the docks for anyone watching, then sprinted between some containers. As he ducked between the towering stacks, two crewmen came around the corner, talking animatedly in a mix of English and what he recognized as Tagalog.

He pressed into the rusted grooves, trying to disappear, his heart hammering harder as they neared. They walked past his hiding place, apparently only interested in their tall tales of the previous night's activities, oblivious to his presence. Finally gone, he breathed a relieved sigh and tried to relax.

Only a few more hours until we leave port.

Once at sea, he would worry about how he would survive. For now, he needed to get out of Peru and back to where he had friends who could help him.

He moved deeper into the maze of containers, then sat on the deck where he was sure he couldn't be seen. He gazed up at the stacks towering above him, the sky barely visible. He said a silent prayer for those he had lost, then turned his attention to the task at hand. He opened his gym bag and surveyed his provisions. Half a dozen bottles of water and two PowerBars.

Three days to Mexico with nothing but your nightmares to keep you company.

The White House
Washington, DC

"William Guthrie, this is Mr. Darbinger, the White House Chief of Staff," said the orientation leader assigned to him, finally introducing him to his boss after a mind blowing two days.

Billy gulped and extended his hand. "It's an honor to meet you, sir."

"Likewise, Mr. Guthrie." Darbinger shook Billy's hand. "I'm not sure if you remember me, but I met you at your father's house about three years ago for his retirement party."

"Of course, sir, I remember." Billy flashed back to that night, desperately trying to remember Darbinger. It had been a whirlwind of disinterest for him, paraded around as the brilliant son who would one day carry on the legacy. It had been the end of an illustrious career for his father, after having served in the Air Force for ten years before turning to politics, first as mayor, state assemblyman, then congressman. His last five years were spent as Speaker of the House, and he had retired when his wife was diagnosed with cancer.

"It was that night I asked your father to have you come work for me when you were old enough." Darbinger regarded Billy closely. "You don't remember that at all, do you?"

Billy blushed and shook his head. "I'm really sorry, sir, but I met so many people that night."

Darbinger laughed. "Don't worry about it. I was a teenager once too." He turned back to the orientation leader. "Get William set up at a desk and make sure he's well looked after." He then turned back to Billy. "If you need anything, feel free to come see me. I told your father I'd look out for you."

"Thank you, sir. I will."

Billy was led to a cubicle and shown the basics, then the orientation leader handed him a ridiculously thick binder to read. "This should take you the rest of the day. It's not to leave the building."

Billy nodded, eyeballing the massive tome, certain it would last him at least a week or two. As he read through the orientation binder, his eyes glazed over and he found himself drifting as the boredom took hold, life at the White House not as exciting as he had assumed.

This is definitely not like the movies.

There was a knock at his cubicle "door" and he flinched in his chair, spinning to see who had interrupted his daydreaming. He recognized the woman, but took a moment to place exactly who and what she was. Once he remembered, he straightened even more in his chair. It was the Chief of Staff's secretary, Sheila Norton

"Hi, William, I've got your first job for you." Sheila flashed a smile and held out a legal-size envelope, "I need you to take this to the president's secretary. Hand it to her personally, and have her sign the receipt."

"Yes, ma'am, right away." Billy jumped out of his chair, taking the manila envelope, and rushed down the hallway. Turning a corner, he ran headlong into Rachel, his fashion critic. He dropped the envelope, and, much to his horror, the cup of Starbucks Café Latte with low-fat skim milk she was carrying, landed right on top of it, spilling its contents.

"You loser! Why don't you watch where you're going?" She picked up the coffee cup and headed to the nearby bathroom to wash off before he could apologize. He retrieved the envelope, his chest tightening at the unfolding disaster, then made a beeline for the men's room to dry it off. Many paper towels later, and several minutes under the hand dryer, were of no use. It was obvious something had spilled on the envelope.

He had to do something, but what, he wasn't sure.

I can't bring the file like this to the president's office!

Panic set in and his breathing increased rapidly. It was still his first week, and he had already screwed up in a huge way. He was about to hide in a bathroom stall until he figured out what to do, when he remembered one of the stops on the intern tour.

The supply room!

He stuffed the file under his sport coat and headed to what he hoped would be his salvation. Finding a matching envelope, he glanced around, then untied the red string holding his now stained one. Inside was a document with several photos clipped to the front. He pulled it out, and was about to put it in the new envelope, when he stopped.

"What the hell is this?" he asked aloud, then quickly checked to make sure no one had heard him. He flipped through the photographs, each of a different person.

They're dead!

His stomach churned. He steadied himself and looked closer. Most had a bullet hole through the head, and all had *Terminated* written across the bottom except the last photo. It showed a man with *Target Status Unknown*. He read the name. *James Acton.* He hurriedly stuffed the photos in the new envelope, realizing he was not supposed to have seen them. His heart raced.

God, please don't let them find out I saw these!

Lesley Darbinger ran his fingers through his hair, then massaged his temple with his thumb as he sat on a couch in the Oval Office, talking to his old friend sitting across from him. "It would be nice, though."

"What?" asked President Jackson.

"To not have to be watching over our shoulders constantly."

Jackson agreed. "Yeah, ten years of hiding in the open. I'm afraid that if this doesn't get resolved before my term is up, they won't hesitate to remove us. They wouldn't dare while I'm in office, though."

"No, *you*, they wouldn't. Me on the other hand…."

Jackson leaned toward his friend. "Don't worry, your position protects you as well. We're too visible to eliminate. Besides, this will be all over soon."

Darbinger nodded. "You know, when you first approached me about stealing the Smithsonian skull, I thought you were mad."

Jackson chuckled. "Yes, but you came around soon enough. You knew it was the right thing to do. The only way to accomplish our goal is to take control of at least three of the skulls." He leaned back and stretched his arms across the back of the couch. "We know from our own history the power of the skulls when brought together. The fire of 1212 was a cleansing fire brought by God. He wants the skulls brought together, and He has chosen us to be His servants."

"Amen." Darbinger hid his discomfort at his friend's increasingly fervent religious beliefs. They had both attended the same church for years, though over the past ten, his friend had let his religion intensely dominate his life. He had taken to praying for guidance on major decisions, much to the annoyance of those around him. Darbinger flipped through the folders sitting beside him, searching for the mission report from Peru. It wasn't there. "Shit, I must have left the report on my desk. I'll go get it. You'll want to read it."

"I'll be here." Jackson rose and returned to his desk. Darbinger headed to his office and rifled through the stack of folders where he thought the missing file should be, but didn't see it. His pulse kicked up a notch, knowing full well if anyone got their hands on that file and leaked it, they would all be going to jail for a long time. He searched his office with more fervor and came up empty.

"Sheila!" His assistant poked her head into his office. "There was a file on my desk, where did it go?"

"I had it brought to the Oval Office just a couple of minutes ago. I figured you wanted it, so I had Billy bring it." Sheila's eyes narrowed. "You didn't get it?"

"No."

"That's odd, he should have been there by now. Do you want me to find him?"

Darbinger's heart sank.

Why did it have to be Billy?

"No, I'll take care of it."

Somewhere on the Pacific

James Acton awoke with a start. He glanced around, looking for what had woken him, but he was alone. It was dawn of the third day. The ship would be arriving in Mexico that afternoon if they were on schedule. He could see the ocean from his vantage point, and they were in a heavy fog, yet the Captain kept the engines at full steam, sounding the horn repeatedly.

Moron.

He checked his supplies, only to reconfirm what he already knew. He was out of water, and had been since early yesterday. The salty air was making him thirsty, and he had finished his supply in half the time he had expected. He needed fresh water, especially since he had to be at his peak when getting off the ship.

Rising from where he had slept, he stretched the kinks out as best he could. He slung his bag containing the case with the skull over his shoulder, and cautiously headed toward the crew tower at the stern of the ship. It took him some time, moving from container to container, careful not to be seen. The chance of any crew being among the containers was slim, but he also had to make sure he wasn't seen from above.

Eventually, he reached the final row, within sight of a tap mounted to the wall he had seen men drink from earlier in the trip. It was tantalizingly close, but also exposed. Opening his bag, he removed two of the empty water bottles. He unscrewed their caps and shoved them into his pocket. With one last glance around, he raced across the open space between the containers and the tap.

He reached the wall without incident, and turned the tap on, placing the first bottle under the stream. The flow seemed impossibly slow, though it was probably his imagination. His heart hammered as he swapped the second for the first, drinking down the filled bottle.

His thirst quenched for the moment, he refilled the first bottle, then turned to leave when a fist slammed him directly on the nose. His eyes watered from the searing pain and he tumbled backward, striking his head on the hard metal deck, darkness overtaking him.

Someone yelled, then Acton reeled from a smack across the cheek. He opened his eyes, the world a blur. He tried to touch the aching spot on his head, but discovered his hands bound to the arms of a flimsy chair.

"You know what we do with stowaways?" yelled the blur in front of him. Acton looked about as his vision cleared, finding himself in a storage room.

More like a garbage room.

Supplies were haphazardly stacked in one corner, the rest of the room littered with various pieces of wood and machine parts. It hadn't seen a broom in years.

Martha'd be pissed.

He recognized his assailant as one of the Filipinos he'd seen earlier. His friend was in the corner staring at the skull. "What is that?" The first one pointed at it. "How much it worth?"

"Nothing," muttered Acton, reading the unmistakable greed in their eyes. "It's just a trinket."

"He's lying." The second man placed the skull on a nearby table and pulled out a long machete. "Now I show him what we do with *lying* stowaways."

His partner laughed and turned his head to look at the skull. Acton had to act fast. Raising his feet off the floor, he kicked the man in both knees, the kneecaps snapping with the blow. The man collapsed, screaming in agony. His partner stared in shock as Acton rose as far as he could in the chair, and propelled himself backward. He slammed hard against the wall, shattering the wood chair into several pieces, freeing his arms.

Acton picked himself up off the floor as the second man came at him with the machete. He ducked to avoid the first swing, and punched the man in the stomach, knocking the wind out of him. As he doubled over, Acton kneed him in the face then pushed him to the ground. Grabbing him by the shirt, he punched the man in the nose several times.

He swiftly bound the now unconscious man and stuffed a rag into his mouth, as the other continued to writhe on the floor. He tied the man's hands, and gagged him as well, before grabbing his case and placing the skull back inside. Putting the case back in his gym bag, he listened at the door, then, hearing nothing, cautiously opened it.

Finding an empty hallway, he made his way along the dark corridor toward what appeared to be natural light coming from a stairwell at the end. He reached the steps and stared up, seeing a door open to the outside and nobody around. As he reached the top of the stairs, an announcement came over the PA system that they would be docking in half an hour. He gingerly touched his head and winced. He would have to evade the crew, as his assailants could be discovered at any moment. Racing across the deck, he again hid among the containers. He pushed as deep into the maze as he could, then sat to rest, closing his eyes for a moment.

And immediately fell asleep, exhaustion and the mild concussion taking over.

He awoke to the foghorn as the ship was towed into dock by the comparatively tiny tugboats. He looked around to make sure he was still alone, then took up a position where he could monitor the gangplank for a chance to escape unseen. It took almost half an hour to dock, but once the all-clear sounded, the crew departed quickly, probably heading directly to the nearest whorehouse to catch or spread some new disease.

And his two attackers were nowhere to be seen.

They must still be tied up.

He took one last look around, then as calmly as he could, walked off the boat, with no one noticing him.

17th Street, Washington, DC

Billy had been trying to forget the events of earlier, but it was no use. His mind was consumed by what he had seen, the photos of the dead people, executed, and the knowledge his own country was involved, his own president. He sat on his couch, staring at the television for hours without watching it, until he finally realized he was starving. He ordered pizza then waited, his feet up on his table, a privilege his mother never allowed him at home, as he watched CNN, distracting himself with new horrors from around the world. Watching the nightly news was a habit his father had drummed into him years ago that he hadn't been able to break, and since he worked at the White House, he felt it was his duty to keep up on current events.

His stomach rumbled. He patted it and checked his watch.

Forty minutes.

Yes, he could have ordered from a thirty-minute pizza place, but quality took time, and a Chicago-style deep-dish pizza was worth the wait.

But forty minutes?

There was a knock at the door. He flew from his seat then gathered himself, trying not to appear too excited. Checking the peephole, he saw the delivery man eying his watch. He counted to three, then opened the door.

"Hello, sir," said the teenager as he handed over the box. "That'll be twelve-fifty."

Billy handed him fifteen bucks. "Keep the change." The kid smiled and took off down the hallway toward the elevator. Billy closed the door, feeling good about the decent tip, the events of earlier rapidly disappearing from his mind, replaced by the aroma of Italian sausage and onions. He sat on the couch, his stomach growling in anticipation. He grabbed the remote to un-mute the television.

And his jaw dropped.

On the screen was a picture of the same man he had seen in the file.

"—developing story. CNN has been able to confirm that Professor James Acton was not among those found dead in Peru. A State Department source is quoted as saying that Acton was not among the

bodies found, and his whereabouts are currently unknown. We will keep you posted—"

He paused the TiVo, the image of the man staring back at him as his face blanched, his pizza forgotten.

St. Paul's University
St. Paul, Maryland

Milton was still in shock from the news of several days before. The phone calls he had made had been the most grueling of his life. He wished he could have notified the families in person, but most of the students who had been killed were from out of state. The nightmares he had experienced the first night had convinced him to not even try sleeping the next two. Every time he shut his eyes, he kept seeing his friend of so many years being killed.

I never should have let him go!

He was exhausted. He took another swig of his double cream, double sugar coffee, the caffeine struggling to keep his systems going. As he shook his head to wake up, the intercom on his desk demanded his attention. Pushing aside the speech he was working on for the memorial service, he pressed the button.

"Yes, Rita?"

"There's a phone call for you, sir, he won't say who he is."

"Take a message, I'm busy." Milton hit the intercom button to end the conversation. A moment later, his cellphone vibrated on his hip. He grabbed it and read the message.

Answer your phone Corky.

He gasped and almost dropped it on the floor when the intercom buzzed again. "Sir, he's really pers—"

"Put him through!" yelped Milton, grabbing for the phone.

"Yes, sir, line one."

He jabbed the button. "This is Dean Milton."

"Hi Greg, it's me, Donald." Milton was confused. Only one person knew him as Corky, an old nickname from their college days together he'd rather forget. And that one person was not named Donald.

It was James Acton.

"Donald?" The voice was Acton's, but he decided he better play along. "Good to hear from you. It's been a long time."

"Too long, my friend. I'd like to meet if you've got the

time."

"Are you in town?" His heart was sprinting now. Something was definitely wrong. "Where can we meet?"

"Remember where we crammed for English Lit finals? Can you meet me there, say eight p.m. tomorrow?"

"Yes, absolutely. Eight p.m."

"Okay, goodbye, old friend."

"Goodbye." Milton hung up and sat back in his chair, confused.

He must have thought someone was listening.

He hit the intercom button. "Rita, cancel all of my appointments for the rest of today and tomorrow." Leaning back in his chair, he closed his eyes as a big smile spread.

Jim's alive!

In a telephone repair van parked just off campus, Agent Lambert nodded. The screen in front of him flashed the confirmation. *98.3% positive match.* "It was Acton all right."

Jasper smiled. "We've got him."

A moment later, snoring rumbled through the speakers.

Somewhere along the Mexican Border

Acton sipped on a water bottle, trying to keep cool, as the car he had hired headed for Nogales in the scorching heat. He had used some of his remaining cash and his near perfect Spanish to take care of a few things, including a ride to the border in a vehicle that redefined the term 'beater.' He adjusted himself for the umpteenth time, seeking comfort in the threadbare back seat, but finally gave up to the spring poking through the cushion. Fortunately, exhaustion won out, and he soon fell into a restless, nightmare-filled sleep.

Visions of his students being tortured, pleading for their lives, watching as their classmates were murdered one by one, tormented him. Robbie trying to save him from the gunman, needlessly dying for his efforts. Of poor Garcia, his crumpled body left in the middle of the camp, never to return to his wife and seven kids.

"I'm sorry!" he cried over and over to visions of his students glaring at him, asking him why he had run and not saved them. Why *he* had survived, and no one else. Acton jerked in his seat, awake. "I'm sorry!"

"Sorry for what, señor?"

Acton looked around him, regaining his bearings. "Where are we?"

"Nogales. We have arrived, señor. The border is just ahead." The driver pointed toward a long lineup of cars.

Acton frowned. He was certain his passport would be on a watchlist, so he couldn't afford to have it scanned at the border crossing. Before he could open his mouth, his driver turned in his seat to face him.

"Perhaps, señor doesn't want to be seen crossing the border?"

How'd he guess?

Acton nodded.

"No problema, señor." The driver smiled broadly, revealing four beautiful teeth. "For a price, I can get you across, no problema."

Acton sighed and pulled out his wallet.

Is it illegal to sneak back into your own country?

New York City, New York

Red shoved the laptop away, clearly pissed. Upon landing stateside, they had seen the reports on every television station about the massacre of American students in Peru, and how their professor, James Acton, was missing.

It didn't match the intel they had been provided by Control, yet once they realized the truth, it fit with what they had seen. Dawson had demanded an explanation from Control, and the explanation had been typical.

"Would it have made a difference?"

"It sure as hell would!" he had replied.

"They were all terrorists, vetted, and on the Termination List. What their educational status was is irrelevant, and would have clouded the situation. If I had told you they were all bricklayers, would it have made a difference? They were terrorists who had killed American soldiers, stolen highly classified materials, and were plotting more killings. The fact they were students was irrelevant. And these were mostly grad students. There were no teenagers here."

The sad thing was that Control was right. It didn't matter who these people were beyond the fact they were murderous terrorists. Yet he was still troubled. Where were the weapons? What was the purpose of the cordoned off section of the camp that looked like something out of Indiana Jones? Why did they act as if they were anything but terrorists?

But then there was Professor James Acton.

It didn't matter if he was an intellectual. He had killed Spaz, severely wounded Mickey, and had acted in anything but an innocent manner. In fact, he and Red were now in a hotel suite near JFK because of Acton's latest actions. They knew from a phone conversation he had earlier, that this was where he was heading—his friend Milton had booked a ticket to New York immediately after the call. They had arrived a few hours ago as an advance team, and had set up a base of operations in a hotel overlooking the airport. The remaining team members were being transported with their equipment by a C17, and would arrive within a couple of hours.

Leaving them lots of time to second guess their mission.

Red folded his arms. "Can I ask you something, off the

record?"

Dawson already didn't like where this was headed, but he and Red had been through too much too many times to deny him at least the privilege of asking the question. It didn't guarantee an answer, however. "Go ahead."

"Off the record…" Red hesitated. "Shit, BD, those were just kids."

Dawson frowned. "You don't think I know that?" Red was about to say something else when Dawson raised a finger to stop him. "We had our orders, and Control confirmed them over the comms during the mission. We follow orders, that's what we do. We can't let age cloud a mission. Remember, they murdered four servicemen."

"I know, but—"

"Remember Yemen?"

"What, when you got hoofed in the balls?"

Dawson allowed himself one chuckle. "Same mission, earlier in it. Who were the hostiles?"

Red nodded. "Kids. Teenagers."

"Exactly. And they had no problem trying to kill us, and we had no problem killing them. And remember nine-eleven? How old were those bastards? Mostly early-twenties? The world is a harsh place, my friend. It's up to us to clean it up a little for Bryson."

Red smiled at the mention of his kid. "I'm never letting him out of the country." His computer beeped at him, demanding his attention. "We've got a hit in the airline reservation system."

"What is it?" Dawson rose from his chair and rounded the table to where Red had several laptops set up.

Red spun one so Dawson could see the display. "Acton just booked a flight from Phoenix to New York, leaving in less than an hour."

"Using his own ID? That's pretty bold. Can you hack the security system and get some eyes on him?"

"Give me a sec." Red's fingers flew over the keyboard, and several minutes later, they were watching the airport security cameras. After a few minutes of scanning, Dawson leaned in and tapped a couple of keys, backing up to a camera angle that had just flipped by.

"There he is." Dawson pointed to the security check lineup. "Zoom in on him."

Red highlighted the image of Acton to enlarge it. They watched him empty his pockets as he went through security. He set the alarm off, and was scanned manually with the wand. Security had him remove his belt and go back through. After he cleared, he put his belt back on then picked up what appeared to be a wallet, watch, and keys. He then walked out of view of the camera.

"Did he check any luggage?"

Red pulled up the baggage claim info in the reservation system. "No, no luggage."

"And he doesn't have a carry-on. Where the hell is the package?" Dawson paced the room. "Backtrack his movements through the airport, see if he handed it off to anyone. We have no idea how big this terrorist cell is, and he could have contacts there."

Red deftly manipulated the camera angles and archival footage to track Acton back from security to the bathroom, the bathroom to the ticket counter, and finally to the taxi drop off outside, where he exited a cab. He wasn't carrying anything the entire time.

"He must have done a handoff to somebody before arriving," said Red.

"Get the ID number off that cab. I want to know if they made any stops along the way, or if the target said anything that might indicate where the package is."

"Roger that." Red hammered at the keyboard, and within minutes, had the number of the cab, the company, and the cabbie's name. Along with the motel he had picked up his last fare at. Red searched a classified database containing the location of nearly every connected camera in the country, and located one across the street from the motel at a bank machine. He pointed at Acton entering the cab, empty-handed. "Maybe he ditched it somewhere?"

"Maybe. Looks like we're going to have to retrace his steps."

Though Acton was at the top of his personal hit list, Dawson's admiration for the man's abilities was growing. He had assumed his opponent was a simple geek professor considering his subject matter, and his weekend warrior status hadn't exactly impressed him, though it was better than what most citizens did. Yet despite his limited experience, he had managed to take out one of his men, wound another, evade capture, and find his way from Peru to Phoenix without being detected.

The man had skills.

And a lot of luck.

Mickey was a lucky hit, and if it weren't for the cave-in, Spaz would have survived. And if they hadn't been ordered out of the area by Control, they would have captured him.

And sent him on to the next damned life.

Yet here stood their target, bold as brass—since there was no way he could know they had been ordered to keep him off the watchlists—getting on a domestic flight, using his own ID, without what appeared to be a care in the world.

Which meant he had done something with the stolen DARPA item that had him certain he was now bulletproof. And he was right. Until they recovered the item, they couldn't kill him.

What would I do?

He racked his brain until something finally clicked. "Can you check the shipping companies to see if they have any packages going from Phoenix using Acton's name?"

"That'll take some time. Would he risk it, though? What if it got lost?"

"It's what I would do if I were him. He's got to know that we're after the package and not him. By separating himself from it, he's betting we won't terminate him until he reacquires it."

And he's right.

"I'll start with the major carriers and work my way down." Red began to access each individual system and scan the manifests for Acton's name as Dawson returned to his seat.

"We're going to need boots on the ground to retrace his steps." He activated his comms.

Time to figure out what the hell he did with that package.

THE PROTOCOL

Somewhere in U.S. Airspace

The men sat solemnly, the roar of the engines doing a poor job of drowning out their thoughts of Spaz. His flag-draped body was in the hold, watched over by his good friend Sergeant Zack "Wings" Hauser. The team had been held at sea for several days until Control had cleared them to return to home soil. Barely a word had been spoken the entire flight until Mickey finally broke the silence.

"How did he get the nickname 'Spaz' anyway?"

Sergeant Tim "Marco" Gere frowned.

That kid talks too much.

Mickey was left dangling for a few moments before Niner finally decided it was best to fill him in. "Ever see Revenge of the Nerds?"

"Who hasn't?"

"When we get back, I'll show you the tape we made at the party celebrating his making the Unit."

"What happened?" Niner didn't answer, so Mickey turned to the others. A smile creased Smitty's face. Mickey looked at him. "Well?"

Smitty, whose own nickname had come from his voracious appetite for pancakes, laughed. "Shit, that's a night he always wanted to forget!" A few of the others chuckled. "Spaz got so floor lickin' pissed, he put Michael Jackson's 'Beat It' on, then started to imitate the dance from Revenge. It was one of the funniest damned things I've ever seen." The chuckles transformed into outright laughter. The nervous tension finally broken, the men reminisced about some of the other escapades they had enjoyed with Spaz.

Marco tuned out the others and got comfortable, trying to get some rack time, when his headset squawked.

"Bravo Transport-One, Bravo Zero-One. Come in, over."

He sat up at the sound of Dawson's voice, as most of the others continued to enjoy the recalled memories, Mickey wincing between laughs and gripping his leg as Sergeant Will "Spock" Lightman adjusted his medication.

"Zero-One, Transport-One. Go ahead, over."

"Transport-One, we need you to land immediately. I want a four-man team in civvies in Phoenix. Further instructions

79

once in position, over."

"Roger that, Zero-One. Will find nearest strip and notify you. Transport-One, out."

Marco headed to the cockpit and notified the pilot, then returned to the passenger area.

"Hey, Marco, where'd you get your name?" Mickey's words slurred slightly from the Demerol.

"Someone found out I played polo."

"No shit?" Mickey laughed. He turned to Spock as he checked his dressing. "And you?" Spock cocked one eyebrow at him. Mickey roared in laughter then passed out.

Marco pointed to Smitty, Niner, and Jimmy. "Gear up for a civvy street assignment, we're going to Phoenix."

The four of them started stripping out of their fatigues as the C17 banked sharply to the left and descended. A private charter was arranged at their drop-off point, and minutes later they were winging for Phoenix, arriving within the hour.

Marco pointed to Jimmy as their jet came to a stop at the airline's private terminal. "Get us some wheels. I'll check in with BD and see what the mission is." Jimmy left the aircraft as Marco contacted command. His comms beeped in his ear.

"Bravo Team Phoenix, Bravo Zero-One. We're sending you the data now. Find this cab driver. We need to know if he made any stops, spoke to anyone, or said anything while in the cab, over."

Marco watched Niner tapping away on his laptop. He glanced up and nodded. "Zero-One, Phoenix. We have the data. Will contact you when target is acquired. Phoenix, out."

Niner hacked the cab company's GPS tracking system, and soon found the cab Acton had taken earlier. "He just left the airport, about ten minutes out."

"Let's go," said Marco.

Niner closed up the laptop, and they disembarked as Jimmy pulled up in an Escalade. Niner shook his head as they climbed in. "What are we, pimps?"

In his best rapper's voice, Jimmy replied, "Yo mo fo, don't you be dissin' my ride or I'm gonna have to take you outside and serve up a can o' whoop ass!"

Niner stared at him. "You're *so* white."

The others pissed themselves with laughter in the back seat as Marco activated the GPS on his laptop, tying into the real-time feed for the cab's locator.

"Let's go. Looks like he's about twenty minutes away."

Jimmy floored it, launching the men into the back of their seats.

Make that fifteen.

New York City, New York

"BD, I've got it!" It had taken two hours, but Red finally had a hit. Dawson jumped from his chair, tossing his comms on the table as he joined Red at the laptop. "A package just left a collection point for the Phoenix airport. It was sent by James Acton to Pedro Gonzalez, Professor of Archaeology in Madrid."

Did he really think he'd get away with it?

"Relay the coordinates to Bravo Team Phoenix and have them intercept the package," ordered Dawson, the adrenaline flowing as all the pieces came together. "Have Clint and Atlas reported in yet? I want them to eliminate Acton when he arrives in New York as soon as we have confirmation of the item's retrieval."

"They're on location already. His flight should be arriving any minute."

"Excellent."

Dawson wished he was at the airport to remove Acton from existence himself, though it wasn't to be—his current job more important. Chirping came from his headpiece on the table, and he reached over to pick it up. Pushing it into his ear, he heard the call repeated.

"Zero-One, Control, do you read, over?"

"Control, Zero-One. Go ahead, over."

"Zero-One, we have a security breach on this end that needs to be taken care of. Send one of your men to Washington immediately, instructions have been sent via secure transmission. Make it look like a mugging. We don't want to tip them off. Control, out."

Dawson turned to Red who nodded. "Encrypted packet just arrived for you." He brought up the transmission on his laptop and spun it around. Dawson entered his password and read the file.

"Holy shit."

"What?"

Dawson held up a finger and finished reading the transmission, leaning back in his chair when he was done. "This thing is way bigger than we thought."

Red's fingers froze over the keyboard. "What do you mean?"

"This terrorist cell, the one we've been having our doubts about?"

"Yeah?"

"They've got one of their own working in the White House, not two hundred feet from the president."

Acton awoke as the flight descended into New York. He stretched his arms and legs in the cramped seating without much success. Putting his shoes back on, having removed them shortly after takeoff, he gave his lap belt a tug as he mentally prepared for what might be next. He was sure he had been watched, and no doubt they had flagged his ID, though the fact he hadn't been intercepted told him whoever was after him, wanted the skull. After struggling overnight through the desert sand and bitter cold, he and his cadre of illegals had made it to a road where his companions hid behind a dune, waiting for a prearranged truck to arrive. Since he was American, he just hitched a ride, and within minutes, was picked up by a rig headed to Phoenix.

Once there, he paid cash for a room at a motel, cleaned up and put on a fresh set of clothes purchased from a nearby thrift shop, then found a store with a FedEx drop-off where he put the riskiest part of his plan into motion, a plan he had developed while on the ship from Peru.

But did it work?

When he had arrived in Mexico, he had Googled the skulls, reading up as much as he could on them, eventually finding an expert who didn't appear to be a quack.

In England.

If they hadn't found the package he sent, then he should be okay getting off the flight.

But if they had?

His heart beat hard against his ribs, adrenaline rushing through his veins as he realized if his ploy hadn't worked, he was about to die. As the plane taxied then stopped, waiting for the gangway to extend, he repeated the same two words over and over.

Stay alive!

Phoenix, Arizona

Jimmy gunned the motor and cut in front of the FedEx van their new orders had sent them to intercept. He slammed his brakes on, blocking their target, as the other three Bravo Team members jumped out with weapons drawn, pointing them at the panicked driver.

"Get out of the truck!" ordered Niner, tapping his gun on the window. The driver raised his hands and climbed out, his blue shorts revealing shaking knees. "Open the back." The driver shuffled sideways to the back, never taking his eyes off the gun pointed at his head. He groped for the handle, and when he found it, twisted it then pulled the door up, revealing hundreds of packages inside. "We're looking for this package number." Niner handed him a tracking number. The driver nodded, still shaking, and climbed into the back of the truck. A minute later, he found the package and handed it to Niner.

Niner double-checked the tracking number and the information shown on the package. Acton's name was written clearly on the label. Looking back at the trembling driver, he raised his weapon and cold-cocked the terrified man on the side of his head, rendering him unconscious. He returned to the SUV, handing the package to Marco.

Marco activated his comms as the rest of the team climbed back in. "Zero-One, Zero-Nine, we've recovered the item, over." Jimmy quickly put several miles between them and the FedEx truck, then Marco had him pull into an area of warehouses and stop. "Everyone out, I have to confirm the contents." The other team members climbed out of the Escalade, leaving Marco alone.

Dawson had cleared him to open the package, though no one else was to see what was inside, by order of Control. As the other team members milled about outside the SUV, he carefully examined the package for booby traps, then used his utility knife to cut open the packing tape encasing the plain brown box. Opening the top, he removed the packing material inside, his heart pounding with the excitement of finally finding out what this entire mission had been about.

What was worth killing all those people for?

He didn't know what to expect, but when he had

removed enough of the packing material to reveal the item, he shook his head in disbelief.

What the hell is this?

LaGuardia Airport
Queens, New York

Sergeants Carlos "Clint" Sanchez and Leon "Atlas" James fell in behind Acton as he left the secure area of the airport. When Clint had been assigned this mission, he had relished in the thought of killing the man who had taken his friend. Spaz had been the one to give him his nickname when he had joined the Unit, both of them loving old movies, Spaz always acting out parts with Clint doing incredibly bad impressions of the characters' voices—one of his worst being Dirty Harry. He smiled at the memory then frowned.

This is for you, buddy.

"Zero-Eight, Zero-One. Do you have him, over?"

Clint tapped his earpiece. "Zero-One, Zero-Eight. Affirmative, moving into position now, over."

"Copy that, Zero-Eight. Eliminate the subject. Zero-One, out."

Clint glanced at Atlas with a nod, their orders confirmed. His heart picked up a few beats as they closed the gap between themselves and their target. Rarely had he killed in revenge, and never for something so personal. Eliminating terrorists in revenge for 9/11 was one thing, but taking out the man who had killed a buddy, who had killed Spaz?

That was different.

Yet he had to keep his emotions in check, otherwise he might blow the mission. Killing him would be easy. Killing him and getting away with it was the hard part.

They were both dressed in suits with long overcoats. Clint had his hands in both pockets, the bulge from his suppressor-tipped weapon now pointing at the target. They quickened their pace. As they did, a man crossed in front of them pulling a carry-on, staring at a map of the airport. Atlas shoved him out of the way as they stumbled over the case, and Clint cursed as their target made eye contact.

Their cover was blown.

Acton turned to see the commotion behind him. One man was on his knees, a case he had been pulling knocked over on the floor. Two men stepped over him without a second glance. Acton saw one of them had his hand in his pocket, a sliver of something metallic showing.

A gun!

Acton looked up at the man and nearly fainted when he caught him staring directly at him. Acton whipped his head back around and picked up his pace, his heart slamming as if he were running a marathon.

Clint was about three feet behind Acton, Atlas to his side and slightly back. Clint slowly squeezed the trigger. There was no way he could miss at this distance, and in the din of the airport, it would barely be noticed. Red had already disabled the cameras in this area, and any footage that might show them would be scrubbed by Ops.

Spaz's murderer was about to die, another terrorist leader was about to answer to his maker.

"Abort, abort, abort!" came Dawson's voice through the comms system ear buds. "Do not eliminate the target!"

Clint tensed as his finger left the trigger. He casually broke to the left as Atlas headed in the opposite direction, disappointment shoving aside the exhilaration he was feeling.

Dammit!

Acton was now panicked and about to run. Blood roared in his ears, adrenaline rushed through his veins, causing his entire body to shake as his heart beat so fast he became faint. Glancing again over his shoulder, he prepared to turn and fight, with what, he had no idea.

He stopped.

Both men were gone.

He looked around, but they were nowhere to be seen. Had he imagined it?

No, that was definitely a gun.

He sucked in several deep, slow breaths, calming himself, then resumed his walk, albeit at a brisk pace, to the car rental counter.

And smiled. So far, his plan was working.

And they definitely don't have the skull.

"The bastard, he must have sent a second package." Dawson's respect for his adversary ratcheted up another notch. It had been close, Marco's reporting of the package merely containing rocks coming in mere seconds before their target was about to be eliminated.

Too close.

He turned to Red. "Run a check, see if you can find another package he might have sent. And I want Atlas on a flight to DC to plug that security hole."

Dawson sat and connected to Control to relay the news. He hadn't anticipated much resistance in Peru, and they certainly hadn't received any except from Acton, an adversary he wouldn't underestimate again. With each clever move by Acton, his doubts on whether they had been sent on a bullshit mission were diminishing. The terror cell had an agent inside the White House, and Acton had sent a decoy package, clearly proving there was an item that needed to be retrieved.

What the hell that item was, he still had no clue, except that it was some type of crystal material.

"You'll know it when you see it."

Dawson shook his head.

What the hell does that mean?

17th Street, Washington, DC

After what had seemed an endless day, Billy was finally heading home. His chest was still tight, his palms sweating as he walked toward his apartment from the corner store where he had grabbed a microwaveable hoagie.

I shouldn't have seen that!

Hearing footsteps behind him, he glanced back over his shoulder. A man walked behind him, staring down the street, perhaps for a cab. He quickened his pace.

The footsteps quickened as well. His heart felt like it would pound out of his chest. He ran. Dodging into an alleyway, he sprinted toward the other end. Checking over his shoulder again, he gulped as the man followed him into the dead end. With his attention on the man behind him, he didn't notice the discarded tire in front of him until he tripped over it, slamming into the ground. As he scrambled to get up, he was hauled to his feet and spun around, his back facing the man.

His assailant growled in his ear. "This is for Spaz, you terrorist piece of shit."

Terrorist?

In one swift motion, his mouth was covered and his head pulled back, stifling his scream. Something slid across his throat then a warm liquid pulsed down his neck onto his chest. It took a moment before the pain registered, and another before he realized it was his own blood pouring from his now slit throat.

He was thrown to the ground, and as he lay there, bleeding out, he stared helplessly as the man took his wallet, keys, and watch. Before he lost consciousness, the man said something.

"Zero-One, Zero-Seven. The target has been eliminated, over."

New York City, New York

Milton exited his cab on 71ˢᵗ Street, his head hunkered down behind the collar of his jacket. He hurried into Central Park, and headed to Strawberry Fields. He glanced behind him then broke into a run. He had flown to New York that afternoon after delivering the eulogy, and had been traveling all day around the city by cab, subway, and foot, in case he was being followed. His intense paranoia had him suspicious of everyone. His chest was pounding, and adrenaline pulsed through his veins, fueling his panic further. Forcing himself to breathe deeply, he slowly calmed down. He eased to a jog, then eventually a brisk walk, catching his breath and cursing his desk job.

Remember where we crammed for English Lit finals? Can you meet me there?

As a grad student almost twenty years ago, he had taken Acton, a promising sophomore, under his wing. They had been inseparable since. They would jog through the park every morning and engage in deep philosophical discussions while sitting on the benches or lying in the various green spaces.

Strawberry Fields lay in the most beautiful section of Central Park. He had discovered it before it became known as that, before Ed Koch dedicated it to John Lennon, before its upgrade, and before people flocked to it. By the time he'd met Acton, that had died down, and it became their escape from the throngs that were New York City.

When he had offered Acton a teaching position at the college four years ago, he had been afraid it would affect their relationship, but it hadn't. Yes, they had their fights, some loud ones—including the one preceding his latest expedition—yet those had only served to strengthen their friendship. Acton was a well-respected archaeologist, and the alumni loved him. He had ended up perfect for the position.

Twenty years ago, I quizzed him for his English Lit finals on that bench.

He came to an abrupt stop and looked around again. No one.

Including Jim.

He eyed the bench where they had sat that night. His

cellphone went off, sending his pulse racing again.

Look under the bench.

He inched toward it and sat. He casually reached under with his left hand and felt around. Something was taped underneath. It came free with a little effort. He hid it in his hand and brought it up, palm inward, shielding it from prying eyes. He crossed his legs, and with his knee now blocking his hand from view, turned it over to see what had been underneath the bench.

A cellphone!

He nearly jumped out of his skin as it vibrated in his hand. Flipping it open, he brought it to his ear as casually as his shaking hands could manage.

"Don't say anything, you're being watched." Milton looked around but couldn't see his friend. "Go and visit our angel, you know where she is, and wait for me to call you there. Cough if you understand."

He coughed.

"Okay, see you soon my friend."

The line went dead.

Milton got up and walked east, deeper into the park, toward Bethesda Terrace. His heart drummed and blood rushed through his ears.

Calm down. Inhale. Exhale.

He tried to ignore the people around him, yet he couldn't help wondering which ones might be following him.

17th Street, Washington, DC

"What have we got?" asked Detective Raymond Wheeler of his partner, Detective Justin Schultz, as he ducked under the yellow police tape. Wheeler's slightly portly figure wasn't the model of police fitness, but twenty-five years on the force often led to that, especially since he hadn't been chasing perps in over ten. Detective work was less physically challenging, though a hell of a lot more interesting. He'd been partnered with Schultz for most of his time in a suit, and, much to his chagrin, Schultz had managed to avoid the spare tire.

"One DB, probably a mugging gone bad," said the Medical Examiner, Mendosa. "I just got here. I'll know more when I get a good look at him."

"Mugging, huh?" Wheeler kneeled and lifted a corner of the sheet draped over the body. "Any ID?"

An officer stepped forward. "No. No wallet, keys, or watch."

Schultz turned toward him. "You were first on the scene?"

"Yes, sir."

"If this is a mugging, then why was this made a priority homicide call?" asked Wheeler.

Mendosa grunted. "Not by me. That was our overzealous friend here." He jabbed his thumb at the officer.

Wheeler stared at him. "Well? Are you just wasting my time, or are you going to speak up for yourself?"

The young officer appeared nervous. "Well, sir, it's like this. I'm ex-Army, did two tours in Iraq, and, well, this doesn't look like a mugging to me."

"What makes you say that?"

"Look at the cut, sir. That's textbook, exactly the way we were trained to take someone out from behind, with no noise."

Wheeler approached the body and pulled aside the sheet once again. He stared closely at the wound.

The kid's right. This was no mugging.

He looked at Mendosa. "What do you think?"

Mendosa kneeled and examined the wound. "Could be. He moves to the top of my list. I'll contact you as soon as I know more, probably a couple of hours."

"Run his prints right away, too. I want to know who this kid was."

New York City, New York

Agent Turner yawned as Lambert stared at the video footage transmitted by one of the trailing agents. "Is that a cellphone he picked up?"

Jasper leaned over Lambert's shoulder as he peered at the monitor in front of them. "Yes, it is. Can we listen in?"

"No. None of our agents in place have a parabolic."

"Shit!" Jasper pointed at Turner. "Take a parabolic and get out there now."

Turner's eyes narrowed. "Won't I look kind of conspicuous, sir?"

"To hell with conspicuous, we need to hear that conversation. Go!"

Lovely.

Turner grabbed the parabolic dish out of an upper cabinet and climbed out of the back of the van. He dodged the heavy morning traffic on Central Park West, and sprinted into the park. He felt like an idiot. There was no way to be inconspicuous while carrying a one-foot diameter circular cone. As he neared the bench where Milton had been, he received instructions over his earpiece as to where the target was now heading. He finally spotted Milton as he reached a fountain. His target looked down at the phone and flipped it open, placing it to his ear. Turner searched for a hiding place.

No damned way am I standing in the open, pointing this thing.

Running behind a nearby tree, he propped the dish on a branch and pointed it toward Milton as he put the headphone in his ear. Static. He aimed more carefully, and he could make out a few muffled words, though little else. Just static.

It's the damned fountain!

Raising his hand to his mouth, he activated his comms. "Sir, I can't hear a thing, the fountain is drowning everything out." He didn't have to be in the van to hear the string of curses at the other end.

"Get back here."

"Can you hear me?" asked Acton.

"Barely, the fountain is pretty loud," replied Milton, relieved to hear his friend's voice again.

"Good, that means they can't hear us either. Listen, old friend, I'm in danger, and so are you just by talking to me, but I had no choice."

Milton's eyes narrowed. "What are you talking about? In danger from whom?"

"I'm not sure. I think they were our troops, some sort of black ops team. They killed everyone at the camp, and they almost got me."

"Our own troops? I was told it was rebels after your supplies or something you had found."

"Who told you that bullshit?"

"Two State Department agents came to my office four days ago and told me what had happened. They said you were missing, and wanted me to contact them if I heard from you. I didn't, of course."

"Good. They may be in on it. Listen carefully. For some reason, I think they're after what we found in Peru."

"What did you find?"

"A crystal skull."

"A crystal skull? Like Mitchell-Hedges?"

"Yes, exactly!" Acton sounded like a teenage boy describing his first car. "It's beautiful! I've seen pictures of them, of course, and had a chance to see the one in London up close, but I've never held one in my hands. It's the most incredible thing I've ever seen."

"I'm sure it is, Jim, but why would they want to kill you over it?"

"I have no idea, but I think I might know who would. Problem is, I need cash."

"I thought you might, so I brought some."

"Listen." His friend's tone became more serious. "They killed everyone, and they're probably after me. If you want out, now's the time to get out. I won't judge you."

"Jim, you've known me long enough to know I don't leave my friends hanging. Now, how do I get this money to you?"

"First, we have to lose whoever's tailing you."

Milton listened to the plan then snapped the phone shut before tossing it in the fountain. He looked around again, trying to spot any pursuers, but gave up. There were too many people in the park. He walked briskly toward the nearest subway station, hurried down the stairs, paid his fare, then made his way out onto the platform. He scrutinized people descending the stairs, though no one stood out.

Too many suits.

His train arrived, and he waited until the last second to jump aboard, hoping he might surprise whoever was following him. He took a seat and tried to appear inconspicuous—not hard considering this was a New York subway car, nobody looking at anybody as they tried to ignore their surroundings and make it to their destination with as little interaction with their fellow passengers as possible. He grabbed a newspaper from the seat beside him and buried his head in it.

Turner and Jasper had both followed Milton into the subway station. When the train arrived, Turner boarded right away, in case Milton tried anything last minute—he could always get off at the next stop if needed.

There he goes.

Jasper smiled to himself.

Predictable.

He made his way back up to the van, and waited for Turner to let them know when Milton got off. In the meantime, they at least knew which direction to travel. "Let's head south."

Washington, DC

"Detective Wheeler, this is Mendosa from the Medical Examiner's Office."

Wheeler stopped chewing on his foot-long hot dog with the works, and handed the pile of artery-clogging fat and calories to Schultz, who stared at it with disdain. Wheeler pulled out his notepad and pen. "What've ya got, Doc?"

"We got a hit on the John Doe's prints."

"He was in AFIS?"

"No, he was in the Fed's Employee database. You're not going to believe who this kid is."

"Who?"

"William Guthrie, son of former Speaker George Guthrie. The kid started Monday as an intern at the White House."

Wheeler scribbled the information onto his pad. "Still think this is a random mugging?"

"No. I've examined the wound, and our young vet was right. This was a professional hit, made to look like a mugging."

"Okay, I'm going to go see the congressman. You keep me posted." Ending the call, Wheeler grabbed the hot dog from Schultz. He was about to take a bite when he lost his appetite. He tossed it into the nearby garbage can and motioned to his partner. "This case just got a whole lot more interesting."

"How?"

"Our victim is a VIP."

Wheeler explained as they made the drive out to Chevy Chase, Maryland. This was the part of the job he hated. They both hated. Telling parents that their kid was dead. It was one thing when it was a gangbanger—it was expected. But a clean-cut kid, barely out of high school, working at the White House for the summer?

It wasn't supposed to happen.

They pulled into the long drive of the Guthrie residence and parked near the main entrance, the house huge.

It's good to be the king.

He often wondered why it was that politicians, no matter how rich or poor they were when they entered office, always managed to leave wealthy.

Couldn't be corruption, of course.

He knew from the papers, Guthrie had married money, so his current situation was clean. But what his son was mixed up in, he had no idea. A professional hit meant either he had dug himself in deep with some bad characters, or this was a hit to send a message to Guthrie, Sr.

Wheeler and Schultz crossed the drive and climbed the three steps of the main entrance, an impressive columned affair with a massive double, carved wood door. Wheeler was about to knock when the door swung open, a man he instantly recognized as George Guthrie, the boy's father, standing there, his eyes red, his face flushed.

"What do you want?"

Anger and pain tinged his voice, and it was clear the poor bastard already knew why they were there.

"I'm Detective Wheeler, this is my partner Detective Schultz, Metro PD. We're here about your son."

The man's shoulders sagged and he turned away from them, leaving the door open as he shuffled deeper into the house. Wheeler looked at Schultz and shrugged, then followed Guthrie.

They found him in a sitting room, consoling his wife and fighting the tears welling in his own eyes. He took a moment to steel his nerves as he placed his wife in a chair and turned to face the detectives.

Wheeler cleared his throat. "I take it you've heard?"

Guthrie nodded, his bottom lip trembling for a moment. "We just received a call from a friend who thought we already knew."

"I'm truly sorry you had to find out that way, sir. As soon as the identity was confirmed, we drove over. In fact, I'm surprised anyone knew before we did."

Guthrie ignored the observation. "All I want to know is how my boy died."

"This may be difficult to hear, Mr. Guthrie." Wheeler motioned to a chair. "It appears to have been a professional job, made to look like a mugging."

Guthrie dropped into the chair, his legs giving out. "Professional? But why? He was only eighteen!" This elicited a wail from his wife.

"It's early in the investigation, sir," replied Wheeler.

"We'll get to the bottom of this."

Guthrie stood and faced Wheeler. "I'm sure you know who I am. I still have a lot of friends in this town. If anyone gets in your way, stonewalls you in any way, you call me. I'll open any doors you need. I want my Billy's killer caught."

"Yes, sir, you'll be the first I call."

Grand Central Station
New York City, New York

Milton hopped off the subway at the last second, again hoping this would help. He had taken the subway daily when he lived in New York, but hadn't been on it for well over a decade. He didn't miss it. The throngs of commuters made it difficult for him to reach the main floor of Grand Central Station. Once finally there, he headed through the Hyatt Hotel entrance, directly toward the main floor bathrooms. One had a yellow sign in front, indicating it was closed for servicing, and he walked confidently toward it then entered. As his friend had promised, he found a piece of wood in the corner. Wedging it between the door and the entrance wall, he tested to make sure it couldn't be opened.

He hurried to the back of the bathroom, climbed up on the counter, and pushed on the window. It swung open easily. Again, his friend had planned this perfectly. Milton struggled out the window, soon realizing his friend's plan wasn't perfect after all.

Jim apparently forgot I sit behind a desk for a living.

The last time he had climbed out a window was after his high school girlfriend's father nearly caught him in her bedroom.

It had been easier then.

Someone tried the door handle to the bathroom. The board did its job. Whoever it was pushed harder, pounding on the door then apparently throwing their shoulder into it. After a few moments of panic, thinking he might be caught, Milton squeezed through the window. Dropping unceremoniously to the floor of a service corridor, he ran toward a door at the end, below a glowing red exit sign. He shoved the handle and spilled onto Lexington Avenue, much to the surprise of a few passersby. He dusted off and looked around. The green Prius he was told to expect was there.

Jim, even running for his life, he thinks of the environment.

He ran over and climbed in. The car sped off before he had a chance to even say hello.

Turner finally broke through the bathroom door as a piece of wood blocking it splintered then snapped. He burst in and noticed the open window. He hopped up on the counter, pulled himself through, then dropped to the ground. He looked for Milton, but couldn't see him. He sprinted to the exit at the far end and searched up and down the busy street as he emerged.

Milton was nowhere in sight.

He radioed in, cursing to himself. "I lost him."

"They shouldn't be able to track us in here."

Stuck in traffic in the Queens-Midtown Tunnel, Acton finally felt safe, despite traveling for hours to make sure he wasn't followed. He had chosen the Prius not for environmental reasons, as he was sure his friend thought, but for the fact the incredible gas mileage meant he wouldn't need to stop for gas, whereas anyone following him would. Also, the terrific pickup from a dead stop meant he could accelerate through traffic quicker than most vehicles.

He smiled at his friend. "Thanks for coming."

"I'm just glad you're alive." Milton faced him. "Now, are you going to tell me what the hell is going on, or am I going to have to beat it out of you? I've never been so terrified in my life!"

"Quite the adrenaline rush, huh?" laughed Acton.

Milton scowled.

"Okay, here's what happened. Last week on our dig, we found some hidden chambers inside a cave. It looks like the Incans bored out a huge chunk of the hillside to make these things. The carvings and whatnot were impressive in themselves, but inside, on a stone altar, was this." He reached into his pocket and took out several Polaroids.

Milton's jaw dropped. They were carefully taken close-ups of the skull from various angles. He held the photos up to examine them closer.

"It's beautiful," he whispered, "in an almost eerie way." He flipped to a photo showing the hollowed out eyes. "This looks just like the Mitchell-Hedges skull." He flipped to another picture.

"Exactly the same as far as I can tell. Completely smooth, no tool marks."

"Where is it now?"

"On its way to London, God willing. When I was in Mexico, I FedEx'd it using one of my student's IDs to an expert on the skulls."

"Who's that?"

"Professor Laura Palmer of the British Museum. She's been studying the one they have for years, and is known as *the* expert in these things. She's apparently examined all of the ones known to exist that are accessible."

"What do you mean by accessible?"

"Some are in private collections." Acton stared ahead as the traffic stirred again. "Okay, we're almost out of the tunnel. You brought the money?"

"Yes." Milton reached into his jacket pocket and pulled out an envelope. "Nine thousand nine hundred dollars, the most I could withdraw without flagging a government inspection." He handed it to Acton.

Acton took the envelope. "I think it's five thousand now."

"What? Are you sure?"

"I think they changed it recently." Acton stuffed the envelope into the inner pocket of his jacket. "You might be flagged, but they're not looking for you."

Milton tried to put on a brave face. "Well, the important thing is you're now flush with cash. I assume you're going to London?"

"Yes, there's a midnight flight."

"How are you going to get through security?"

"They're not after me, they're after the skull. They must know by now that I don't have it, so I'm probably safe for the moment."

"Let's hope so." Milton nodded toward the pocket Acton had put the envelope in. "There's also a new Visa and bank card from the university in there. If you have an emergency, use them. Hopefully, they won't think to trace them."

"Hopefully, but these guys are pros."

"Any idea who they are?"

"I don't know. They must have been some type of Special Forces. They came in by helicopter, were well armed, state-of-the-art equipment, well disciplined. I shot one and pistol-whipped another. That one I spoke to, his English was perfect Bronx."

"You're sure they were ours?" Milton shook his head. "I can't believe that. Why would our government want to kill you over this?"

"I don't know, but don't forget, our *government,* as you put it, doesn't always know what these black ops guys do. It could be some rogue element that the administration doesn't even know about."

Milton was still shaking his head. "I just can't believe it. You're sure it wasn't the Shining Path or some other rebel group? They've killed a lot of people."

"No, they don't have equipment like this." Acton checked his rearview mirror to see if they were being followed. "I think we lost them." He took the exit for JFK.

"You're not worried about them knowing you're on the plane?"

"A bit. I'll just have to hope they're not willing to shoot down an airliner full of people. They're after the skull, regardless, and right now they don't know where it is. I'll try and lose whoever is waiting for me in London. I can't believe they'd want to risk an international incident at the airport. My guess is they haven't even notified the regular authorities to watch for me, since that would raise too many questions."

Arriving at the airport, Acton battled his way to the departure drop-off area and jammed into a spot as another car pulled away. He turned to Milton. "I don't want any more help from you. If they ask you questions, tell them the truth."

Milton shook his head again.

"Listen, I don't want you to get hurt," pleaded Acton. "Too many have died already. Promise me."

Milton sighed. "Okay, Jim, I promise." With that, Acton popped the trunk and left the car. Milton climbed out as well. Acton gave his friend a quick one-armed thumping hug, grabbed a duffel bag from the trunk, and strode into the terminal, not looking back, silently praying his friend would be okay.

Entering the terminal, he studied the boards to confirm the midnight flight to London. It was on time and leaving in two hours. He approached the counter and purchased a ticket. He could be tracked on this flight since he had to use his passport, so he used his credit card, preserving the cash for when he arrived in London. His ticket bought, he headed for customs to find several of the scanners down and the crowds getting frustrated. Finally cleared, he took one last glance over his shoulder, and could have sworn a man was staring directly at him as he talked into his wrist.

"Zero-One, One-Two. Subject has cleared customs, over."

Red grinned as he accessed the reservation system, Dawson packing up their equipment, having correctly guessed Acton was heading out of the city by air. They had pre-positioned teams at all the major airports, then it was just a matter of him showing up at one of them.

And he had, as predicted.

"Recall the other teams. Have them rendezvous at the base. We'll head out once you find the reservation. And signal the JFK team to tie up that loose end. Control says he's on the Termination List."

"Roger that."

THE PROTOCOL

As Milton guided the Prius through the chaos that was the JFK loading and unloading zone, he shook as the realization of what he had been through sunk in.

Get a grip!

He reached into his jacket pocket, pulled out a handkerchief, and wiped the sweat from his forehead.

Someone stepped in front of his car and he slammed the brakes on. The person, dressed in a dark suit, flashed a badge as he walked up to the passenger door. He knocked on the window, pointing at the lock. Milton reached for the switch, then hesitated.

"Open the door, sir," said the man in a firm tone.

I have to get out of this alive.

He glanced in his sideview mirror and saw a gap in the traffic. With the car still in drive, he took his foot off the brake and hit the gas. The car's electric motor thrust it into traffic with a force he hadn't expected.

Maybe that's *why Jim chose this car.*

Dodging in and out of the lanes, he put as much distance as he could between him and his would-be passenger, whom he could no longer see in his rearview mirror. As he left JFK, he breathed easier.

I've got to ditch this car.

He didn't see the black Ford Expedition following several car lengths behind, his would-be passenger inside, watching on a laptop the red blip from the tracking device stuck to the Prius' door.

Milton found a car rental place outside the airport and parked the Prius in a lot a couple of blocks away, walking back. As he entered the rental office, the Expedition pulled in and parked, its tinted windows blocking a view of the interior. Within minutes, he was waiting out front for the car to be brought around for the customary inspection. He signed the paperwork and climbed into the Ford Focus. He gunned the motor and left the parking lot, disappointed in the power after having experienced the extra torque available in the Prius' bottom end.

The SUV pulled out and followed. Milton drove for

about half an hour, then pulled into a gas station. Inside, he bought several candy bars, a bag of chips, and a couple of Diet Cokes.

Just for the taste of it.

He asked for the bathrooms, and the attendant pointed to the rear. Milton left his bag on the counter and headed to the back. He didn't look back as the chime sounded at the opening of the front door.

Entering, he grimaced at the pungent odor of stale urine. He used his foot to kick the lid up, not wanting to touch anything, and relieved himself.

Man, I've been needing this!

He was about done when the door to the bathroom opened. He glanced over his shoulder, surprised, as he was certain he had locked it.

"I'll just be a minute."

No response.

He zipped up his fly and was about to turn when he heard two slight popping sounds, then felt a searing pain. He fell to the floor, one hand gripping his back, the other trying to hold on to the sink. A few seconds later, he was prone on the floor, bleeding out. The man calmly walked out of the bathroom, the chime on the door signaling his departure.

The life draining from him, Milton reached for the phone on his hip and pulled it loose. With his last few ounces of strength, he typed a message into it, pressed *Send*, then collapsed, the device landing in the now large pool of blood. Bright spots of light flashed before his closed eyes as the life-sustaining oxygen stopped reaching his brain.

Then nothing.

THE PROTOCOL

Classified Airstrip

On a military airstrip twenty miles away, in a closed hangar at the end of the runway, members of Bravo Team loaded equipment into a Gulfstream V, while nearby, Dawson studied the screen of one of Red's several laptops.

"Confirmed, BD, he just boarded."

"Okay, wheels up in five."

Outside, the wind whipped around as a Black Hawk helicopter touched down. The massive doors of the hangar opened, and it taxied through. The Bravo Team members who had been tailing Milton hopped out and ran toward the G-V. The computers were packed up, stairs stowed, and the door sealed, leaving empty tables and a lone helicopter.

The G-V's engines powered up, filling the cabin with their whine as they taxied out onto the airstrip. Dawson peered out the window to see a flatbed truck pull up to transport their chopper back to base. There would be no record of it having been there. He laid his head back on the leather seat and let out a deep sigh, preparing for a few hours of rack time.

Who knows when I'll get the next chance?

Around him, his men did the same. Looking at the two new members of his team, Sergeants Vince "Stucco" Stewart and Danny "Casey" Martin, he nodded in approval. He hadn't worked with them before, though knew from their records they would make fine additions. Mickey would be hard to replace—he was so gung-ho and loyal, he would execute orders without question, now that he had learned his lesson with the Smitty incident. He was relieved to have found Mickey alive in the cave when they returned to search. It would take months of recovery, but he'd make it back—he was tough.

Spaz was another story. Just thinking of the kid's name made him smile.

That guy was the life of the party.

He had already told Spaz's wife about the unfortunate training accident. He hated lying to the families, but it was necessary for operational security. What made it worse was they knew they were being lied to.

Though if all went well, they would have their revenge by

tomorrow.

The thought had a smile spreading, and he was asleep before they reached cruising altitude.

THE PROTOCOL

Somewhere over the Atlantic

Acton stared at the seatbelt warning light, waiting for it to go out as the plane climbed toward thirty-five thousand feet. Finally, the gentle gong rang through the cabin. Acton whipped off his seatbelt, rose, and approached the nearest flight attendant. "Do you have any Internet terminals that I could access?"

"Yes, sir, on the upper deck there are several." She pointed to a curving staircase a few feet away.

"Thanks," he said as he rushed toward them. In Mexico, he had about fifteen minutes to find out to whom he should send the skull. Once he had found out Professor Palmer was the foremost expert, and was in London, he had headed for the courier's office. Now he needed to complete his research.

As he neared the top of the stairs, he noticed a row of terminals lining one wall. All were taken except one. He quickly sat in front of it. He brought up Google and typed in *professor laura palmer british museum*. Google responded with 197,000 hits.

Shit.

He scrolled through the entries until he found who he was searching for. One click brought up a picture of a woman with her hair tied back and sleeves rolled up, working on a dig site in the desert.

Not bad.

He scanned the biographical information. Dr. Laura Palmer had several degrees, including Archaeology, Ancient History, and Literature. She was a Professor of Archaeology at University College London, had held a position at the British Museum for over ten years, and was well respected in her field. She lectured all over Europe and North America, and was currently on a dig in Egypt.

Egypt!

He scrolled through the document to find the date it had been written. Two years ago. More searching confirmed she was currently at the university, lecturing as he had thought. He spent the next few minutes entering notes into his cellphone on contact names, numbers, and addresses he might need. When he was done, he turned it off, knowing he wouldn't get a signal here, nor when he'd have a chance to recharge the battery. Next, he pulled up a map of the Heathrow terminal.

Now to figure a way out.

Fifteen thousand feet above him, Bravo Team slept in their G-V. Several thousand feet below, and about an hour behind, followed a C17 with their heavy equipment, and six hours behind everyone, Jasper and Lambert sat in US Airways coach, trying to sleep while a baby wailed in the seat behind them. Finally, Lambert gave up and opened his complimentary bag of mixed nuts. As he munched away, he realized he was thirsty.

Salty.

He flagged the attendant and asked for a Pepsi.

"Is Coke okay, sir?"

He nodded.

Same shit, different flies.

She brought back a half-size can of soda, poured it into a glass of ice, then placed it on his tray table. "That will be three dollars, sir."

Now he realized the scam. He fumbled for his wallet and paid her, grumbling the entire time. Finishing his peanuts then his sippy-cup-sized Coke, he searched for more things to entertain himself with. He turned to Jasper. "Sir?"

Jasper opened his eyes without raising his head and stared at his younger partner. "What?"

"Any idea why Acton would run to England if he were innocent?"

"No."

"Do you think he had something to do with it?"

"No."

Lambert grabbed the in-flight magazine and flipped through it for a couple of minutes. "Sir?"

"What?" This time Jasper sounded slightly exasperated.

"Uh, nothing, go back to sleep."

"You've woken me now, what is it?" Jasper was clearly frustrated.

"I was just wondering something."

"What?"

"Have you ever been to England?"

"When I get my gun back, I'm gonna shoot you."

"Yes, sir."

THE PROTOCOL

Washington, DC

Detective Wheeler had never worked on a case this high profile before, but now appreciated all the resources it granted him. They had worked through the night, and were now running on adrenaline and Red Bull. Every minute of video footage from every store in the area had already been pulled and reviewed. They had the killer on tape, but his pulled-up collar, pulled-down baseball cap, and blacked-out shades, rendered him impossible to identify. This had at least confirmed it was not a random mugging.

Billy had been targeted.

One wall Wheeler had run into, however, was the White House. They had refused to give him any information regarding the boy, until he had placed a call to Guthrie. Fifteen minutes later, Wheeler had an appointment with Billy's boss.

After clearing security, Wheeler and Schultz were led to a waiting area where they sat for several minutes before being shown into an office where they were greeted by the victim's supervisor.

"Lesley Darbinger." He pumped both of their hands in a double grasp. "Pleased to meet two of Washington's finest." He motioned toward a pair of chairs in front of his desk as he leaned on the edge of it.

Wheeler sat in the chair and looked up at Darbinger.

Classic assertion of power technique—always be higher than your opponent.

"We're here about the death of one of your interns, William Guthrie."

"Billy's dead?" Darbinger's shoulders slumped as his jaw dropped. "But I just saw him yesterday!"

"You didn't know?" asked Schultz, surprised.

"No, I've been in closed-door meetings all day." Darbinger stared at the floor, shaking his head. "What will I tell his father? Does he know?"

"Yes, we've already notified the family," replied Wheeler.

"How did he die?"

"He was murdered."

"Murdered!" Darbinger appeared caught off guard. "Do you know who did it?"

Wheeler shook his head. "Not yet, but it appears to have been a professional hit."

"Professional? What do you mean?"

"Military style," explained Schultz. "Head held back exposing the jugular. Throat slit, left to right, deep. He bled out within a minute."

Darbinger shook his head in disbelief. "This is terrible. Does his father know?"

"Yes, sir, as I said, I've met with his parents already."

"Of course you did, sorry. I'm just a little shaken up. How can I help you?"

"Well, sir, Mr. Guthrie had started here Monday, and within his first week, he is killed in what looks like a professional manner. We believe that's too much of a coincidence," said Wheeler. "Was he exposed to anything here that maybe he shouldn't have seen?"

"No, he's just an intern. He wouldn't have clearance to see anything."

"Well, just the same, we're going to need to talk to everyone. We'll conduct the interviews here to make things easier for you."

Darbinger nodded. "Of course, I'll see you get full cooperation."

THE PROTOCOL

USAF 48th Fighter Wing, RAF Lakenheath
Lakenheath, England

"Welcome to RAF Lakenheath, sir. I'm Sergeant Berkin. The Base Commander has ordered me to take care of all your needs while you're here."

Dawson acknowledged the sergeant who greeted him at the bottom of the G-V's steps. Since Dawson was dressed in civvies, he forgave the "sir" and surveyed their surroundings. They had taxied to the far end of the tarmac, separate from the other air traffic and prying eyes. "Status, Sergeant?"

Berkin pointed to three Humvees waiting nearby. "These are yours to use while you are here. In the hangar behind us are the civilian vehicles you requested, a civilian chopper, and we've freed up this building over here for your men to stay in." He pointed at a beat-up building several hundred yards away. "It's unoccupied, but includes a rec room, comms room, and small infirmary. I've had it fully stocked. Should accommodate any of your needs."

"Very good, Sergeant. Notify me when my C17 arrives." Dawson grabbed a handful of the gear the team had already unloaded, and headed to one of the Humvees. Berkin ran after him.

"A C17, sir?"

"Yes, a couple of hours out. Make sure you have enough men available to unload it as well as assemble and arm an Apache." Dawson was impressed—only a brief moment of shock registered on the sergeant's face. He would have been told to follow orders, no questions asked, then to forget they were ever there.

He's probably wondering what the hell black ops are doing in England.

Dawson threw the equipment in the back of one of the Humvees then returned to the plane for another load. He glanced at Red as he approached carrying satellite communications gear. "When we're done, have Stucco and Casey take one of the civilian vehicles in that hangar and locate the target."

Red nodded. "We'll be up and running in fifteen minutes."

Berkin watched as the men unloaded the plane. One

walked by with a case of grenades. "My God, are we invading?" he muttered.

"Sergeant!"

Berkin spun toward Dawson.

"Are you just going to stand there, or are you going to use those two God-given hands to help us?"

Berkin gulped, rushing toward the pile of off-loaded equipment. "Right away, sir!"

THE PROTOCOL

Heathrow Airport
London, England

The delay seemed interminable as Acton waited for the doors to open so the passengers, already jostling for position, could disembark. He sat quietly in his seat, waiting for the mass to flow forward. Eventually, the door opened, and the passengers began their shuffle toward it.

Like cattle. No wonder it's called steerage.

Acton eventually exited the aircraft, and headed to baggage claim. After another eternity, his duffel bag emerged. He battled through a senior's tour to get to the carousel, grabbed his bag, and tossed it over his shoulder. He finally cleared customs, then headed toward a bathroom, resisting the urge to look for pursuers. He wanted to give the impression he didn't think he was being followed—though he had little doubt he was.

Once inside, he locked himself in a handicapped stall and unzipped the bag. He quickly changed his clothes, donned a hat and sunglasses, then took out several large shopping bags. He folded the duffel bag as small as he could, then placed it inside one of the shopping bags. Stuffing his old clothes into the remaining bags, he left the stall, went to the sink, and washed his hands.

Then he waited.

It didn't take long for someone to leave one of the other stalls and approach the sink. The well-dressed, slender man stood in front of the mirror adjusting his tie.

"Excuse me," said Acton. "Would you happen to know how to get to Buckingham Palace?"

The man stared at him, surprised the universal etiquette of never talking in a men's washroom had been violated. He replied in a thick French accent. "Sorry, but I am a touriste ici as well."

"Really? Where ya from?" Acton walked out of the bathroom with the man, trying to make it look as if they were old friends to anyone who might be watching.

"I am from Nice," replied the man, not making much effort to hide his displeasure at the situation.

"Really?" Acton was uncharacteristically animated. "I've never been to France, myself. Don't speak the language, you

115

see." As they walked out of the terminal together, the Frenchman approached a cab. The cabbie popped the trunk and helped him load his luggage, then looked at Acton.

"Are you traveling together, sir?"

The Frenchman appeared horrified.

"Sure, why not?" Acton handed over his bags before the Frenchman could protest, then climbed into the back seat. "Come on, *mawn amy*! Let's get a move on!"

"The Dorchester, s'il vous plaît," the Frenchman ordered with a scowl.

Much to his further horror, Acton looked at him with an astonished expression. "Dorchester? You're kiddin' me! I'm stayin' there as well!"

The cabbie pulled out into the early afternoon traffic, stifling a smile. The Frenchman buried his face in the glass. Acton had a big, childlike grin.

"This is gonna be great!"

Inside the terminal, a man in a business suit entered the bathroom he had seen his target disappear into several minutes before. He searched the opened stalls, then peered over the tops of the closed ones, much to the annoyance of those inside. Not finding who he was looking for, he ran out of the bathroom, raised his wrist to his mouth, and activated his comms. "He's gone! The subject is not in the bathroom."

The White House
Washington, DC

Rachel sobbed when Wheeler told her about Billy's death.

"Did you know him well?" Wheeler was worn out. They had been interviewing staff and interns all morning, and he was already exhausted from being up all night. The drab, windowless room provided, was not helping.

"N-no," she sniffed, "I didn't. Actually, I feel terrible about this, but the last time I saw him, I called him a loser."

"A loser? Why?" asked an equally tired Schultz.

"He had bumped into me in the hallway and spilled my coffee."

"How'd that happen?" Schultz was now thoroughly bored.

Spilled coffee? How much more of this crap do we need to listen to?

"He came running around the corner with a file and ran right into me. I yelled at him and went to the bathroom to clean up."

Wheeler stifled a yawn. "Why was he running?"

"I don't know. He had a priority file in his hands, so I guess he was making a delivery."

"Do you know what was in the file?"

"No, but I do know it was covered in coffee when I last saw it." Rachel blew her nose. "I think he changed the envelope, though, because when I came out of the bathroom, I saw him leaving the supply room."

Wheeler perked up. "Do you know who the file was addressed to?"

"No, but that hallway leads directly to the president's office."

Control Actual slammed his fist on the desk.

This is getting out of hand!

On the screen, the two detectives excitedly talked to each other about what they had discovered.

This needs to be stopped, now!

He reached for the communications gear to contact Dawson, when he hesitated. So far, he had convinced the Delta team they were dealing with a terrorist cell that needed to be eliminated, and they had bought it. But to murder police officers was an entirely different thing. He frowned. If he tasked them with this, he might end up causing them to question their orders, and he couldn't risk it.

He still needed them.

No, this required a different asset, one where morality didn't come into play.

One he had encountered during darker days.

He sent a secure message with the details to an old "friend," and waited for the reply. His phone vibrated.

Consider it done.

THE PROTOCOL

The Dorchester
Park Lane, London, England

As they pulled up in front of The Dorchester hotel, a porter in a crisp white uniform opened the door, and the Frenchman, whom Acton had learned was named Serge, bolted from the cab as if freed from a cage. Acton was still talking, and the cabbie was still struggling to keep a straight face, as he climbed out to help with the luggage.

"Do you have dinner plans tonight, *Surge*?"

"No, I mean, yes, I do. I am sorry, but I already have plans!" yelped Serge, wincing at the massacred pronunciation of his name.

"That's too bad." Acton was enjoying himself thoroughly. "Perhaps tomorrow?"

"Perhaps," answered the Frenchman, following the porter into the hotel lobby with his luggage. Carrying his three shopping bags, Acton entered behind him.

No way I can afford this place!

He gaped at the intricate woodwork and marble running throughout, everything in immaculate condition, only its 1930s architecture revealing the true age of the hotel.

He walked up to the check-in counter and interrupted Serge talking to the desk clerk. "Excuse me, where are your bathrooms?"

The clerk pointed. "Over there, to your right, sir."

"See you in a few minutes *Surge*, nature's callin' again!" Acton flashed Serge a grin then raced off toward the bathroom.

"You said you have a reservation, Monsieur Savard?" asked the desk clerk. "One moment while I look that up for you."

Serge stared at the departing American, then turned to the clerk. "I'm sorry, but there has been a terrible mistake. I'm at the wrong hotel." He motioned to the porter to bring his luggage, and walked toward the exit as fast as he could, muttering, "Je *déteste* les Americains!"

Acton entered the washroom and laughed for the first time in almost a week.

Now that was fun.

He checked himself in the mirror, then reached for his cellphone. Turning it on, he pulled up the number for the British Museum. As he scrolled through the details he had input earlier, it vibrated in his hand. A text message. He pressed the button to read it.

they got me tell wife daughter i love them bye old frnd

Acton's chest ached as he collapsed back against the wall and fell to his knees in shock. The cellphone slid from his hand and onto the floor as he put his head in his hands and sobbed, his shoulders shaking as his stomach hollowed out. His best friend was dead, and it was his fault, of that there was no doubt.

I never should have brought him into this.

As he gasped in ragged breaths between sobs, he recalled meeting Milton for the first time in college. Milton had been working on his PhD when they met at a cross-country meet. Even with "Corky" settling down, getting married, and having a kid, and Acton gallivanting around the world on one archaeological dig after another, they had always remained close. He had even been named godfather of their daughter.

Those bastards. They have to pay!

His sorrow soon turned to anger, a warm rage building inside him as his breathing came under control, the salty tears slowing as he became consumed with the thought of bringing those responsible to justice—and death. He was now determined to find out what was going on. With nothing left to lose except his life, which at the moment didn't feel much worth living, he picked himself up off the floor, retrieved his cellphone, then washed the tears from his face.

The White House
Washington, DC

"Glad I caught you gentlemen before you left."

Wheeler and Schultz were still filling their pockets and holsters with the various accouterments of their trade they had been forced to check upon their arrival, when Darbinger jogged up to them.

"What can I do for you, Mr. Darbinger?" asked Wheeler.

"Just wondering if you found out anything. Any leads as to who may have killed our Billy?"

Schultz opened his mouth to speak when Wheeler cut him off. "No, dead end for now, I'm afraid. But we'll keep looking."

Darbinger frowned. "That's too bad. Well, I'm sure no one from here is involved." He opened the door for them. "You gentlemen have yourselves a great day."

Schultz followed Wheeler to their car, turning to his partner. "What do you think?"

"I think he knows more than he's saying."

Schultz agreed as he unlocked the doors. "But how the hell do we accuse the Chief of Staff of the President of the United States of holding out on us?"

Wheeler shook his head. "I don't know, but I do know who to call next."

"Guthrie?"

Wheeler nodded as he reached for his phone.

Triarii Headquarters
London, England

Over the intercom system, the collection of members sitting around the table listened intently.

"The subject was identified leaving his flight, but was lost when he went into the bathroom," related the voice on the other end of the line. "A review of the security tapes show that he left the bathroom in disguise with another man, then got into a taxi with him."

"So, he has a contact here already?" asked one of those around the table.

"It would appear so, sir. We're trying to track the cab to see where they went. We'll also backtrack the contact to see what flight he came off, and get his name. We should have that information shortly."

"Contact us when you do."

"Yes, Proconsul."

The room fell silent. Everyone looked to the Proconsul of the Triarii, sitting calmly at the head of the table. He tapped the ashes off the end of his cigar, a frown spreading. "This is the first time that two skulls have been in the same city since that BBC cock-up, and those were fakes," he finally said, recalling their closest call in years.

The BBC had done a documentary on the skulls, bringing two of them to England for scientific study. The Triarii had managed to replace the London and Smithsonian skulls with fakes before they were shipped. The resulting embarrassment had forced the British Museum to remove the skull from display. Unbeknownst to them, the skulls had been switched back to the real ones upon their return.

"A bullet was definitely dodged there," agreed the woman to his right responsible for the Paris skull. "We've always relied on the holders of the skulls to either jealously guard their secret, or be considered barmy. Now we have a professor in London with the final missing skull, far too close to another genuine skull, and we don't know what his intentions or that of his accomplice are."

"We should take immediate action to remove the British Museum skull," said another. "Since it's my responsibility to protect, I'll put my plan into action to have it removed, tonight. Agreed?"

There were nods around the table then all turned to the Proconsul. Unlike the others, he wasn't convinced there was foul play afoot. He had no doubt as to what President Jackson and his Special Forces were up to, but not so when it came to the professor. And as long as the professor had the skull, he felt they were safe, at least for the moment.

He shook his head. "Not yet. Let's wait and see what our centurii find out."

"Yes, Proconsul."

J. ROBERT KENNEDY

Institute of Archaeology, University College London
Gordon Square, London, England

Acton entered the lobby of the Institute of Archaeology at the University College London campus, still carrying his shopping bags, and walked up to one of the students milling about.

"Can you tell me where Professor Laura Palmer is?"

"Yes, sir, she's lecturing right now, I believe. Room two-twelve, up those stairs, to the right."

Acton thanked the young man and headed toward the stairs, quickly finding room 212. His heart thumped with the final part of his plan hopefully about to come together. And the fear of knowing that either way, he had no idea what to do next.

He peered through the window and was taken aback when he saw her, realizing she was much more attractive than she had appeared in the desert. She was holding up an old earthenware jar with a slender, alabaster arm partially revealed by a cardigan that had slipped up to her elbow. He followed the arm to her hand and noticed with a satisfaction that surprised him at a time like this, that there was no ring on *the* finger.

Finally, he tore his gaze away to look at the jar. It appeared Babylonian, about 2000 BC.

Impressive.

He knocked on the door.

She looked over and saw him through the window. An immediate light of recognition showed, along with a smile that could stop hearts—and it did. She rushed over, opened the door, and stepped into the hall.

"Professor Acton, I've been on pins and needles waiting for you!"

"You received the package?"

"Yes, this morning. I was gobsmacked to receive something from you. I had just finished reading your article on surviving Incan culture in Archaeology magazine last week. And the spread they did on you in National Geographic last year, when you were on the Yucatan Peninsula, is still one of my favorites. When your parcel arrived, I was so excited, but then when I read your note not

124

to open it until you arrived…I was gutted."

Slightly embarrassed though also flattered, Acton lowered his voice. "I need your help."

"You need *my* help? I'd be happy to, but first I must introduce you to the class." She turned back toward them, but he grabbed her arm. Startled, she swung around and stared at him.

"Nobody can know I was here. I need to show you what was in that package. Is there a place we can talk?"

"Yes, my office. But what is this about? I'm in the middle of a lecture."

He leaned over and whispered in her ear. "I found another skull."

She poked her head through the open door. "Class dismissed, I'll see you all next week!" She grabbed his arm and rushed him toward another wing of the building. Not a word was said between them until they reached her office, where she closed the door behind them, locking it. He pulled down the blind to cover the door's glass, then they both closed the horizontal blinds on the other windows. He looked around for any other means passersby could use to see into the office as she unlocked a filing cabinet and lifted out a box. Satisfied no prying eyes could watch them, he joined her at the large oak desk occupying the back of her office.

"Show me!" Her voice quivered with excitement as she placed the package on her desk and pushed it toward him.

He unlocked the case and carefully unwrapped the skull. She cooed in awe as he held it up in the light. "It's brilliant!" He hadn't had time to examine it closely since he'd been on the ship, and nodded in agreement. It *was* beautiful, in an eerie way. Translucent, it was a life-size, heavy, solid piece of crystal that took both hands to hold.

As he turned the skull, light from the room shimmered and reflected off it, sending a kaleidoscope of patterns onto the walls and ceiling, surrounding them much like a prism. The skull had a myriad of strange lines within it, giving it a vein-like appearance, whereas the facial structure and jaw were clear. It was as if the sculptor had wanted to give the appearance of a brain, of intelligence. The veins in the crystal distorted objects on the other side like an eerily beautiful funhouse mirror. The hollowed out eyes and grinning face made him shiver.

"Where did you find it?" she asked as he handed it to her.

"At a dig in the Andes in Peru."

She ran her expert fingers over the smooth cranium. Acton knew she was feeling for the telltale marks of a carver's tool, and equally knew she would find none. She adjusted a desk lamp to get more light, and continued her inspection as he related the story of the dig in the mountains.

"They were ancient Incan ruins, a fairly large community from what we had unearthed so far. Everything was pretty routine, but fascinating nonetheless." He sat in one of the guest chairs as she examined the skull. "The first unusual thing we found was evidence of thirteenth-century European nobility."

She glanced up from the skull. "What? That's impossible. That area wasn't discovered until early sixteenth century."

"I know, that's what didn't make sense, but there was no doubt about it. First, we found clothing and some trinkets that clearly dated from that era. If it weren't for the clothing, I could have believed that the other items were just heirlooms that some Spaniard had left, but nobody in sixteenth century Spain would wear thirteenth-century British garb."

She sat in her leather chair, momentarily distracted from the skull. "How could this be? We've known for years now that Columbus wasn't the first to discover America. The Vikings had discovered Newfoundland five hundred years before."

"And we know that European fisherman for at least a couple of hundred years fished the Grand Banks in secret, not wanting people to know where they got their easy catches from," added Acton.

"But we've never had evidence that Europeans had gone to South America, certainly not Pacific coast South America."

"I know, which is why I thought maybe this was some fluke, some shipwreck or something that had washed up on shore and they found the items and brought them back to their city." Acton paused. "But then we found the skeleton."

THE PROTOCOL

London, England
AD 1212

Lord Richard Baxter surveyed the curious scene in front of him. The four walls of what was once the council's strongest and most secure building were flattened, all outward, as if some great force from within had knocked them all down as it tried to escape. The night sky was filled with smoke as fires still burned in the distance, this particular area already devastated with little left to burn. As he looked about him, it became evident that whatever had caused this disaster had originated here.

He had been in the council chambers, the celebration of the skull's arrival still going strong, when word had come of the strange noise it emitted when placed on a pedestal with its companions. He had thought little of it when their most learned scholars were dispatched to investigate. Moments after this report, the explosion had occurred.

The skulls in their charge had already been recovered and taken to their backup site under heavy guard. He had ordered them kept separate upon their arrival at their new location, in case their union had caused the terrible event. At first, he couldn't believe it, though seeing how the walls had been knocked down as if from within, and how the skulls had remained untouched in the center of the chamber, he realized it must somehow be.

He shook his head and spun on his heel, heading to a meeting with the surviving members of the council. The memories of his fallen wife and daughter's screams were still fresh in his mind, though his mourning would have to wait. He knew what must be done, but it would be hard to convince the others.

He entered the room, finding the others—the few that remained—already seated. He took his regular place, and when the meeting was brought to order, he rose to be recognized.

"My fellow council members, this is a difficult time. We have all lost loved ones, but more, we are directly responsible for the destruction of our beloved city of London, and nearly half its loyal, innocent residents." Heads bobbed around the table, the faces long with shame and anguish at the

127

knowledge. "There is nothing that can be done to undo what has happened, however there is a way to prevent this from ever occurring again."

"What is it you propose?" asked his good friend Jonathan.

"I propose that this new arrival, the third skull, be taken away, and permanently disposed of." Protests erupted from around the table, and Richard held up his hand to quiet them, if only for a moment. "And any future skulls that may be found."

"And just how would you dispose of them?" asked Jonathan, their friendship being tested.

"I propose that this third skull, and any further skull, be sailed to the west and over the edge of the Earth, so it may never harm another living soul."

"Absolutely not!" Jonathan's fist slammed into the table. "We have been protecting the skulls for over a thousand years. What you propose is preposterous. Blasphemous!"

Richard shook his head. "No, Jonathan, it is the only way." He looked around at the others sitting at the long table. Some bore injuries from the fire, many having lost family like he had—his was not the only devastated, and he was determined to prevent it from ever occurring again.

"When our ancestors came here with the original skull, we believed it to be the only one. Then centuries later, a second was discovered, and this was considered a great gift. Now a third has been delivered to us, and look what devastation it has wrought. No man here can look me in the eye and deny that the third skull is responsible for this."

There were several nods and grunts of agreement, though no one yet was willing to back him verbally.

"But we are sworn to protect the skulls. What you propose goes against the very purpose of the Triarii," Jonathan protested.

"No," said Richard softly, trying to calm Jonathan down. "That is where you are wrong. We were sworn to protect the original skull by the Emperor, not the others. Our predecessors took it upon themselves to extend that oath to all other skulls that may be found, when we discovered the second skull. Once we realized there may be more, a decision was made to actively seek them out and protect them, but it was not our original mission."

This finally elicited a response from William, one of the oldest surviving members of the council, official records keeper, and chronicler of the deeds of the Triarii.

"He's right, Jonathan. According to the scrolls, when the second skull was discovered, the council decided to actively seek out any other skulls that may exist, and protect them from the unworthy. If that council could change our mandate, then this council can change it yet again."

"Thank you, William," nodded Richard.

"But what he proposes…." Jonathan was quieter now that William had spoken, though still shook his head. "It's madness!"

"It would be madness not to."

"But who would undertake such a mission?" asked another.

"I volunteer. I have nothing left here except my duty and honor. And I can think of no greater duty or honor than preventing a disaster such as has befallen us, from ever happening again."

Jonathan leaped from his chair. "But you would never return! It's suicide!"

"It is my life to give and God's to take." He placed a hand on his friend's shoulder. "I propose that this council pass my resolution forthwith, so that I may leave without delay."

The nods of agreement were unanimous this time, though few had the courage to meet his gaze, knowing what they were agreeing to meant the death of their companion.

Chevy Chase, Maryland
Present Day

George Guthrie shook his head. "I can't believe it. Lesley Darbinger?" He sat in a high back leather chair in his den, the two detectives sitting across from him.

"Yes, sir," said Wheeler. "We both got the definite impression that he was holding out on us. That, and the fact your son worked for him and was carrying a coffee-stained folder into a supply room, then was later seen with a matching folder that didn't have coffee on it, leads us to believe that he stumbled onto something he shouldn't have."

"How?"

"He must have switched envelopes and seen what was inside when doing so," explained Schultz. "We think that this switch was discovered, and they had him eliminated."

Guthrie sank back into his chair. "Where was the file heading?"

"It looks like the president's office."

"Do you have any proof?"

Wheeler shook his head. "No, and I'm not sure how we can get any. If this was indeed something sanctioned from within the White House, you can bet they've covered their tracks."

Guthrie sighed. "So, my son's killer may go free." He clenched his fists and slammed both of them into the arms of the chair he was sitting in. Taking a deep breath, he reined in his anger. "Okay, I'm going to make some calls. If Darbinger did this, I'm sure Stew—I mean, the president—didn't know. I'll see if I can get in touch with him. If all else fails, I'll call in some markers and have a damned Senate investigation into the matter convened. I won't stop until we get to the bottom of this." He stood and herded the two detectives toward the door. "I'll call you as soon as I have something for you."

"Thank you, sir."

Wheeler headed out the door, toward their car. Schultz looked at him.

"You realize if Darbinger is behind this, we'll never be able to touch him."

"Perhaps. But Guthrie still has a lot of pull in this town."

"Maybe, but he's liable to get himself killed just for nosing in. This kid saw something he shouldn't have, and they killed him for it. They obviously think they're untouchable. Guthrie should be careful."

Wheeler tossed the keys to Schultz. "You drive, I forgot to ask Guthrie about how Billy got hired in the first place."

"How's that important?"

"I want to know if it was general knowledge whose son he was." He headed back to the door as Schultz climbed in the driver's seat and turned the key. The car turned over a few times, but didn't start.

Wheeler heard this and spun around. "No!"

Schultz didn't have time to react to the warning before he turned the key again. This time the car started, the engine overwhelmed with a gut-wrenching roar of hatred as an explosion tore through the vehicle, the flames rushing out from under it, sending a shockwave that had Wheeler flying back toward the entrance of Guthrie's house. Shrapnel from the gutted car tore through everything in its path, including a small piece that sliced Wheeler's arm. He picked himself up as Guthrie ran out of the house, his mouth agape, offering a steadying hand.

"Are you okay?"

"Justin!" cried Wheeler at the now roaring fire that was his partner. He fell onto a porch bench, grabbing his head and pulling it down toward his chest as he tried to control the sobs that desperately wanted to be heard. Several of Guthrie's staff ran toward the scene, one with a fire extinguisher that proved of no use.

They're too late.

Wheeler stared up at Guthrie, rage written all over his face. "They have to pay."

"And they will."

The Ritz
150 Piccadilly, London, England

Serge toweled off in front of the window as he stared out at the London skyline. The view was magnificent, and he was now convinced switching hotels was not such a bad thing. He tossed the towel over his shoulder and was about to head back to the bathroom when there was a knock at the door. "Who is it?" He had ordered a massage to unwind from his experience with the American, but was told she wouldn't arrive for hours.

"Room service, sir," replied the muffled voice.

"But I did not order anything." Serge pulled on a bathrobe.

"It's champagne, sir, compliments of the hotel."

Ahhhh, excellent!

He unlocked the door, and as he turned the knob, the door was shoved open from the other side, knocking him to the floor as two men rushed in. One quickly closed the door and locked it, while the other stuffed a rag in Serge's mouth before he could protest. They then bound his hands and feet with plastic ties, and in less than a minute, he was sitting in a chair, terrified, as the men searched his room.

One of them stood in front of him, staring through his sunglasses, before ripping the gag from Serge's mouth. "Where's Acton?"

"What? What are you talking about? What is an Ac-ton?" Serge trembled in his chair, desperately trying not to urinate.

"Don't bugger about. We saw you meet him at the airport and get in a taxi together. Now, where is he?"

Serge's eyes widened. "That stupid American from the aeroport? I've never met him before today!"

"Bollocks!" The man removed his sunglasses and leaned in. "I guess we do this the *hard* way."

Serge pissed himself.

Merde.

THE PROTOCOL

"He knows nothing, sir," said the voice over the speaker. "The professor apparently approached him in the bathroom and ingratiated himself upon Mr. Savard."

"Could he be lying?" asked the British Museum member.

"No, ma'am, I'm quite certain he isn't lying. As soon as I threatened him, he urinated himself and told us everything. He even switched hotels to avoid him."

"Very well, keep us posted." The Proconsul hit a button, cutting off the conversation. "I'm not convinced there's malevolence here."

The British Museum member counted off her points on her fingers. "He never reported his find, he's actively hiding from us, he's been using disguises. What more evidence do we need? He is trying to either bring the skull to someone for their own purposes, or he has a purpose of his own. Either way, we can't take the risk that three or more skulls may come together. The Protocol is clear. If two or more skulls are at risk of coming together, then the Triarii Council must take action to prevent this."

The Proconsul listened quietly, then leaned forward. "You are right. Three skulls together have resulted in disaster in the past. We cannot risk an unknown rogue element with an unknown agenda to have access to the skulls." Nods of agreement circled the table. "I do, however, think it is premature to activate The Protocol." He turned to the British Museum Member. "We should, however, switch your charge. You proceed tonight."

"Yes, Proconsul."

Professor Palmer's Office, University College London
Gordon Square, London, England

"Skeleton?" Laura Palmer shook her head in disbelief, as though unsure she had heard him correctly. "You found a thirteenth-century European skeleton at an Incan dig in the Andes?"

"Yes, Professor," grinned Acton. "It was incredible, but there was no doubt. He was buried in a combination of Incan and European traditions. He was wrapped, but there was also a golden cross buried with him, held in his hands on his chest."

"He was buried as a nobleman?"

"Yes."

"Incredible. And please, call me Laura."

Acton smiled, relieved to finally talk to someone about what had happened over the past week. "Call me Jim."

"Thank you." She smiled back, then lifted the skull. "Now, how does *this* fit in with your story?"

"Well, I noticed that the body was oriented pointing directly at a recently discovered cave entrance on a nearby hillside. At first, I didn't think much of it, but had one of my students do some exploratory digging."

"And this was inside?"

"Yes, deep in the cave there was evidence that dirt had been packed by hand against the far wall, so we had one of our guys start to dig at it. It took a couple of days, but he finally broke through to a chamber on the other side and then saw this. Scared the shit out of him." Acton laughed, recalling Garcia's panicked ranting. The memory of the proud father cast a shadow over his face.

"What's wrong?" asked Laura softly.

"When I saw what we had, I realized we might have a problem. If word got out, we could end up with every nutjob on the planet swarming our camp, which would draw too much attention from rebels and other elements. So, I shut down the dig for the day and had everyone go to Lima for some R and R. I completed the excavation myself, and put the skull into that case then locked it in my cabin. They arrived the next night."

"Who?"

"The men in the helicopter. They had to be military, probably Special Ops guys, Delta Force or Navy SEALs maybe. I saw them take out our guards before they landed, probably with a sniper. I took the case, and tried to draw them away from the camp, but it didn't work."

Laura put the skull down and walked around the desk. "What did they do?"

"They—" Acton's voice cracked. "They killed everyone."

"But why?" She pointed at the skull she had placed on the desk. "Why would they kill for that? It's just a piece of quartz crystal."

"I have no idea, but these guys were professional, well-armed, well disciplined." Acton paused. "And they've killed again since then."

Laura sat in the chair beside him. "Again?"

Acton nodded. "My best friend, Dean Gregory Milton." He pulled out his cellphone, scrolled to the message, and handed it to her. Her hand darted to her mouth as she read it, tears filling her eyes.

"I'm so sorry, James." She passed the cellphone back. "How did you escape?"

"Myself and one of my students, Robbie—he'd been standing guard at the cave entrance—hid in the chamber where we found the skull. He tried to save me by telling them I wasn't there, but he was shot. I took the guy out with a pickaxe. I used his gun on another one, then some grenades to collapse the cave entrance."

Laura looked on wide-eyed. "You killed one of them?"

"I had no choice, I just reacted. It was him or me. I did a stint in the Guard when I was younger, so it was just the old training coming back. Anyway, I found a hidden passageway that led to another entrance in the side of the hill. When I got out, I found the camp empty and everyone dead, executed. The supply truck arrived shortly after, and I was able to get to Lima.

"Whenever I'm on a dig, I get a safety deposit box at a local bank, and put all of my papers and some emergency cash in there, so I picked up that stuff and stowed away on a ship for a few days until it docked up the coast in Mexico. I sent the package to you, snuck across the border, and in Phoenix sent a decoy package. From there, I went to New York and made contact with Greg. I caught a flight to

London, ditched them at the airport, and came here."

"Amazing." She paused. "I must confess something." She reached under a pile of papers on her desk and pulled out a newspaper. She flipped a few pages in, then pointed out an article to him. *Archaeological Team Massacred by Rebels*. "You've been big news. It says you were missing and presumed dead. When I got the parcel and realized it was from you, I wasn't sure whether or not I should contact the authorities."

"You—"

"No, I didn't," reassured Laura. "Against my better judgment, I decided to hear what you had to say. As I said, I've followed your work for years, and couldn't believe you had anything to do with what happened. Now that I hear your story—I'm not sure what to think."

"You don't believe me?"

"No, it's not that, I do believe you. I've just never met anyone who's gone through this type of thing, and I have to admit, I'm scared just having you here."

"You're right." Acton rose. "I shouldn't have involved you. I don't know what I was thinking. I'll leave now."

She grabbed his arm and pulled him back into the chair. "No, that's not what I meant. I mean, I'm scared, but I want to help, if I can. Which brings me to my question: Why me? Why did you contact me?"

"Because according to what I've read, you're the one expert on these things who isn't considered a quack."

She laughed. "Some of my colleagues might disagree."

"What can you tell me about the skulls? Why would someone kill over one?"

"Well, let me say, that this wasn't the first time someone has died because of the skulls."

THE PROTOCOL

Maria leaned against the doorframe, closed her eyes, and sighed.

I'm the one who needs the massage.

She was exhausted from fending off a group of Japanese businessmen, who thought all massages should have happy endings. She opened her eyes and looked down at the Do Not Disturb sign on the door, then at the room number.

Right room.

She checked her watch.

A little late. Perhaps he fell asleep?

She knocked anyway, rather than risk getting in trouble for not showing up for an appointment. There was no response. She knocked harder and called into the door. "I'm here for your six p.m. massage, sir." Still no answer.

Or was there?

She thought she heard a moan. She pulled out her access pass and swiped it, opened the door, and peeked inside.

"I'm here for your massage!" she called out again. This time she definitely heard a noise. She pushed the door all the way open and lifted her massage table through. As she cleared the frame, she let the door close behind her, and walked into the room. She saw no one, but heard the moan again from the bedroom. Her thoughts were of another perverted client. She peered around the door of the bedroom and screamed at the scene that greeted her, dropping the massage table onto the glass table in the center of the room, shattering it.

There was blood everywhere. Spattered on the walls, the ceiling, the carpet. So much that she couldn't believe whoever it belonged to could have survived. Her heart thumping, she backed out of the room when she heard the moan again. She rushed for the suite door, afraid whoever had done this was still there. Reaching the door, she stopped.

What if they need help?

She inched toward the bedroom. Again a moan. Peering around the doorframe, she saw a man. He was tied to all four posts of the bed, naked and bleeding from his eyes, ears, nose, mouth, arms, chest, legs, feet, even genitals. He had a rag stuffed in his mouth and was barely conscious. She removed it, and he turned his head to her.

"Bloody hell!" she exclaimed. "Who would do such a thing?"

"Ac-ton," he whispered.

"What? What did you say?"

"Ac-ton," he said, a little louder.

"The man who did this was named Acton?" He stared at her then passed out. She lifted the phone and called reception. "Call nine-nine-nine, someone has been hurt very badly in room six-one-two. Send an ambulance immediately." She paused a moment then added, "And the police."

Detective Chief Inspector Hugh Reading entered the bedroom of the suite and whistled at the scene before him. A tall, large-framed man, he cut an imposing figure to those who didn't know him, though those who did, knew he was intensely loyal to his subordinates—and had a legendary penchant for tea.

After serving over twenty years, he was nearing retirement. Not that he wanted to retire. He loved his job. It would be a true *forced* retirement. It was his life. Divorced long ago, he had decided ruining his life by devoting it to the job was better than ruining the lives of an entire family, so he hadn't remarried or even tried. He had seen a lot of things over the years, yet this was something new. He could tell this would consume him for the coming days.

The staff member who had phoned it in was sitting on a chair, a female constable comforting her as the coroner's staff zipped up the body bag, preparing to transfer it to a gurney. Blood was everywhere.

The poor bastard never had a chance.

He looked at the floor to make sure he wasn't stepping in any of it, and was surprised to see there wasn't much, just the odd spatter the crime scene guys had already marked and photographed. Surveying the room, he examined the spatters on the bed, ceiling, walls, and lamps.

There's something odd about all this.

"Okay, what do we know?" he asked the room in general.

Detective Inspector Chaney approached him. His slight yet athletic frame made him seem tiny compared to his supervisor. "His name is Serge Savard, French national, arrived on an Air France flight today at eleven-thirty a.m. Miss Barnaby here discovered the victim when she came to give him a scheduled massage at six p.m. TOD was several minutes after that."

"After?"

"Yes, guv. He was apparently alive when she found him."

Reading looked around the scene again. "Somebody survived this?"

"Not for long, guv. According to her, before he passed out, he said a man named Acton did it."

"Acton?" He glanced at Miss Barnaby, then approached her. He motioned for the constable sitting with her to leave, and sat beside the distraught woman. "Miss, my name is Detective Chief Inspector Reading of Scotland Yard. I'm leading the investigation into Mr. Savard's death. Can you please tell me again exactly what happened?"

She relayed the story to him, ending with her phone call to the police.

"And he said a man named Acton did it?"

"Yes."

"Those were his exact words? 'Acton did it?'"

"Well, not exactly. I said something like 'Who did this to you?' and he said 'Acton.' He said it twice to me before he died," she replied confidently.

"That's all he said? Acton. Just that one word?"

"Yes, sir. All he said was Acton, twice."

"Thank you, Miss." He patted her on the knee and got up, heading over to the bed where Chaney was examining the plastic ties that had bound the Frenchman.

What happened here?

"The coroner said that this went on for hours," explained Chaney. "You can tell by the blood spatter. Some of it's dry, some of it just starting to congeal. The dry stuff is from the beginning of the torture, the fresh stuff toward the end. Whoever did this certainly knew what they were doing."

"What do you mean?"

"Well, to keep somebody alive that long while torturing them with this much blood loss, they would have to be professionals, wouldn't they? I mean, one wrong cut and you hit an artery. Then he's dead and of no use. This guy was still alive when he was found."

Reading nodded, impressed. "Did you notice anything

else?"

"Such as, sir?"

"The blood spatter."

Chaney looked around the room then back at his boss, shaking his head.

"If no arteries were hit, why the spatter?"

Chaney's jaw dropped. "I can't believe I missed that. Could there be a second victim?"

"Possibly, however, my guess is the spatter was part of the torture. Your victim needs to see blood, to think he's going to die. Small, precise cuts, especially where the victim can't see, don't scare once the pain is gone. See how there's a pillow under his shoulders so his head is tilted back? He can't see what's happening. Cut the person, and whip your scalpel toward the wall, the blood spatter is there for him to look at the entire time. Keep doing that for hours, and you get a scene like this."

Chaney winced, clearly disturbed by the image. "Sir, how—"

"How do I know this?" He smiled slightly. "I wasn't always a copper." With that, he swung around and left the room, Chaney scurrying after him. "We need to find this Acton person. He's the key to this. Let's trace the victim's movements, starting with how he got here. We need to figure out what happened between him getting off the aircraft and arriving here. Somewhere along the way, he met this Acton person, who either killed him, or knows who did."

THE PROTOCOL

Jasper leaned back in the rear seat of the cab and closed his eyes, exhausted from their long flight. And from his partner's incessant chatter. "Scotland Yard." The cab immediately pulled out as Jasper sank further into the seat.

Lambert, though tired, was apparently too excited to rest. He pressed his head to the window, eagerly taking in as much as he could. "Have you ever been to London before, sir?"

"No."

"Did you know that it's actually called New Scotland Yard?"

"No."

"Yeah, the original burned down, so they had to build a new one."

"Lambert?"

"Yeah, boss?"

"You *do* know that I will get my gun back eventually?"

"Shutting up, sir."

Jasper managed to catch a few minutes of peace before the cabby announced their arrival. Lambert paid, and they grabbed their luggage, entering the large, bustling facility. They presented their credentials to the Desk Sergeant.

"You the Yanks we've been expecting?"

Lambert nodded as the man called up to the Detectives' Office. A few moments later, he put the phone down.

"Sorry, sirs, but the Chief Inspector isn't available at the moment. Would you care to wait?"

"Wasn't he expecting us?" asked Jasper. "The State Department was supposed to arrange a meeting to discuss a very important matter."

"Yes, sir. Your people called here earlier, but the Chief was called away on urgent business. Don't worry gents, shouldn't be long. I'll have a cuppa brought for you."

"Coffee, please. And lots of it."

The Desk Sergeant frowned, his thoughts clear.

Coffee? Uncivilized!

Professor Palmer's Office, University College London
Gordon Square, London, England

As Laura explained the little known about the skulls, the overcast sky had turned into a heavy downpour, and sheets of rain driven by gusts of wind rattled the windows. A lone desk lamp cast a gentle glow on the office.

"Most of the skulls we know about are fakes," she said, "believed to have been made by European craftsmen in the eighteenth and nineteenth centuries, including the ones located here and at the Smithsonian."

"The one here is a fake?"

"Yes. According to tests performed for a BBC documentary, it's one of those that was created in Europe within the past two centuries."

"You sound doubtful."

She sighed. "James, I studied that skull for years, and I swear the things they said about it during the study just don't match up with what I've seen."

"Such as?"

"Well, they said that you could see the tool markings from polishing equipment that dated from the past two centuries. I've examined it for years, and never found even the minutest trace of any markings. I also studied the one at the Smithsonian years ago, and found it to be the same."

"So, how do you explain it?"

"Better equipment? Incompetence maybe?" She shrugged. "I don't know. Anyway, here's what we do know. Most of the skulls that are considered genuine were found in Mexico, and Central and South America. It is believed that they are some sort of ancient religious icon from the Mayan, Aztec, or Incan civilizations, or maybe even from more than one."

"We were at Incan ruins, so that would fit."

"Yes, it would," she agreed. "The indigenous people of the area believe that the skulls have magical healing powers, but nobody really knows what they were used for. Some claim that if you bring them together and shine certain colors of light at them, they give off energy patterns that match the human brain and can even affect time as we know it."

"You're kidding!"

"Remember those quacks you talked about?" Acton laughed as she continued. "The lore surrounding the skulls is varied and most of it unbelievable. Some believe there are twelve genuine skulls, others thirteen, and that bringing them together will mark the dawn of a new age. Others believe that bringing them together will destroy the world. Still others believe it will send a signal to aliens. The fact is, nobody knows what they do, because nobody really knows where they came from."

"But I thought they came from the Aztecs, Mayans, and Incans?"

"That's where many of them have been found, but those cultures didn't have the technology to create them." Acton stared at her, puzzled. "In fact, even today we don't have the technology to create the genuine ones."

"What do you mean?"

"I mean just that." Laura got up from her desk and stepped over to one of the bookcases. Turning on a switch that lit the beautiful oak shelves from end-to-end, she scanned several volumes, pulled out a binder, and returned to the desk. "In 1970, the most famous skull, the Mitchell-Hedges skull, was given to Hewlett-Packard to do some testing on it. Their labs in Santa Clara, California, were renowned for crystal research and leading experts were involved in the testing. What they found was astonishing."

Acton leaned in. "What did they find?"

Laura smiled at his eagerness. "As you may be aware, crystal has a natural axis. This axis is the natural orientation of the molecular symmetry of the crystal. When carving crystal, modern carvers will always determine the natural axis of the crystal, and carve *with* it. If you carve against it, or against the grain if you will, the crystal will almost always break, especially a piece the size of one of these skulls. The genuine skulls are all made of a single piece of crystal, which in itself is quite amazing, but even more so, the genuine skulls were carved *against* the axis, which is unheard of. No one to this day has been able to duplicate this. Not even with the use of lasers."

Acton let out a low whistle. "Amazing. How do they explain this?"

"They can't. But that's not all they found. They also determined that there were no markings whatsoever on the skull to indicate that any kind of tool had been used in the carving. They hypothesized that it could have been roughly carved with diamonds and then a solution of silicon sand and water used for the detail work. There's only one problem with this explanation though."

"What's that?"

"It would have taken over three hundred years to complete."

THE PROTOCOL

Rodney Underwood stared down at his friend Clive, who lay motionless on the floor with an astonished look still on his face. He hated doing this to him, Clive truly a good friend, yet he had no choice—it was his duty. He picked up Clive's chair then sat while examining the monitors. At the back gate, a truck pulled up to the loading dock. He hit a few keys on the console, and the large metal door of the loading dock rolled open, the truck driving in seconds later. He watched on the monitors as it followed the ramp down into the underground shipping and receiving area. It backed up to a platform, then bumped the lip. The door to the back opened, and six men exited, the driver remaining in the truck. Rodney closed the front gate and watched on the monitors for the other guards patrolling, then radioed the go ahead as each area was clear.

The team rapidly made its way to one of the storage rooms then waited for Rodney to enter the code to open the door from the control room. The door buzzed open, and the men entered, closing it behind them. Two headed directly to the third row of shelving, another two grabbed a wheeled ladder and followed them. The remaining pair covered the door.

"There it is." The first man pointed to the fourth shelf, about twelve feet up. The team with the ladder locked it in place, and two men rushed up the steps. The first to arrive grabbed the box and handed it to the other. He opened the top to make sure what they were searching for was inside. Underneath the velvet wrapping, the grinning face of a skull stared up at him. He shivered. Covering it back up, they transferred the skull into a backpack, then replaced the original with the fake used in the BBC documentary. No one would know they had been there. They descended and ran to the door, the second team placing the ladder back where they found it, then they waited for the all-clear signal.

Rodney rechecked the halls then sent the signal. The team raced back to the loading dock, boarded their truck, and left the underground garage through the doors Rodney opened for them. When they were clear, he closed the doors, relieved.

Done!

Looking around to make sure there were no signs of what had happened, he rose from his chair and turned his attention to Clive. He removed the tranquilizer dart from his friend's chest, placed the chair on its side again, then hid his gun in his bag. He took out another weapon and stuck it in his belt behind his back.

Kneeling beside Clive, he slapped him gently on the face. "Clive, wake up."

Nothing.

He slapped him harder. "Clive, wake up!"

This time Clive moaned.

"Wake up. You fell out of your chair and hit your head."

"Wh-what happened?" Clive groggily rubbed his eyes then stared up at Rodney. "You shot me!" He grabbed at his chest, searching for the wound as he panicked, scurrying backward on the floor.

Rodney laughed. Pulling the gun out from his belt, he pointed it at him. He squeezed the trigger and a flag snapped out with Liverpool F.C. emblazoned on it. "I'm sorry. I guess I scared the shit out of you on that one. You fell right out of your chair and hit your head pretty bad. You've been out for almost fifteen minutes."

"Really?" A bewildered Clive rubbed the back of his head, wincing when he felt the lump that had formed. "I could have sworn…." He checked his chest, seeing he was clearly not shot. Still confused, he extended a hand. "Help me up, you wanker."

Rodney laughed again and pulled his friend to his feet.

"Complete success, Proconsul. Nobody will ever know we were there. Our inside man will wipe the tapes showing our presence."

"Very good, Centurion," said the Proconsul, looking at one of the cameras showing an image of the team leader. The operation at the British Museum had been monitored by the council through camera feeds from their agents' headgear, and it had gone like clockwork. "Move the item to its secondary site and await further instructions."

"Yes, Proconsul, we're on our way—"

The view from the camera shifted unexpectedly as the team leader lost his footing. Shouts of confusion rang out as the truck swerved wildly, tossing around the men in the back. They were all thrown forward as the vehicle screeched to a halt.

"What's going on there?" The Proconsul pressed a button in front of him, and the view split to all of the different camera angles available.

"I'm not sure, Proconsul," was the reply. "What the hell is going on up there?" the team lead shouted into his mic to the driver. There was no answer. The camera showed him getting up and approaching the back doors to the truck. He was about to open them when they exploded outward. Three men standing in jeans and plaid shirts with balaclavas over their faces rained gunfire into the truck.

In the Triarii chamber, the onlookers watched, stunned, as each camera view either went dead or dropped to the floor, the entire scene unfolding in less than a minute.

Then there was silence.

Dawson climbed into the back of the truck and looked around, his gaze landing on a bag he thought might contain what they were searching for. Stepping over the bodies, he approached the rear. When one of the occupants to his right moaned, Dawson put a bullet in his chest. He opened the bag.

Are you kidding me?

The words from Control Actual echoed in his head. *"You'll know it when you see it."* But this wasn't it. At least it shouldn't be. Acton still had the item from Peru as far as they knew. And this appeared to be some carving belonging to a museum.

Why the hell did I just kill seven men over a crystal skull?

Under orders from Control, when they first arrived, his men had set up surveillance on the apparent headquarters of Acton's terrorist cell. When his team reported the vehicle leaving, he had ordered it followed. This had proven a wise move, allowing them to ambush the terrorists as soon as they left the museum. Yet nothing was making sense. The skull fit the loose description of knowing it when seeing it, and being made of crystal, but he refused to believe his country would have him chasing trinkets.

Though if these terrorists are actually a cult, it might make sense.

Perhaps they were stealing crystal objects, including the DARPA project, all over the world? At the moment, he couldn't care less about what was in the bag, beyond that Control had instructed they retrieve whatever was stolen.

It's as if they knew exactly what was going to happen.

He took the bag and left the truck, his men jumping into the two SUVs they had arrived in, leaving in opposite directions. They would meet up later after switching their vehicles and clothing to confuse London's cameras.

"What the hell just happened?" asked one of the council members.

"We've been betrayed," said another. "How else could they know what we were planning and when?"

"Who would kill our men so coldly?"

"We know who." The Proconsul leaned back in his chair. He stubbed his cigar out in an ashtray on the table in front of him, the taste no longer pleasing. All eyes were on him now. "We've known this day could come when the one who betrayed us once would betray us again."

"Are you sure?"

"Did you see their tactics?" asked another. "They had to be Special Forces. Those outfits were for the benefit of the cameras on the street."

"There's one way to know for sure." The Proconsul punched a button on the control panel in front of him. "Get me our friend in Washington."

"Right away, sir."

The room waited in anticipation, no one saying anything, all fearing their worst case scenario was about to be confirmed.

"Go ahead," said a disembodied voice through the speaker. It would have been chilling if he didn't know who he was talking to, the subterfuge necessary, however, as not all at the council table knew who was speaking, and if there were any uninvited listeners, their contact's safety was paramount.

"This is the Proconsul."

"Yes, sir."

"Seven of our men were killed minutes ago. The British Museum skull has been lost."

"I know, I just heard. The operation was carried out by his forces."

"What are his intentions?"

"I believe he intends to bring the skulls together."

"If that *is* his intention, he may need to be dealt with."

"I understand."

"We will speak again." The Proconsul severed the connection.

"You *do* realize who you're talking about killing, don't you?" asked the Paris member.

The Proconsul nodded as he took in a deep breath.

"Anyone who gets in our way is forfeit if necessary."

The Dorchester
Park Lane, London, England

Chaney stopped and gaped at the surroundings as Reading walked purposefully toward the front desk of the Dorchester. Savard's plane tickets had been booked through an agency, and a quick phone call had determined he was originally scheduled for a stay here, and not the Ritz where he was found. Chaney was about to comment on the opulence to his boss, when he noticed he was now standing alone. He rushed to catch up.

Reading flashed his warrant card to the clerk behind the desk. "DCI Reading, Scotland Yard. This is DI Chaney," he said, glancing at his tardy underling. "We were wondering if you've seen this man today." He motioned to Chaney who pulled a blow up of the Frenchman's passport photo out of a manila envelope and showed it to her.

She shook her head. "I'm sorry, sir, I haven't. May I?" She reached for the photo.

"Of course." Chaney handed it to her. She took the photograph and walked away, showing it to several others. Another man nodded and returned with her.

"This is Michael. He says he saw him earlier."

"DCI Reading, DI Chaney," repeated Reading as he took back the photo and held it up. "You saw this man?"

"Yes, sir, this afternoon. I took his bags in from a taxi and waited with him while he checked in. Then he said he was at the wrong hotel and rushed out. I followed him with the bags and put them in a taxi for him. Then he left."

"He said he was in the wrong hotel?" asked Chaney.

"Yes, sir, quite strange if I do say so, sir."

Reading turned to the desk clerk. "Can you confirm if a Mr. Serge Savard had a reservation here today?"

She punched a few keys on her computer. "Yes, Inspector, he had a reservation for the next three nights, booked a fortnight ago." She hit a few more keys. "It looks like the check-in process began and then was stopped for some reason. The agent who was on duty is on break now. Do you want me to get him?"

Reading nodded, and she rushed off. He turned back to the porter. "Was there anything else unusual about his behavior that you can think of?"

The porter thought for a moment. "Well, I thought it kind of odd that he left his friend here."

Reading stopped. "His friend? You mean he wasn't alone?"

"No, sir, he came with someone else, an American, I believe. He asked where the toilets were, then went off in that direction." The porter pointed toward the bathrooms. "It was then that the gentleman in the photograph left."

The desk clerk approached with another in tow. Before she had a chance to speak, Reading cut her off. "Do you have security cameras here?" She nodded. "We'll need to see the tapes from this afternoon immediately."

They were led to the security room, a cramped affair with one lone occupant who was quickly filled in on the situation. Within moments, he had the lobby footage from the time of the check-in displayed.

"That's him there." Chaney pointed at the image of the Frenchman in the lobby. "And that must be the man he arrived with." Again he pointed to the screen, this time at a man carrying shopping bags and heading toward the bathrooms. A couple of moments later, the Frenchman scurried toward the doors.

"Okay, show me the entrance camera for a few minutes before so we can see how they arrived," ordered Reading.

"No problem, mon," said the security technician, a white man with a thick Jamaican accent and dreadlocks tucked into a Rastafarian Tam hat. He punched up a different camera view and time code.

"There they are." Reading pointed at the two men entering the building. "Back it up." The image reversed, and they saw the men climbing out of a cab. "Stop it there. Zoom in on the taxi, I want the number." The image froze, and the tech zoomed in on the top of the cab. "Got that?" Reading asked Chaney.

"Yes, sir." He jotted down the cab number and company name. "I'll call right now and find out where the pickup took place." He stepped to the other side of the small room to place a call from his cellphone.

"Okay, now move it forward inside the lobby and see if we can spot our mystery man leaving."

The tech laughed. "Mystery Mon, yaw, gud name for

eem!"

Reading grabbed the back of the man's chair and swung the startled tech around to face him. "This man is wanted for questioning in the brutal murder of someone earlier today, so you will excuse me if I fail to see the humor!" Reading glared at the cowering tech.

"Sorry, sir," replied the tech in perfect English, without a hint of his Jamaican accent. "I didn't know." He switched the camera view back and played the image at double-time. A few minutes later, they saw the same man with the shopping bags heading toward the doors. The tech switched the view to the entrance, and they watched as he got in a cab. He looked up at Reading sheepishly. "Would you like the taxi number, sir?" Reading nodded. The tech zoomed in on the cab number, and Reading jotted it down.

"Can you give me a printout of his face?"

"Yes, sir." He backed up the image frame by frame, searching for a good face shot. When he found one, he zoomed in on it and hit a button. It appeared in the printer tray moments later. Swiveling in his chair, he grabbed the photographic paper off the tray and spun back toward Reading. "Here you go, sir."

"Thank you." Reading stared intently at the picture.

Who are you?

Chaney flipped his phone closed and turned to Reading. "Got a hit on the taxi, guv. They were picked up at Heathrow."

"Okay, tell them we're on our way and to have the videotape ready." Reading strode toward the door. He tore the other cab number off his pad and handed it to Chaney. "And find out where this one went."

THE PROTOCOL

Dawson and his men parked their SUV in an alleyway and climbed out. Two of his men opened a manhole cover, then they all descended into the London storm drainage system, walking several hundred feet before Dawson looked up at the next access point. Climbing the metal rungs, he tentatively pushed the manhole cover up and carefully surveyed the surroundings. Seeing everything was clear, he pushed it aside and looked up.

A vehicle was parked directly overhead. He climbed up a few more rungs, then knocked on the bottom. An access door opened and Smitty stared down at him.

"Pardon me, sir, but do you have a reservation?" he asked in a fake British accent.

"Yes, it's under Hugh, Mr. Eff Hugh." Dawson handed him the bag. Smitty smiled and took it, then grabbed Dawson's hand, hauling him into the truck. Dawson sat on one of the benches that lined either side, the second team, led by Red, already there. The rest of the men rapidly exited the drainage system, and soon the manhole cover was replaced, and the hatch closed. Once out of the city, they would take a quick detour into some woods where their chopper would take them back to base.

Nothing but a routine exercise.

He checked his watch then looked at Red, sitting directly across from him at the back of the truck. "Timer set?"

Red nodded. "Yup. Should make for one hell of a demonstration."

Dawson banged on the side of the truck. "Let's go. We need to clear the Ring of Steel before that detonation."

The truck's engine roared to life, and they slowly pulled away, leaving Dawson to dwell on his thoughts. He considered himself a moral man. He had killed for his country before. Many times before. He had even been forced to kill civilians occasionally, though they were never innocent bystanders. They had been in his way, sheltering a target, lying to him, whatever. They were always guilty of something. This was the first mission, however, where he had serious doubts. When Acton had fled to England, Control had provided further intel on the terrorist cell.

Apparently, their main base of operations was in London, the US cell simply that—a cell—one small part of a much larger organization aimed at bringing down the West.

Yet he still had a hard time reconciling that homegrown terrorists could be organized across continents, with so many willing participants.

And the man at the hotel? He had tortured targets for information before, but this man knew nothing, despite Control Actual insisting he did, ordering the initial torture, and the final, brutal acts that would have haunted him for the rest of his days if he had followed through.

But he hadn't. There were certain lines even he wouldn't cross.

His morality was being challenged, though every time he felt guilty about what he was doing, he was forced to think back on what had happened to this point. The terrorists in Peru were on the Termination List—and you didn't get on that by accident. Acton had killed one of his men and seriously wounded another, then fled not to his university and the authorities, but to the very city his terrorist cell was centered in—London. And he had sent a decoy package, which proved he was hiding something—if he weren't, there would have been no need for a decoy.

As well, his cell had managed to insert an operative inside the White House, feet from the president himself, which had to mean they had more contacts on the inside. And now a group of armed men had left the very headquarters Control Actual had briefed him on, and committed armed robbery, stealing a sculpture from a museum.

It was this skull that now gnawed at him. Control had said in the initial briefing the object was a top-secret crystal, part of the Structural Amorphous Metals project, stolen from DARPA while in transit. It was moldable, making it unique—a new form of crystal that had incredible military applications.

"There isn't a government on this planet that wouldn't kill to get their hands on it."

The entire idea of moldable crystal had sounded like BS to him, though it wasn't his job to question the science. It was his job to recover the item. And now, for some reason, he had a crystal skull sitting in a bag between his knees, seven more were dead, and he had more doubts than ever.

"Problem, BD?" asked Red quietly. Dawson knew Red could tell this mission was eating at him. It was eating at all of them. He rarely gave any sign of his true feelings in front of his men, but Red could read him like a book.

Dawson shook his head. "No, just tired."

Red nodded. "You and me both."

Dawson could tell his friend wasn't convinced.

Heathrow Airport
London, England

Detective Inspector Chaney pulled the car up in front of the administration building of Heathrow airport. He and Reading climbed out and headed toward the entrance, both taking a moment to stare up at the never-ending flow of planes landing and taking off. The smell of jet fuel filled the air from the over one thousand flights per day Heathrow handled. They flashed their warrant cards at the guard and entered the building. As they approached the reception desk, a man called to them.

"DCI Reading and DI Chaney?"

"Yes," replied Reading, "and you are?"

"Jeffrey Tilson. I was told by the Chief to escort you to the security center." He gestured to an electronic pad on the reception desk. "I'll need you to sign here, then stand over there for your picture to be taken."

Chaney signed the pad and stood for his picture, Reading following. A moment later the guard at the reception desk handed them two laminated security passes with VISITOR emblazoned across them. "These must be visible at all times, and you must have an escort at all times."

Tilson laughed as the detectives clipped them in place. "We have over sixty-eight thousand employees and can't recognize everyone!" He motioned toward the elevators. "This way, gentlemen." Tilson broke into a jog as he rushed to hold an open elevator. He held the door for them, waving off a few people who tried to board. Swiping his security card through a card reader, he punched a code and pressed the button for *B3*. An LED readout scrolled *"Restricted Access. Doors Will Not Open Again Until Level B3"* as the elevator began its descent.

When the doors opened again, they were met with glaring artificial lights and two heavily armed guards who inspected their cards. They swiped them and continued. Tilson led them down the long corridor and into a glass-walled room filled with hundreds of monitors watched by as many personnel. Leading them over to a side office, he knocked on a door that read Chief of Security.

"Enter!" a voice boomed from the other side.

THE PROTOCOL

Tilson opened the door and the three men entered. A large, well-built man in his fifties rose from behind his glass and chrome desk, approaching them with a polite smile.

"DCI Reading, DI Chaney, may I present Mr. Arthur Pleasance."

"A pleasure to meet you, gentlemen." Pleasance extended his hand first to Reading then to Chaney. "Have a seat please." He motioned to two chairs in front of his desk. "Do you have time for tea?"

Chaney was about to answer no when Reading interrupted. "There's always time for a cuppa." Pleasance nodded to Tilson who left the room, closing the door behind him.

"Do you have the tapes ready for us?" asked Reading.

"Yes, I do. I had my people pull the footage for the entrance where you said the taxi picked him up. Our facial recognition software matched someone to the photo of your man you sent us." He hit a few keys on the keyboard and gestured toward the large screen on the wall. "Here are your two subjects getting into the taxi."

Chaney nodded in agreement. "That's them all right."

"Can you back it up and see where they came from?" asked Reading. Pleasance tapped some keys. The footage showed the men leaving the cab, unloading their bags, then walking backward toward the entrance of the airport. He switched views again, and they traced the men back to a bathroom where the image showed them exiting together.

"Do you have cameras in the loos?" asked Chaney.

"Of course not, that would violate privacy laws." Pleasance tapped a code into his keyboard. A view of the bathroom popped up. He reversed the tape, and the two men could be seen talking before the Frenchman headed backward toward a stall. The other man waited at the sinks for a couple of minutes, then backed into a stall.

There was a tap on the door.

"Enter!" roared Pleasance. Chaney flinched.

Tilson entered with a tray holding a tea service for the three men. "Ahh, thank you, Jeffrey." Tilson put the tray on the Chief's desk and left the room. After serving his guests, Pleasance turned back to the monitor.

The Frenchman entered the bathroom after their John Doe, who then walked out of his stall backward. "Wait," said

Chaney. "He's changed his clothes, and is carrying some sort of large bag there. The later footage shows him with three shopping bags and definitely wearing something different."

"You're right." Pleasance reversed the footage further and switched the view back to the entrance of the bathroom.

"Can you track him back to which flight he got off of?" asked Reading.

"Yes." Pleasance smiled. "Watch this." He hit a few keys and the system zoomed in on the face. It plotted the required facial recognition points, then the software followed the subject back through the various camera angles, through the main concourses, security, the baggage claims area, the arrivals area, and finally right to the gate he first appeared at.

Reading gave out a low whistle. "Impressive. Now, what can you tell me about that flight?"

Pleasance switched to another computer and entered the time and gate number. "It was a British Airways flight from New York. One moment and I'll pull up the manifest information." A few more keys and the list appeared on his screen. He scrolled through the names then frowned. "Savard was not on this flight."

Reading shook his head. "No, we have him arriving on an Air France flight around the same time. And judging by the footage we saw and the witness statements we've taken, I don't think he knew this man at all."

"And you were also looking for someone named Acton?" Reading nodded.

"Here he is. James Acton, US citizen."

Reading slapped Chaney on the shoulder. "Now there's a break!" He turned to Pleasance. "What more can you tell us?"

"Nothing, I'm afraid. That's all we're given by the airlines. It will take a court order to get the rest. You guys can run him through Interpol probably quicker."

Chaney eyed the screen, disappointment evident. "He's obviously trying to hide from somebody. He changed his clothes and bag."

"Yes, I agree." Reading rubbed his chin and thought for a moment. "Now, if you were following me, and I went into a bathroom and never came out, what would you do?"

"I'd go in to see if you were still there."

Reading turned to Pleasance, already tapping away at his

keyboard. "Way ahead of you." A few more keystrokes and he looked up at the display. The video advanced, showing Savard and Acton leaving together as if they were best friends. A few more passengers came and went, then another approached, glanced around as if to see if he were being watched, then tentatively pushed open the door. Pleasance switched the view, and they could see the man search the stalls then run out of the bathroom. Pleasance flipped the view again, and they saw the man leave the bathroom and put his wrist up to his mouth, his eyes wide and lips moving quickly.

"He's being followed!" exclaimed Chaney.

"Yes," agreed Reading, "and since he's talking to someone, by more than one person. Can you get me a picture of his face, please, and email it to my DI's mobile?"

Chaney handed Pleasance a card with his number.

"Wait a minute, who's that?" Chaney pointed at the screen. Another man emerged from the same bathroom and activated a comms.

"Someone else was following him!" exclaimed Pleasance. "What the hell makes this guy so popular?"

"I don't know, but one of these groups found Monsieur Savard," said Reading.

"But how?"

"Just a second." Pleasance furiously typed away at his keyboard. When he found what he was searching for, he leaned back in his chair as his eyes widened in shock. "Someone broke into the surveillance system!"

"Well, that explains how they found Monsieur Savard. Can you trace it?" asked Reading.

"No, and that's not the only thing. It was hacked by *two* different people within minutes of each other."

"Then the question is—" began Reading.

"Who found him first?" finished Chaney.

Professor Palmer's Office, University College London
Gordon Square, London, England

Acton sat back in his chair, flabbergasted. "Three hundred years!"

Laura smiled. "Amazing isn't it?"

"I'll say. So, basically what you're telling me, is that either some ancient civilization had a method more advanced than lasers to create these things, or each was created over ten generations?"

"Or aliens brought them."

"Haw."

"Some people believe that. Some even believe the skulls are millions of years old, left over from some ancient precursor civilization that we've yet to find a trace of. Still others believe they were sent by God to test our faith."

"So, essentially, nobody really knows. What do you believe?"

Laura paused for a moment, then answered carefully. "Over the years, I've come to believe that some things are not meant to be understood until we're ready. As a scientist, I'm not much of a believer in religion, the church, and the Bible, but part of me believes there is something out there that is greater than us. Whether these skulls were put here by a so-called god, or were created by people from Atlantis, I don't know. I do know, that we have no idea why they are here or why they were created, but maybe someday we will reach a level of technology or evolution where we will know. When that day comes, all will be revealed."

Acton looked at her, expressionless. She stared back at him, waiting for a response.

Does he think I'm off my rocker?

Acton inhaled slowly and adjusted his position in his chair. "Well, Laura, I've only been around this thing for a week, and all *I* know is that I want to get as far away from it as I can. It has cost me the life of my best friend, the life of over a half-dozen of my students and helpers, and almost my own life. Either someone wants this thing at all costs, or they want it and *me* at all costs, I don't know. But until I do, I can't risk losing it, because it could be my only bargaining chip for staying alive."

Laura nodded. "And you have no idea who it could be?"

"No. In Peru, they definitely seemed to be American Special Forces of some type. My friend Greg said that agents from the State Department had been in his office. We know he was followed to New York because he's now dead. I can only assume that I'm being followed, but the fact that I'm sitting here alive, talking to you, tells me that for the moment, they don't know where I am."

"For the moment," repeated Laura. It sent chills down her spine. Associating with Acton could put her own life at risk, yet at the same time, she was drawn irresistibly to either him, or the skull sitting on her desk.

Or both.

He reminded her of her brother, someone she trusted without question. "What about going to the authorities here? You're far from the States now, maybe they can help you?"

"What am I supposed to say? That I think the United States government is trying to kill me and everyone I know because I found a skull that came from outer space? They'd help me all right, straight into the loony bin!" He shook his head in frustration.

Laura stared down at the floor. "I'm sorry, I just thought…."

"No, I'm sorry, I didn't mean to blow up," he said in a soft voice, leaning toward her. "You're the first person I've been able to really sit and talk to about this, and all of my emotions are starting to come out. I've needed to vent and ask questions and yell and cry and everything else that someone should do in this situation, but instead, I've been running for my life for almost a week now."

She looked up at him and smiled. "I understand, I guess I forgot what you've been going through and why. You're right, of course. The police wouldn't believe you for a second. We need to try and find out who is after you."

Acton let out a deep sigh. "God, I'm so exhausted. I haven't slept properly in a week. I've only showered twice, I think, and you know what? I don't think I've eaten in three days other than that rubber thing they called chicken on the flight."

Laura laughed and stood. "We need to get you cleaned up and rested. Let's go back to my flat, and we'll figure out what to do from there. First, let me grab a couple of books for research."

"Are you sure you want to get involved any further than you already are?"

"Absolutely." Laura grabbed several books off the shelf and turned to him. "I want to find out who killed those poor kids, and why these skulls that I've spent my career studying are worth killing for if they're supposedly fake."

THE PROTOCOL

"Extensive bruising and surface abrasions, along with minor cuts over most of his body, as well as almost every bone in both hands broken," explained the coroner to Reading and Chaney, standing on the opposite side of the autopsy table containing the body of the Frenchman. "But, most interestingly, the bones were broken one at a time. See?" He moved toward an X-ray of the hands. "You can see that they're broken in different places. If they had been broken together, there would be some pattern, a line, that the breaks would follow. In this case, however, the breaks are all over the place, as if someone wanted to cause the most amount of pain possible, and knew exactly how to do it."

"A professional?" asked Chaney.

"Definitely someone who has been trained in torture techniques, or had enough medical knowledge to do this," agreed the coroner. "Now, the bruising and broken bones aren't all." He pointed toward cuts made on the chest, arms, legs, and scrotum. "These were made deliberately shallow enough to cause pain when the nerves were hit. They're barely scratches. You said he couldn't see what was happening. I think it was all psychological. Whoever did this knew exactly what they were doing."

"I thought the cause of death was loss of blood?"

The coroner shook his head. "No, it wasn't."

"But there was blood everywhere."

"We tested it. Pig's blood. Like I said, this was psychological. He was given a good beating and his fingers were broken, but none of that would kill him. The rest was for show, to make him think he was going to die if he didn't cooperate."

"But he *is* dead."

"It's all sort of puzzling, if you think about it. You torture somebody for what I believe was three hours, you obviously have the expertise to do this without killing him, why don't you just finish him off and slice his throat or something? Why would the person who did this risk letting him live long enough to tell someone who did it?"

"Sadistic whacko maybe?" offered Chaney. "He's a nutter

who doesn't care if he's caught or doesn't think that he can be?"

"Maybe," said the coroner.

Reading motioned toward the table. "So, what did kill him?"

The coroner smiled. "Ahh, that's the strange part. I detected an overdose of morphine in his system."

"You're joking!"

"I don't joke."

"Why would he torture someone for so long then put them out of their misery?" asked Chaney.

"Almost as if he began to feel some compassion for his victim," replied Reading.

"But the torture. You'd have to be off your nut to do something like that."

Reading shook his head. "No, you're ignoring the fact that we know the man he was with earlier in the day was being followed by more than one person." He pulled the photo out and pointed to it. "He was talking to someone. That means there are two people or more involved, which suggests this is not some psychopath working alone. These are professionals. This level of torture is professional, government. They didn't care if he survived because they knew there was no way in hell we could ever trace them. The morphine suggests they were doing a job, it wasn't personal. When they had what they wanted, they ended his suffering."

"Can I see that?" The coroner pointed at the photo and Reading handed it to him. He glanced at it for a moment. "Follow me, you're not going to believe this."

He pulled off his latex gloves and tossed them into a garbage can as he headed out the double swinging doors, Reading and Chaney following. They walked down the hallway and entered the crypt, all shivering at the cold. Inside, there were seven bodies, still bagged.

"What the hell happened tonight?" asked Chaney.

"You guys haven't heard? There was some sort of gang massacre. All seven of these guys were ambushed and shot in their van." The coroner stepped over to the fourth body and unzipped the bag, revealing the head. "Look."

Reading and Chaney approached the body and stared down at the face. The coroner held the photo up to it. It was the same man.

THE PROTOCOL

Palmer Residence
London, England

"I don't think anyone followed us," said Acton as he peered down at the street below Laura Palmer's apartment. Located within walking distance of the university, it had taken barely fifteen minutes to arrive, with a single umbrella to shield them from the rain. Acton closed the blinds and returned to the entrance. Laura flipped on the light as he stepped out into the hallway and took one last glance down the stairwell.

"Good! Then maybe they don't know where you are right now."

He removed his shoes and jacket. "For now, at least."

"Tea?"

"Sure."

Laura headed to the kitchen, leaving Acton to survey his surroundings. It was a small, two-bedroom apartment, tidy, and nicely decorated with artifacts and furniture from around the world. The couch appeared incredibly inviting.

Laura entered the living room where Acton had sat. Smiling, she took a seat beside him, curling her leg up so she could face him. "You look exhausted. The shower is over there." She pointed toward a hallway. "Why don't you freshen up, change your clothes, and I'll order us some Chinese."

Acton nodded. "A shower sounds great." He sighed then took an exaggerated sniff of his armpit. "I think I need one."

Laura laughed and playfully slapped him on the shoulder. "Go clean up, stinky, and I'll order some food. Anything in particular you'd like?"

"If they've got a good moo shu pork, I'll take that, otherwise anything is fine, as long as there's some meat in it." He got up and patted his stomach, heading for the bathroom. "If it's all vegetables, I'll just be hungry again in half an hour." He closed the bathroom door and ran the shower as he stripped out of his clothes. He took a whiff and gagged, sending a silent apology to all who had been exposed to him since he left Phoenix. He took his time, not sure when his next opportunity might be, and when done, luxuriated in the heat for a few minutes, simply leaning against the wall as the water gently massaged him.

There was a knock on the door that snapped him back to reality.

"Is it safe to come in?"

"Yes."

The door opened, and Laura leaned inside. "I found some clothes for you. Hopefully they fit."

"Thanks."

The door closed and Acton shut the water off, quickly toweling dry, then donning the fresh clothes laid out for him.

Definitely not her style.

They fit surprisingly well, and after admiring himself in the mirror for a moment, he exited to find Laura at the door paying for the food. He quickly stepped back so the delivery boy wouldn't see his face. When the door closed, he rounded the corner and met her in the kitchen.

"Well, don't you look better." Laura leaned in and sniffed. "Smell better, too."

Acton laughed and looked around. "How can I help?"

"Go sit in the living room, I'll take care of it."

Acton headed to the living room and took the same seat on the couch. He was still exhausted, but clean. "Whose clothes are these?"

"They were my brother's," she said as she appeared around the corner. "He kept some stuff here for when he visited."

"Where is he now?"

"He died three years ago when we were on a dig in Jordan," she answered as she put the food down on the table and took a seat across from him.

"I'm terribly sorry. I didn't mean to pry."

"It's okay, it's not your fault. There was a cave in, he was killed instantly." She finished setting up the food and continued. "About a year ago, I finally boxed up his stuff, but could never bring myself to donate it to charity."

Acton nodded. "It's tough to lose someone you love, especially under tragic circumstances."

Laura shook her head for a moment. "Okay, enough talk, let's eat and try to figure out what to do next."

Acton agreed and took a taste of the moo shu.

Soooo good. But raw cow would probably taste good right about now.

New Scotland Yard
London, England

"We're looking for this man." Jasper handed over a folder, Chief Inspector Manning finally seeing them after several hours of waiting. "His name is James Acton, and he arrived from New York today."

Manning opened the folder and put his glasses on. "Acton, huh? That sounds familiar for some reason."

"Our office would have already sent you the name earlier," offered Lambert.

"No, that's not it. Just a moment." Manning rose and left the office. Jasper watched as the door closed behind him.

Now what?

He was getting frustrated. And tired. The coffee wasn't helping anymore.

A few minutes later, the door opened, and Manning entered, frowning as he handed a file over to Jasper. "I knew the name sounded familiar."

Jasper opened the file. "What's this?" Lambert leaned in to look as well. It contained an Interpol printout on Acton.

"We ID'd him just a short while ago from some footage taken earlier today," explained Manning. "He's wanted for questioning in regards to a murder that took place, today."

"Murder?"

"Yes. As a matter of fact, the DCI in charge of the case will be back shortly. I'll put you in his office and have him come see you right away."

Jasper nodded his thanks as he processed this new information.

Murder? Could he have been involved in those deaths in Peru?

"Okay, so one of the people looking for our John Doe character was topped tonight in a gangland-style shooting, along with six of his mates," said Reading as he and Chaney entered New Scotland Yard.

"That's what it looks like," agreed Chaney.

"There was nothing gangland style about this shooting, gentlemen," said a young man rushing toward them. DI Nelson, the detective originally assigned to the shooting, was rising quickly through the ranks, and Reading could tell he wasn't pleased about losing the case.

It's not all about credit, lad.

Nelson handed Reading a folder. "As you can see from these stills from the security cameras, this was a professional hit."

Reading opened the folder and flipped through the pictures as Chaney glanced over his shoulder. "I'll need to see the video."

"No problem, guv, if you'll come with me, I'll bring you up to speed." He headed toward the elevators with Reading and Chaney following. Minutes later, they were huddled around a screen, the video playing before them both brief and shocking. It showed a white box van enter the frame from the left, then get cut off by an oncoming SUV. Four men with automatic weapons jumped out of the SUV and killed the driver, then took up covering positions as a second SUV entered the frame from the left, behind the box van. Four men appeared, three setting up position at the doors as the fourth placed something on the back door and hurriedly moved to the side of the truck, out of view.

There was a flash, and the doors swung open. The three men opened fire for about ten seconds. When they stopped, the one in the middle climbed into the back of the truck and reappeared a few moments later carrying a black bag. All eight men jumped into their vehicles and left in opposite directions. The box van was left sitting in the middle of the frame.

Reading squinted. "Were you able to pull any faces off this?"

"No, guv. They were all wearing balaclavas. Numbers were obscured, but I doubt they would have led anywhere."

"Have you tracked them?" asked Chaney.

"We're in the process. We're also tracking back the box van to see where it came from. You'll want to see this." He gestured at a table behind them. On it were laid out body armor, weapons, night-vision equipment, cellphones, radio headgear, and much more.

Chaney grunted. "Looks like they weren't so innocent. Were they on their way to a hit and got hit themselves?"

"Like I said before, the blokes in the four-by-fours were pros. You can tell by the way they took up their positions. It was done with military precision. The victims were equipped as well as any military unit I've ever seen, so I don't know what the hell is going on." Nelson picked up one of the guns. "And look at this." He removed the magazine, ejected one of the bullets, and handed it to Reading.

Reading held up the bullet, a bullet that appeared more like a needle. "What's this?"

"Tranquilizer dart. All of them were armed with these. They had no live rounds on them. These blokes weren't killers."

"Their enemies certainly were." Reading handed the dart back to Nelson who returned it to the table. "Any gangland tats or other markings on the victims?"

"They all had this tattoo on their inner left wrist." Nelson handed them a photo of a tattoo on one of the victim's hands. "It's actually very small, about half an inch wide." The tattoo was two short horizontal lines with a thicker, slightly wider third line, curving upward.

Reading stared at the photo.

I've seen this somewhere before.

"Have you run it through the database?" asked Chaney.

"Yes, nothing."

"Any ID?"

"We're running their faces through all of our databases, hopefully we'll have something by the end of the day," said Nelson. "Oh, that reminds me. Upstairs asked me to give you this." He reached into his stack of folders and pulled one with Reading's name on it. "They were delivering it to the morgue the same time I got there, so I said I'd give it to you." He handed the file over to Reading. "Apparently, there're two Yanks here who want to talk to you about him as well. They waited for the Chief for several hours, and now he's handed them off to you."

When Reading flipped it open, he found the complete Interpol file on one Professor James Edward Acton. Reading smiled.

Now I know who you are.

"Professor James Edward Acton," announced Reading. He handed the folder over to Chaney. "He had to register in Oman for an archaeological dig six years ago, which means his face made it into Interpol's database. We know who he is, the questions now are, why is he here, who is following him, and why was Monsieur Savard tortured and killed?"

"And how does the ambush of the van fit in?" added Chaney.

Reading nodded. "Nelson, I want you to find out where that van came from and where—"

"Sir!" yelled one of the men manning the Yard's central communications system. "They've just found the first getaway vehicle!"

"Send armed response units immediately," ordered Reading. "Surround them, but wait until we get there."

"Yes, sir!" The man returned to his station and plugged back into the network, relaying the orders.

Reading was already heading toward the door, Chaney following him. Nelson stood there, not sure what to do. Reading, without looking back, called, "Coming, Nelson?"

Nelson smiled. "Yes, sir!"

Acton woke with a start to find himself half-lying, half-sitting on the couch, covered by a blanket. He checked his watch and was surprised at how early it was until he realized he had forgotten to set it to local time. He searched for a clock. *12:45 a.m.*

"Have a good sleep?" Laura sat on a chair across from him, reading one of her books, a single lamp on an end table providing the only light.

Acton stretched. "Yeah, thanks. How long was I out?"

"Just a few hours. You really should take the spare bedroom and get some rest. This will wait until morning."

Acton shook his head. "No, I'm fine, and besides, I don't think they're waiting."

She nodded. "I think I may know who *they* are."

Acton leaned forward, fully alert. "What have you found?"

"I've been going through these books. I knew there was something in one of them that I just couldn't remember, and it was driving me nuts. And I think I've found it." She opened one of the books to a page she had marked, and handed it to Acton. "This is a rather obscure text filled with mostly conspiracy theories, but quite often they're based on a kernel of truth, so I held onto it. Last paragraph on the left."

Acton read the passage:

> *Many ancient relics that were deemed to have power handed down by God or a pagan god, have had groups organize as a result, that either worshiped the item or swore to protect it. One obvious example is the Holy Grail, apparently protected by the Knights Templar. The Crystal Skulls were no different. It has been documented, that over two thousand years ago, Emperor Nero assigned a legion of his best troops to protect what was described as the Oracle of Jupiter. Discovered in what is now modern-day Israel, it was delivered to the Emperor as a gift. Nero became obsessed with the skull, and believed it was communicating with him, convinced it was the voice of the most powerful Roman god, Jupiter. Nero ordered the Thirteenth Legion to take the skull as far away from Rome as possible, and to guard it with their*

lives. It is thought this Thirteenth Legion fought its way north, trying to reach modern day England, the farthest the Empire's domain had reached. During this struggle, most of the first line and second line troops were lost. The third and most experienced line, the Triarii, is said to have disappeared, never to be seen again. Rumors of their existence persist to this day, with some believing they did reach their ultimate destination, and settled anonymously in England, their descendants now fulfilling their ancient promise.

Acton closed the book and sat back in his chair, in fascinated disbelief. "Do you really think that the people after me today could be descendants of a two-thousand-year-old Roman legion?"

"I know it sounds fantastic, but think about it. How long have the Masons been around, the Knights Templar, the Illuminati, the Catholic Church for that matter? All are organizations created around a central theme that has sustained them for centuries if not millennia.

"This skull was believed to be handed down from the gods. Just the belief that something has divine powers is an extreme motivator. If a grilled cheese sandwich that looks like the Virgin Mary can sell for $34,000 on eBay, then imagine the influence a crystal skull could have that your Emperor has told you spoke to him.

"Then imagine that more started to show up over the generations. As each one appeared, it would only serve to renew your faith. Even here in England, to this day, there are Druids and others that worship pagan gods. Monotheistic religion has not taken complete control."

Acton let out a deep breath, trying to reconcile what Laura was saying. "It's incredible to think that people could worship something for so long, but then again, we've seen it time and again throughout history, especially among primitive societies. I guess it's not that much of a stretch for people of two thousand years ago to believe that this was sent by God, and then to indoctrinate their descendants with the same beliefs."

"Yes, and if they are indeed here, today, their original mission of protecting the Oracle of Jupiter may have expanded to include all of the skulls," continued Laura. "They must think that you are some kind of threat to them because you found a skull that appears to have been missing for over seven hundred years."

"I don't understand, though, why so many people have to die because of it." Acton thought of the last text message from his friend. "So many have died, that someone has to pay. Two-thousand-year-old cult or not, they need to be brought down before others get hurt."

Laura's face grew concerned. "How do you think you can single-handedly take down an organization that has lasted over sixty generations? It could be huge."

"Every snake has a head. Cut it off, and the body dies. If I remember my Roman history, the Triarii were the third and final line of defense in a legion. They were the most seasoned, experienced troops, and there was only a small number of them. If they've kept the same structure, there may only be a dozen or so of them at the top, with the rest mere underlings with no real power or knowledge. Wipe out the Triarii, and everything stops."

Laura appeared worried about where this was heading. "How would you ever find them?"

Acton held up the skull. "I have bait." He looked at Laura for a reaction. Her expression wasn't what he had expected.

She looks almost…horrified!

He couldn't understand why she wouldn't want to take down an organization that had killed so many innocent people.

"How are you going to 'wipe them out?'"

"I'm not sure, but first we need to identify them, then try and get them on tape, I guess, admitting their guilt. After that, we could take the tape to the authorities and let them take action." The more Acton explained his plan, the more ridiculous it sounded.

There's no way in hell they'll admit what they did on tape!

He sighed. "Okay, maybe we need a better plan."

"We?"

"Well, I guess I just sort of assumed…."

"Oh, of course I'm in. Not necessarily for the same reasons you have, but for a more selfish reason."

"What's that?"

"Self-preservation. People around you have a nasty habit of turning up dead, and I don't intend to be one of them."

Fleet Street, London, England

Reading climbed out of his car and approached the mobile command set up out of sight of the discovered SUV. "Is everyone in position?"

"Yes, *sir*," replied the Armed Response Unit commander. "Just waiting for *your* orders, *sir*."

Reading could hear the disdain in the man's voice. He didn't blame him.

God knows there's enough glorified DCIs about that have never even shot a gun.

"Do we know if anyone is in the vehicle?" asked Chaney.

"Can't tell, *sir*. Cameras showed people exiting the vehicle, but the windows are all blacked out, so there could still be someone inside."

"And the other team?" asked Reading. En route, word had come of the location of the second SUV.

"They are in position as well, awaiting *your* orders, *sir*."

Reading chose to ignore the attitude.

For now.

"Proceed, Commander."

The ARU Commander spoke into his mic. "All units, stand by, proceed in five... four... three... two... one... *Execute!*" From down the street, yelling erupted, and ARU agents raced out from around the corners of buildings, surrounding the SUV.

"Occupants of the vehicle, armed police! Open the doors and come out with your hands in the air!" ordered one of the men over a megaphone. There was no response. "This is your final warning. Come out with your hands raised immediately!" Again, no response.

He pointed at one of his men, and he advanced on the driver's side door at a crouch, all the while aiming his weapon at the window. Suddenly the alarm started to go off, and the officer froze, quickly backing away moments before the vehicle erupted in a massive fireball. The officers surrounding the van were hurled backward, as if tugged by ropes attached to their backs, and Reading watched in horror as they skidded across the pavement, the truck launching itself almost ten feet straight into the air, before collapsing back to the ground.

"Team Two, abort! I say again, abort!" shouted the ARU Commander into his mic. There was no response. "Team Two, this is Team Leader, what is your status?"

There was still no answer, then a burst of static erupted. "Team Leader, this is Two, some sort of detonation has occurred. My men are down! I repeat, my men are down!"

Reading was already on his phone calling for medical support to both sites, and a bomb disposal unit, while Chaney and Nelson ran toward the downed men.

"Be careful of secondary explosions!" He turned to the ARU Commander. "Commander, set up a perimeter, half a mile in all directions. Nobody gets in or out without being spoken to." The commander nodded, showing more respect. Reading saw the change in attitude and smiled. "Falklands War. I've been around guns since you were popping pimples."

"Yes, sir," stammered the Commander. "Sorry, sir."

"Execute your orders."

"Yes, sir!" He snapped to attention, then ran off to organize the arriving backup units.

Reading strode toward the flaming wreckage that was the SUV.

How many more have to die, and why?

The Triarii chamber was rocked by what felt like a sudden earthquake, sending a momentary panic through the room until the noise died down and they realized they were still intact. The Proconsul stared up at the ceiling with an eye to seeing if it were about to come down on them. Plaster dust filled the air, small cracks evidence of the stress the structure had been put under, though nothing suggested impending doom.

He looked to the man on his left. "Find out what happened!"

The man leaped to his feet and ran to the chamber doors. As he left, the phone rang, echoing through the now silent chamber, all eyes turning toward the device.

This was something that never happened.

The Proconsul stared at his display, confused.

Who would have this number?

He hit the intercom button to put the call on speaker.

"Did you get my message?" a disembodied, electronically

altered voice said on the other end.

"What message?"

"I think you know what I'm talking about. I wanted to remind you that I know where you are."

The phone went dead.

He pressed the button, cutting off the dial tone as everyone stared at each other in stunned silence, several lips trembling in fear, his own chest tight with the implications.

The doors to the chamber flew open, and the previously dispatched member ran back in. "There were two car bombs, one across the road, the other a half-mile away." The breathless man returned to his seat. "Apparently there are a lot of police casualties."

The Proconsul frowned then pursed his lips as he let out a heavy breath. "I believe we have a bigger problem than we thought. It is obvious now that we must take immediate action." His eyes traveled the room as he made certain every single one of the council realized the importance of the words he was about to say. "Implement The Protocol without delay."

All of the members stood and bowed to him, then left. Remaining seated, he contemplated the situation and wasn't pleased. He had lost one skull under his watch tonight. He couldn't risk any more. They had to be taken into safekeeping for now, until this crisis could be resolved.

He feared, though, what that might involve.

Reading clenched his jaw, anger seething inside him as the ambulance personnel loaded the injured men onto gurneys. They had been lucky. Damned lucky. Nobody had been killed, but several had been severely injured. The only thing that had saved them was the alarm going off beforehand. If that hadn't happened…

He shuddered to think of it.

We need to find Acton!

"Guv," said Chaney behind him. Reading turned. Chaney was covered in blood, having saved one man by sticking his fingers in a wound and pinching a ruptured artery. Sometimes Reading forgot Chaney had once gone to medical school then dropped out. After seeing so many bodies come through the ER, he'd decided he wanted to be out on the street preventing the crimes that sent the victims to the doctors. "Nelson just got a call. They found out where the box van came from."

"Where?"

"The British Museum. We have footage of the vehicle leaving there ten minutes before they were hit. We're still backtracking where they originally came from."

"Okay, you and I will go to the museum and see what they were doing there," said Reading.

Chaney nodded, then popped the trunk to their car and fished out a change of clothes. He disappeared into an alleyway as Nelson ran up.

"Sir, I just talked to one of the bomb squad guys." He pointed at the smoldering wreck. "He says we didn't get lucky."

Reading's eyes narrowed. "What the bloody hell does that mean?"

"He said that the charges were shaped so that the bulk of the blast was directed downward. It wasn't designed for mass casualties."

"But it was booby-trapped!"

Nelson shook his head. "No, they found a detonator. It looks like it was set on a timer." He turned to stare at the truck. "I don't think we were meant to be here, and this time of night, there's not a lot of pedestrian traffic."

Reading pursed his lips, surveying the surrounding buildings, little damage evident. "Then what the hell was the purpose?"

Nelson shrugged. "Somebody was sending a message, maybe?"

Reading grunted. "But to who? Who the hell is behind all this? These guys kill seven without hesitation, then set their vehicles to detonate so they minimize casualties? Something's not adding up here."

"I know, it makes no sense."

Chaney reappeared, looking prim and proper. Reading turned to Nelson. "You take command of the situation here and keep me posted. We're heading to the British Museum. Maybe we'll find some answers there."

"Yes, sir!"

The British Museum
London, England

"Look." Clive Obrock pointed to the monitor showing a car pull up and two men getting out. They watched the younger one approach the doors and peer through, knocking on the glass as he reached into his pocket and pulled out a warrant card. He held it up to the nearby camera.

Rodney Underwood pressed a hand to his stomach. "Coppers!"

Clive glanced at his friend.

What's eating him?

He leaned into the intercom system. "Who's closest to the Great Russell Street entrance?"

There was a crackle then a voice responded. "Paul here, I'm about twenty meters away. What's the problem?"

"There're two coppers at the door. See what they want."

"Roger, I'll check it out."

A few moments later, Clive and Rodney watched Paul jogging toward the doors. He inspected the cards through the window and lifted his radio. "They're coppers, all right, and they want in."

"Okay, just a moment." Clive pressed a few keys and watched Paul open the door. The two men entered, and Paul closed the door behind them. Clive reactivated the locks as he and Rodney watched the three men. They spoke for a few seconds, then Paul lifted his radio again.

"They said there was some sort of murder tonight that involves the museum, and they want to review the tapes. I'll bring them up to the control room."

Rodney turned pale as the three men disappeared from view.

Clive noticed. "What's wrong? You look like you've seen a ghost."

"No, nothing, I'm just feeling poorly. Maybe something I ate. I'm going to the loo." With that, he left the control room.

Clive chuckled and stared back at the monitors, watching Paul escort the police to the control room.

A murder?

He rubbed his chest where the Liverpool flag had hit him

and was surprised at how much it still hurt.

How hard did he hit me with that thing?

Rodney sprinted to the bathroom and entered a stall where there were no cameras. He pulled out his cellphone and dialed. When the line picked up, there was silence. His heart was hammering, his attempts to calm his nerves so far having failed. The system would allow him two attempts to get the code right before blocking his number from ever calling again. As calmly as he could, he said, "Seventy-Four Sixty-Two Oh One." There was a pause then ringing as the call was directed elsewhere. He breathed a sigh of relief. The next pickup had a human at the other end.

"Yes?"

"I need guidance, something has gone wrong."

"One moment." Again, the call was redirected.

"Yes?" said the new voice.

"The police are here, something about a murder. They want to review the tapes."

"Have you had time to erase them?"

"No, not yet. The plan was to wipe them over the rest of the shift, but Clive hasn't left his post yet."

"Very well. Our team was eliminated by outside forces after they left."

Rodney's jaw dropped. "Eliminated? As in topped?"

"Yes," replied the coldly calm voice. "There is nothing more you can do there. I want you to leave immediately."

"Yes, ma'am." The line went dead, and he put the phone back in his pocket.

Now I need to get Clive to open the rear entrance so I can get out of here.

Clive looked over as Rodney returned, still not looking himself. "Hey, buddy. Feeling better?"

Rodney nodded.

Clive motioned to the two guests. "This is DCI Reading and DI—. Sorry, I'm terrible with names."

"Chaney."

Rodney shook the proffered hands. "Rodney Underwood."

Clive brought him up to speed. "Apparently a truck left the museum tonight and was attacked. I told the detectives that they must be mistaken, as we haven't had any deliveries or pickups tonight. Here's the footage for the loading dock." The tape raced backward, the time code in the bottom of the screen counting down.

"Stop!" said Chaney. "Back it up a bit." Clive let the tape play forward more slowly, and they could see a box van exit the loading dock. "There it is."

"I'll be—" Clive checked the time code.

That was when I was out cold!

He rubbed his chest and glanced at Rodney, who appeared nervous.

What is going on here?

"Let's see the rest of the footage," said Reading. "I want to know what they were doing here."

"Yes, sir." Clive turned back to the monitors. He brought up the footage, and they all watched as it played out in reverse.

"What room is that?" asked Chaney as they watched the men disappear for several minutes inside a room. "Are there any cameras in there?"

Clive shook his head. "No, sir, it's a storage room for the archaeology department. The only way in or out is that door, so we have no cameras in there."

Reading pointed at the screen. "Show me that room."

"Rodney, you show them the room. I have to call the Archaeology Head to let them know so they can come down here to see if anything is missing."

"Yes, okay." Rodney opened the door. "This way, gentlemen." Reading and Chaney followed Rodney out of the room as Clive grabbed a binder of emergency numbers, and found the home number for the Archaeology Head. He was relieved Rodney was out of the room and with the police.

Something isn't right here. He had to have let them in.

Again he felt the pain in his chest.

He found the number and dialed. He was surprised when the phone picked up right away, and the person sounded wide awake. "Sorry to disturb you at this hour. This is Clive Obrock, I'm security chief for the night-watch at the museum. It appears there has been a break-in at the archaeology storage room, and we'd like you to come down here, right away. The police are already here." He listened to the response on the other end. "Okay, we'll see you in fifteen minutes, Professor Palmer."

Paris, France

It was a beautiful, quiet night on the Seine in Paris. The restaurant hummed with quiet dignity, and no loud drunken conversations ruined the evening. A string quartet played in the corner, loud enough to be heard, yet low enough to not be intrusive. The lighting was just right for an evening of romance, which is exactly what Henri was hoping for. He gazed across the table at his beautiful date, not believing his luck. She was way out of his league, yet that was usually the case with him.

Shoot for the stars!

It meant near constant rejection, but on occasion, those stars did align, as they had tonight. It was a blind date, which were his favorites. It meant he had a chance to make a good first impression. He sported his only tailored suit, a few dabs of his finest cologne, and a tie he had found abandoned in the washroom where he worked. He was looking dapper, and she had appeared relieved when he introduced himself.

And now, he was blowing an entire week's pay on this one meal, in the hopes he might convince this beauty to join him for a nightcap.

Patience, Henri!

He sipped his wine, returning the glass to the table, then leaned in to run a finger over hers, when his phone vibrated. He frowned. "Excuse me." He fished the interruption from his pocket and took the call. "Hello?"

"Thirty-two. Sixteen. Oh Seven. Execute Red."

"I'm sorry, but you've got the wrong number." He hung up as his heart sank. It was a call he had never expected to come, not in his lifetime, though now that it had, he was torn between duty and booty. The woman across the table from him was gorgeous, and after a couple of bottles of expensive wine, perhaps receptive. He might never have another shot at her—if tonight's date didn't seal the deal, he couldn't afford a second one.

If she only knew I was a janitor.

He sighed, knowing duty had to win, absentmindedly scratching the tattoo under his watch. He forced a smile across the table. "I'm sorry, but I've got to go."

He rose and headed for the door, stepping outside and

taking one last look at his date as she stared at him through the window, clearly stunned at this turn of events. He couldn't believe what he had given up, his hopes for a steamy evening shut down by something his grandfather's grandfather had gotten the family mixed up in.

He climbed into his car and pulled out into traffic, smiling as his date rushed out the front door, hailing a cab, while a waiter at their table shouted, likely about the bill not being paid.

A quick drive, and he was soon at the Museé du Quay Branly parking lot. He gunned his two-stroke Citroën up the small ramp and parked it on an angle, taking up two spots. Grabbing a bag from the trunk, he slung it over his shoulder, approached the employee entrance, and waved his pass at the guard. The guard, his head buried in a newspaper, didn't even look up as he reached to push the buzzer.

"Hey, Henri."

Henri smiled. "Hey, Jacques. How did you know it was me?"

Jacques flipped a page and refolded the paper. "That piece of shit you drive can be heard a kilometer away."

Henri smiled. "Sorry, my friend, but it's all I can afford on this meager janitor's salary."

Jacques shook the paper. "If you'd stop turning down the promotions, maybe I'd have some sympathy for you."

Henri laughed and headed to the employee locker room. When he arrived, he opened his locker, put his coveralls on, then walked casually to the janitor's storage and retrieved his cart. Emptying garbage cans and ashtrays along the way, he eventually made it to one of the antiquities storage rooms. He ran his pass through the swipe lock, and it opened. Pushing his cart inside, he closed the door then lifted his bag out of the cart and strode to a row in the back. He opened a cardboard box on the bottom shelf, and moved the packing material aside. A grinning skull stared up at him.

He shivered.

He opened the bag, revealing another skull. He swiftly switched them, then put his bag, with the genuine skull in it, in the garbage bag on his cart. He left the room whistling, and finished his rounds, thinking of the beautiful woman he had left on the Seine.

I wonder if I called her, would she meet me for a late coffee? The poor girl must be so disappointed.

Palmer Residence
London, England

Laura hung up the phone and turned to Acton. "There's been a break-in at the museum. I have to go down and identify what's missing."

Acton got up off the couch. "I'll come with you."

"Are you sure that's wise? What if someone sees you?"

"If they knew where I was, they'd have been here by now, and I don't think it's safe to stay in one place for too long. But we do need to hide this somewhere." Acton held up the bag containing the skull.

Laura smiled. "I have just the place." She walked to the living room table and kneeled beside it, pointing to the end nearest Acton. "Press those two corners in." They were of a different color wood, but didn't look like they should move. Acton pressed on them. They didn't. Laura pressed on the two at her end, and with a click, all four corners came free. He pushed them down as far as he could at the same time Laura did. This turned out to be about two inches. Laura then grasped two sides of the tabletop and twisted clockwise ninety degrees.

"Grab this side and pull up and toward you when I do." She moved to the left and grasped the edge of the table opposite Acton. "Ready?"

Acton nodded.

"Now." They both lifted, and the tabletop split in the middle as it rose, then came outward toward them.

Acton stood, amazed at the sight of the two-foot square hole in the center of the solid block of wood that made up the body of the table. "Incredible!"

Laura smiled. "It's ancient Chinese. The wood is thick enough that it won't sound hollow, but you can hide a fair amount of stuff inside, like important scrolls, jewels, or in this case"—she paused as she held up the artifact—"one crystal skull."

Acton smiled as she put the skull into the cavity. They reversed the procedure and returned the table to normal.

"Nobody will find it in there." She stood. "Now, let's get to the museum. I'll be able to show you the other one as well."

The Himalayas, Nepal

The only noise in the monastery was the heavy breathing of the sleeping monks. Eight in a room, they each had a simple wooden bed with a blanket to keep the cold at bay. A small stove near the far wall provided welcome warmth. Chen lay on his bedroll when a sudden vibration coursed through his body, waking him. It was as if his entire skeleton pulsed from the spine outward, and it took him a moment to realize what it was. He glanced around to see if anyone was looking.

All clear.

He reached under his bedroll and removed the satellite phone hidden there. He unfolded the antenna and hit the *Talk* button.

"Forty-four. Sixteen. Oh Three. Execute Red."

Chen's heart pounded as he hung up and hid the phone among his robes. He had known this day might come, though had never expected it to. Standing, he walked down the long passageway leading from the sleeping quarters to the main temple. Inside, he found the Lama kneeling in front of a large golden statue of the Buddha. He knelt beside him, clasping his hands, giving reverence to that which had guided him for so many years.

"Father, I am so sorry to interrupt, but I must."

The revered monk beside him remained facing forward. "What is it, my son?"

"I cannot explain why, but I must take the Crystal Oracle. It is for your protection and its preservation."

"I understand, my son. If this is your destiny, then you must fulfill it. Go in peace, with my blessing."

Chen nodded and rose. He entered one of the side chambers, and approached the Crystal Oracle sitting on a pedestal, surrounded by candles. Taking a burlap bag from under his robes, he placed the sculpture inside, then walked directly out of the temple and began the long trek down the mountain, unsure when, or if, he'd ever return.

THE PROTOCOL

The British Museum
London, England

Rodney waved to the camera when they reached the storage room door, and a buzzer sounded as Clive let them in. The three men entered and looked around. "Doesn't look like they took anything," said Rodney.

Reading and Chaney continued to look, apparently unconvinced.

"Maybe it was a security drill?" he suggested. "In the morning they'll fire us all for having failed?" He laughed nervously.

The only response was a grunt from Reading. They walked up and down the aisles and saw nothing out of place. As they made their way back to the entrance, Reading stopped and pointed to the floor by the rolling ladder. "Look."

Chaney bent over. "What is it?"

"The marks on the floor look fresh, like someone forgot to take the brake off." He kneeled and picked up some of the shavings from the concrete floor, rubbing them between his fingers. "How often is this room cleaned?"

Rodney stared at the floor. "I'm not sure, once a week maybe?" Reading stared back at him. "I'll find out." He turned away and called Clive on his radio.

"How's it look in there?" asked Clive.

"Everything looks fine. They want to know how often the floors are cleaned."

"Every week, you know that. You let them in last night."

"Oh, yeah, I forgot, sorry. I'll let them know."

"Okay, and tell them Professor Palmer will be here any minute to check over the inventory."

"What?" Rodney shouted into the radio. He glanced over uneasily at the detectives.

"Is there a problem?" asked Chaney.

"N-no, just nerves, I guess." Rodney turned back to his radio and whispered. "Why did you call her?"

"Procedure. I'll have Paul bring her to you."

"No!"

"What?"

He tried to calm his voice. "No, I'll go get her, I'm not

that far from the entrance." He glanced at the detectives, forcing a smile as he raised his voice for their benefit. "I think we can trust the police alone in the room for a couple of minutes."

Chaney nodded at him, appearing more patient than his older partner.

"Fine, but you better hurry. Looks like she's here." Clive paused. "That's strange, she seems to have brought someone. Just a min—"

Rodney cut him off. "I'm on my way!" He headed to the door and glanced at Reading and Chaney as he fumbled with the handle. "I'll be back in five minutes." He closed the door behind him then sprinted down the hallway.

Laura and Acton approached the security entrance and pressed the buzzer. The rain had let up, though a heavy mist still dampened the night air. A moment later, a voice came over the intercom. "Security."

"This is Professor Palmer. Apparently there was a robbery?"

"Yes, Professor. Who is with you?"

"A colleague from the United States."

"Name please."

She looked at Acton and whispered, her head turned away from the camera, "They can't possibly be looking for you here." He nodded. She turned back to the intercom. "Professor Acton."

"Very well, your escort will be there momentarily. Please wait." The connection fell silent. They only had to wait a moment before they heard a buzzing sound then the door flew open, causing them both to jump back.

Rodney almost flew into the two people standing at the door.

"Sorry, Professor Palmer," he stammered. "Just a little excited you know, what with the police here and all." His hand trembled as he offered it. "I'm Rodney." She shook his hand, and before she could introduce the other man, he cut her off. "Nothing seems to be missing. I'm not sure if you're even needed." He noticed the man standing beside her. "Professor Acton! What are you doing here?"

The two professors exchanged wide-eyed glances. "How do you know who I am?"

Rodney had made a terrible blunder, but it was too late now. "I, um, I must have seen your face...shit, just a minute." He walked away from them and dialed his cellphone. His radio crackled.

"Rodney, what's going on down there? Why aren't you bringing them in?"

Rodney reached down and turned off his radio.

"Yes?" said the voice.

"Acton is here!" hissed Rodney.

"What?" It was the first time Rodney had heard his contact convey any emotion. "Are the police still there?"

"Yes. What do I do?"

"The police are looking for the professor in connection with a murder. You must warn him and see if he'll come in."

"Okay, I'll try." The line went dead. He turned back to the two professors. "I'm sorry about that."

"How do you know who I am?" demanded Acton.

"That doesn't matter." Rodney approached them and lowered his voice. "The police are inside. They believe you have something to do with a murder."

Laura's eyes shot wide. "A murder? Whose?"

"I don't know, but at least seven people are dead tonight in connection with this place." He could tell by their expressions they knew nothing about it. "Professor Acton, I suggest you come with me."

"Bullshit. Why would I go with you?"

Laura took his arm and drew him closer to her.

"Because we can protect you."

"Who's we? And how can *you* protect *me*? People have been dying all around me for a week now. How do I know your 'we' aren't the ones doing it?"

Rodney moved his watch band and showed his tattoo. "Because we are the Triarii."

"Triarii!" exclaimed Acton.

"Yes. We are the final line of defense to protect the world from the potential disaster that could occur if the skulls are brought together." The stunned expressions told him they knew what he was talking about.

"The Triarii? You mean you're part of the lost legion?" asked Laura.

"Yes, Professor, I and my brethren have been guarding the secret of the skulls for almost two millennia. When

Professor Acton found the final missing skull, he set into motion a series of events that can no longer be stopped."

"What do you mean," asked Acton, "the final missing skull?"

"I don't have time to explain here, but if you come with me, I'll tell you everything."

They didn't budge.

"Your lives are in danger."

"Is hers?"

"We weren't aware she was involved until now, so she should be safe."

Laura faced him. "James, what are you suggesting?"

"The cops are expecting you." He took her hands in his. "You go in, otherwise they'll get suspicious of you. I'll go with him and find out what he knows, and we'll meet up later where we had Chinese."

"Are you sure? I don't feel good about this."

"Come, now! We don't have time!" urged Rodney.

"How do I explain where you went?"

"I'll run away. Professor Acton, you chase me. Once we're on Montague, we're out of camera range. Professor Palmer, you go into the museum and tell them that I ran away and your friend pursued me. Make up a name for him. I'll never be coming back here again."

Acton looked at Laura and whispered, "Go, I'll be okay."

Rodney took one last look at the museum, then bolted toward the street, Acton giving chase.

THE PROTOCOL

Salem, Virginia

Madely's cellphone rang, waking him out of a deep sleep. Feeling guilty, he checked his watch. *4 a.m.* He shouldn't be sleeping, but the old lady never, in the six years he'd been observing her, left her house until 9 a.m. unless on a tour. His partner was in the passenger seat, his head cocked backward, leaning against the window. His mouth was wide, his snoring loud enough to wake the neighborhood.

I guess I'm not the only one.

He answered the phone.

"Twelve Twelve Oh Five, Execute Red."

His pulse raced, and adrenaline rushed through his veins. He punched his partner on the shoulder. "Johnson, wake up!" Johnson snorted a couple of times then came to.

"What?" he asked groggily. "What's going on?"

"We've been ordered to execute Plan Red."

Johnson bolted upright in his seat and straightened himself. The two men got out of the car and approached the house they had had under surveillance down the road. Walking to the doorstep, Madely rang the doorbell.

Four in the morning!

It took a few minutes, but eventually a light came on deep in the house, and footsteps approached then stopped at the door. Someone unlatched the lock and opened it. The ninety-something lady who greeted them was by no means frail. She traveled the world on a regular basis, and through observing her for years, they knew her to be very independent.

"Ahhh, my shadows."

Madely and Johnson stared at each other, dumbfounded.

"Come in, come in." She backed up, opening the door wider. They entered the house, and she closed the door behind them. "Can I get you something, some tea perhaps?"

"No thank you, ma'am, I'm afraid—"

She cut him off with a wave of her finger. "You've come for my daddy's skull, haven't you?"

Madely was shocked. "How did you know?"

She chuckled. "Your group, the Triarii, isn't it? Your group has been following me since I found the skull in that cave in 1927. It's about time you said hello."

Madely's eyes widened. "I don't know what to say,

191

ma'am."

"Well, I came to the determination long ago that you people weren't here to hurt me." She smiled. "I guess I came to feel that you were my protectors."

"How do you know about the Triarii?" asked Johnson.

"In my over ninety years, I've picked up a few things along the way," she smiled. "Now, if you're here for the skull, I assume something has gone wrong?"

"Yes, ma'am," said Madely. "I'm afraid we must take it, at least temporarily, until the situation is resolved."

"And will it be resolved?"

"I hope so, ma'am."

She frowned, but walked over to a cabinet. Taking a key from around her neck, she inserted it into the lock and opened the doors wide. Inside, the skull rested on a small, velvet-covered pedestal. She picked it up gently, gave it a little kiss on the forehead, then handed it to Madely, tears filling her eyes. "Be careful with my baby."

"Yes, ma'am, we will." Madely placed the skull in the case Johnson held. He pulled a card out of his pocket with the Triarii symbol embossed on it, and nothing else. "If anyone comes looking for the skull, give them this. It will protect you."

She nodded. "Thank you, my dears."

With that, the two men left, leaving the old lady feeling more alone than ever before.

THE PROTOCOL

Leroy bolted upright, listening for what had woken him. He strained his ears, hearing nothing at first, then finally a tapping sound from the front of the house. He checked his wife, sleeping peacefully beside him, then gently climbed out of bed. He tiptoed out of the room, avoiding the floorboards that creaked, and the tapping got louder as he neared the front entrance.

Opening the door, he found the source of the noise was the screen door blowing against the frame in the gentle desert breeze. He reattached the latch then closed the front door and locked it, something he rarely did. There was no need to. The only time people came into the house uninvited, was if they needed to borrow something.

He headed back toward the bedroom when something made him stop. He stared at the bookshelf where they had their collection of artifacts. All of the skulls were lined up as they were whenever they were home. The only time they were moved, was when he and his wife traveled to conferences around the world to show off their collection. They had found skulls all over the world, even in markets in New York City. Gripping the crystal that hung on a leather chain around his neck, he closed his eyes, seeking wisdom from the skulls.

Why do I feel uneasy?

He opened his eyes again and saw it. The last skull, an orange tinted one, was facing the wrong way. It was turned to the right instead of the left. His wife would never have done that. His heart raced, and he ran to the safe in the office. He turned on the light, and his heart sank. The safe was open.

And empty.

He dropped to his knees and cried.

Those government bastards!

Montague Place, London, England

Rodney and Acton reached Montague, then sprinted for about half a mile. Rodney dodged into an alley and Acton followed. As he turned the corner, he was grabbed. In a moment of panic, he turned to swing at his assailant.

"It's okay, Professor, it's me."

Acton relaxed at the sound of Rodney's voice. "Okay, time to talk. Tell me everything about the Triarii and the skulls."

"Fine, but wouldn't you like to go some place warmer? This could take some time."

"No. Here's fine."

"Very well." Rodney leaned against the wall. "Nearly two thousand years ago, in ancient Judea, the Roman Garrison found a crystal skull. It was thought to be so unique by the Prefect, that he sent it to the Emperor, Nero, as a gift to show his loyalty. The Emperor was so fascinated by the skull, he placed it at his bedside. He then began to hear voices and have visions. These terrified him, and he became convinced it was his god, Jupiter, communicating with him through the skull, trying to warn him the Roman Empire was doomed if he did not get the skull as far away from Rome as possible."

"Probably syphilis," interjected Acton.

Rodney chose to ignore him. "He ordered his best legion, the Thirteenth, to take the skull as far north as possible, and to make sure it never came near Rome again. As history shows, he was right. The skull came from Judea where the weak Christian god originated. When Rome converted to Christianity several hundred years later, it signaled the beginning of the end of the greatest empire to ever rule the Earth. The Emperor couldn't stop the tide of Christianity, even though he tried to have all of its followers and preachers killed. With every death, they seemed to only grow stronger. In the end, the empire was doomed."

"But that took half a millennium. What became of the Thirteenth Legion? Why did you continue to protect the skull?"

"Our ancestors, the progenitors of the Triarii, were men loyal to their Emperor and their gods. Remember, in those times, the Emperor was considered a god. He never actually died. He simply left Earth to join Jupiter and the other gods. These men made it to England and settled there, took wives, had families, and handed down the teachings.

"Over generations, we protected the Oracle of Jupiter, making sure that it was never returned to Rome. It took over one thousand years for the Roman Empire to collapse. By that time, dozens of generations had been raised thinking we had succeeded. Around the time of the Empire's collapse, however, a second skull was found, this time in Greece. It was found in ruins that we now know predated the fall of the Greek civilization, therefore it was assumed that this skull had brought the downfall of another empire. A team was dispatched to retrieve the skull and bring it back to the Triarii for safekeeping."

"Who had the second skull?"

"The Caliphate, the ancient Muslim empire that ruled from the Atlantic Ocean in Spain to the Pacific Ocean in the Philippines, the greatest empire to exist since the collapse of the Roman Empire."

"How could you possibly expect to take it from them?"

"The Crusades, of course. The Crusades were not just to try and take back the Holy Land, they were also a secret mission to retrieve the skull. By this time, the Triarii, though secret, were extremely powerful, and we had made inroads into all walks of life and power, including royalty. We were able to convince the King to fund a contingent of Triarii during the Crusades. We had ulterior motives of course, but simply appealing to his deeply religious beliefs, along with the fact that one of his daughters was married to a senior Triarii member, assured our funding.

"We sent a group of knights with the main force, and after years of searching and fighting, finally found and retrieved the skull. Once we brought it back to England, it was hidden away as well. It has become known as the Oracle of Zeus."

Acton shook his head in disbelief. "That's quite the story. You're saying that some of the most important events in history are tied to the skulls?"

"We've used events to our advantage. The Crusades were not because of the skull. There were legitimate reasons for them at the time that went far beyond the skull. We merely used them as cover to fulfill our needs. It wasn't until the thirteenth century that we discovered the power of the skulls. That's when the first true disaster struck."

The British Museum
London, England

Laura shivered against the chill and the light drizzle that had started to fall, huddled as close to the building as she could while she waited to be let in. A few minutes passed before a buzzer sounded.

A confused guard opened the door. "Where'd Rodney go?"

"I don't know. He did a runner when I asked him if he knew anything about the robbery." Laura entered the building and started following the guard. "My friend is chasing him now."

"Really? Should I radio for help?"

Laura thought for a quick second. "Yes, that's probably a good idea."

He activated his radio. "Clive, this is Paul, can you tell the coppers that Professor Palmer's friend—" He stopped and turned to Laura. "What was his name?"

Laura tried to remember if they had said Acton's name yet. "James—Jamison," she stammered. "Rick Jamison."

He raised his radio as they made their way toward the storage area. "Mr. Jamison left in pursuit of Rodney." He then lowered his voice. "Rodney ran when they asked him about the robbery. Do you think…?" he trailed off, as if not wanting to say something over the radio.

"Take her to the Archaeological Storage Room, that's where the police are waiting for her," came the reply. "Tell them about, who did you say, Jamison?"

"Yes, Jamison."

"I thought his name was Acton?"

He turned to Laura with a questioning look.

She shrugged. "He must have heard me wrong."

"No, it's Jamison, I just confirmed it." They rounded a corner to find a none too pleased man in a suit.

"What the bloody hell is taking so long?" He eyed the guard. "And where's the other bloke?"

"He did a runner, sir, that's what took so long. Professor Palmer's friend, a Mr. Jamison, is chasing him now. Can you send for help?"

The man pulled out his phone. "Which way did they go?"

"West on Montague." They had gone east, but she figured it would buy them time to find a place out of sight to talk. She was still anxious about him.

She didn't trust the Triarii.

At all.

"What does your friend look like?"

"About one-hundred and eighty centimeters, slim, early forties, brown hair."

He nodded and turned back to his phone. "This is DI Chaney, I need units in the vicinity of Montague on the lookout for two males, first is one-hundred-eighty centimeters, slim build, early forties with brown hair, the other same height and build, mid-twenties with black hair, wearing a security guard uniform." After listening on the other end for a moment, he hung up. "Your friend was foolish to chase that man," he said to Laura. "A lot of people have died as a result of this robbery."

Laura's heart dropped into her stomach.

I should never have let him go alone!

They entered the storage room to see an irate older man. Chaney made introductions, then explained about Rodney and the chase. This calmed Reading down only a little.

"Well, Professor, there appears to be nothing amiss here, yet a guard has run away, and we've seen footage that clearly shows an armed group of men entering this room and then leaving a few minutes later." Reading pointed to the markings on the floor. "These scrapes, with fresh shavings from the floor, seem to indicate that this ladder was moved since the room was cleaned last night. Would anyone have been in here today?"

Laura stared at the floor then scanned the rows of artifacts on shelves. "No, I would have been notified." She knew exactly where she wanted to check. This had to do with the skull, and she desperately wanted to see if it was still in place, yet it would seem too obvious to go directly there. She walked up and down each row, deliberately taking her time, pretending to examine the artifacts.

Chaney trailed behind her. "Don't you need some sort of list or something?"

"Detective, I know this room like the back of my hand. Everything in here has been inventoried by me countless times over the years. If anything is even out of place, I'll know it." She arrived at the spot where the skull was stored. "Like that." She pointed at the box. "It's on the wrong shelf."

Chaney looked up at where she was pointing. "What's in it?"

"Just a fake sculpture." Laura called to the doorway where her escort was still standing. "Can you bring me the ladder?"

"Yes, Professor," came the reply from several rows over. A moment later he appeared, pushing the ladder. Positioning it, she relocked the wheels and climbed up. She took the box and opened it, moving aside the packaging. It took everything she had not to gasp in disbelief.

This is not *the skull I documented! This is definitely a fake!*

The carving was rough, amateurish in comparison to the original. With her bare hands, the slight imperfections caused by the carving wheel were obvious. It appeared to be the skull described by the BBC documentary.

The Triarii must have switched the skull before the documentary and then put it back! Now they've switched it again!

A huge weight lifted off her shoulders. The embarrassment of that event washed away as she realized what had happened. She had been right all along.

The BBC tested the wrong skull!

She carefully wrapped the skull back up, returned it to the shelf, then descended the ladder.

"Well?"

"Nothing, I guess I was mistaken." She moved on. After finishing the rest of the aisles, she returned to the entrance. "As far as I can tell, nothing has been taken."

Reading frowned, heading to the door. "Okay, let's go to the control room again and look at that footage."

Outside Riyadh, Saudi Arabia

Faisal stretched out the kinks from a long night's sleep. He kissed his wife on the forehead and headed to the bathroom. As he relieved himself, he peered into the mirror, admiring his mustache, then flushed the toilet, giving little thought to the fact he had wasted more water than most of his countrymen used in a day, then turning on the gold plated faucets adorning the marble sink, he pushed the plunger down. Leaning in, he carefully washed his face and hands, then reached for the towel hanging to his left, pressing his face into it. Once dried, he opened his eyes and gasped.

In the mirror were two masked men, both dressed in black, pointing handguns at him.

Faisal swung around to face them. "What do you want?"

"Open your inner office."

Faisal hesitated.

The man pointed the gun directly at Faisal's forehead. "You have five seconds, or he kills your wives, one at a time."

Faisal blanched, thinking of his wife in the next room who had bore him three strong sons, and was pregnant, he hoped, with a fourth. He knew they would kill her first, as she was closest.

He nodded slowly and raised his hands, dropping the towel to the floor. The man led him to a wall lined with hanging silks. Reaching forward, he moved the silk sheets aside, revealing a keypad. He entered his code, and there was a clicking sound. Pushing with his shoulder, a door, previously hidden, opened. The two men shoved him inside.

"Give us the skull."

Faisal was stunned. There was several million dollars' worth of currency, gold, and jewels in here.

Why would they want a skull made of crystal?

It had been handed down for over a thousand years, from father to eldest son, and except for the sentimental, it didn't have any real value. He couldn't believe he would be the one who finally lost what had been in his family since his forefathers lived on the desert plains. He walked to a shelf and took down the skull, handing it to them.

They must be from another clan, here to shame my family.

The men carefully placed it in a case and started to leave the room. One turned around and faced him. "Sorry." He raised his gun and fired. Faisal grabbed at his shoulder as he felt the impact. He looked down, puzzled by the lack of blood, then collapsed.

Somewhere on the Atlantic
AD 1212

Lord Richard Baxter lay on the deck of the boat, propped up against a barrel that had once contained life-sustaining water. His throat parched, lips cracked, and skin badly burned, his once proud body had withered to an emaciated skeleton. If anyone happened upon his ship, they could have been forgiven for thinking he was dead. And he should have been, but he willed himself to stay alive, knowing he couldn't die until his mission was accomplished.

He had left England months before, determined to sail himself, and the skull that had killed his beloved family, over the edge of the Earth. The voyage had taken far longer than anyone had anticipated, and when it became evident the end of the world was farther than expected, he had begun strict rationing to prolong the voyage. That had only extended their provisions by a few weeks, however, and if it weren't for a fortunate heavy rain that had partially replenished their water supplies four weeks earlier, they would have been dead by now.

But that water was gone. His trusted friend and companion, Jonathan, had died two days ago, and now only he and three crewmembers remained. All were in as bad a shape as he was, and the ship was now essentially sailing itself. He prayed for the edge to come before he lost all strength and succumbed to the inevitable death that awaited him. He must ensure the skull went over the edge so no one else could be killed by it.

As he lay in his near-death state, he heard a roaring sound. At first, he thought he was hallucinating, but then the other men stirred. They had heard it too. The sound grew louder and louder.

The edge!

He forced himself to his feet, realizing the roar must be the great waterfall at the edge of the world. He was resolved to sail over it at the prow of his boat, crying the names of his wife and child as his life ended.

Yet what he saw stunned him. He had to rub his eyes several times, and was convinced he must now be hallucinating, but one of his men who stood with him

202

pointed at it, too.

"It be land, Lord Baxter! How can it be?"

Richard's shoulders slumped in defeat.

How could we have been so wrong?

He looked up again and watched as the waves crashed, not over the edge of the world as had been foretold, but against the shore of a mysterious new land.

"What sort of disaster?" Acton was enthralled by the tale being told. As he processed the information provided by Rodney, history as he knew it was being rewritten in his head.

"You've heard of the Great Fire of London?"

"Of course, 1666 wasn't it, killed over thirty thousand people?"

"No, the *first* Great Fire was actually in 1212. The city was nearly lost. It was forgotten by history, so the 1666 fire became incorrectly known as the Great Fire of London. Before that time, the fire of 1212 was known by the same name. And we were responsible for it."

"Responsible? How?"

"When the second skull was discovered and subsequently recovered, we realized there may be others. We dispatched teams all over the known world to look for the skulls, mostly by monitoring religious ceremonies. It was around AD 1200 that we found the third skull. It was retrieved from a mosque in what is now Tehran. Our operatives brought it back to London. When it was put into the same area for safekeeping as the other two, a humming sound was heard. Our scientists were immediately summoned, and during the examination, the three skulls were placed together.

"It is thought that natural light shone down on them and then an incredible explosion or release of energy occurred. All the scientists were killed, along with many innocent Londoners. The fires that ensued destroyed a large part of the city."

"I remember the fire now. I've read about it, London was nearly lost. How do you know that it was the skulls that did it? Couldn't it just have been a coincidence?"

Rodney nodded. "Yes, it could have been, but when we were able to get back into the area at nightfall, we found the skulls in the center of a blast wave. We separated them, realizing their true power."

Acton eyed Rodney skeptically.

"I know this sounds far-fetched, Professor, but all of it is documented in our archives. Almost two-thousand years of painstaking journals and drawings. When you come in, I will show them to you."

"Yeah, well, we'll see about that. Okay, so you nearly blew up all of London. How the hell did I find a skull in Peru?"

"We knew this new skull must not be anywhere near the other two. It was decided that we must get rid of it so there would be no chance of it ever coming into contact again. A group of volunteers took the skull and sailed it over the edge of the world. It had been assumed they were successful. That, of course, was before we knew the world was round." Rodney smiled.

"I didn't think people still believed it was flat then."

"Well, with our lineage being Roman, not Greek, it unfortunately proved popular to discount their mathematicians at times, and in the early thirteenth century, with the Crusades and religious fervor at a peak, literal translations of the Bible were popular."

"And after these things I saw four angels standing on the four corners of the Earth."

"Exactly, Revelations. How can a round world have four corners? The first to sail were led by a nobleman, Lord Baxter. They sailed southwest to avoid the ice packs to the north, and were supposed to go off the edge with the skull. Instead, they discovered America. *South* America to be exact."

"How do you know?"

"Because, Professor, the skull you found is that third skull."

"How do you know it's the third skull? I thought there were lots of these things all over the world?"

"Yes, there are, but there are only twelve genuine skulls that we know of, the last one having been discovered in Nepal in the early twentieth century. We keep track of all of the skulls very closely, watching to make sure that no three ever come in contact. This has meant that our organization is now spread throughout the world. We have people shadowing the owners of all the skulls, all of them, that is, except the last of the lost skulls."

"Lost skulls?"

"After the disaster in 1212, we began sending all the skulls, except for the original two of course, across the Atlantic, with the intent that they would be lost over the edge of the world. When science replaced religious dogma, we returned to the belief the world wasn't flat.

"What scared us the most, was that we had sent out four skulls across the Atlantic. If those four were to come into contact somehow, we had no idea the level of destruction they could bring. In 1492, of course, the New World was formally discovered, and when news of this reached us from one of our operatives on the Pinta—"

"Wait a minute," interrupted Acton. "You had an operative on one of Columbus' ships?"

"Several actually. It was going to be a long, tough voyage, so we couldn't rely on only one man. Martin Alonzo Pinzon, the commander of the Pinta, was actually a member of the Triarii."

Acton shook his head in amazement or disbelief—he wasn't sure which.

"Needless to say, with this news, we sent more people on expeditions in search of the skulls. It took hundreds of years, but eventually, three were recovered and placed into the hands of people that could be trusted, without them even knowing why, to keep them safely separated."

"How could you rely on them to do this? I've heard many of these are in private collections."

"Yes, but over the years, we've had many fakes created and spread throughout the art world. As well, we've discredited some serious owners such as the British Museum and the Smithsonian, most recently by rigging a switch for a BBC documentary that then proclaimed them frauds. Many of the real skulls are now believed to be fakes, therefore no one has any interest in them anymore except as oddities. Others, who hold the real skulls, are terrified to actually let them be tested in case theirs too may be proven fake. It's the perfect situation.

"Most people think the skulls are fake, therefore they don't draw any attention to themselves, and the others don't want to find out that what they own is fake, so they remain quiet. There are a few that believe what they have is real, and tour around the world showing them off, but we always have people watching them and protecting the skulls. And, much to their annoyance, discrediting them. There's a reason why many are considered off their rockers. We strategically place people in the crowds at these events to ask loaded questions, give tainted interviews and whatnot, just to make the whole thing look like a carnival."

"But, why? Why not just collect them all and seal them away in separate locations so that no one can bring them together?"

"Part of our belief system is that these skulls were indeed placed here by the gods or God. We believe that they were sent as a message to mankind, and that when we are ready to understand it, we will. We have come to believe that if the skulls are all locked up and hidden away from humanity, they will not be able to have the influence on people that they are supposed to. By allowing them to move through the population, with more and more people being exposed, we believe that eventually mankind will evolve to the point where the message will be revealed."

"Funny, I've heard something like that before," commented Acton, thinking back on his conversation with Laura. "Okay, so your group, the Triarii, essentially track the movement of all of the skulls and take action when necessary to make sure that they don't come in contact?"

Rodney nodded.

"Okay then, who's trying to kill me?"

Rodney's expression turned grave. "A former member of our group."

When Acton heard who it was, his heart sank.

J. ROBERT KENNEDY

Moscow, Russia

Alexander quietly entered one of the many damp storage rooms in the basement of the Lubyanka building. The former KGB Headquarters' purpose might have changed—albeit slightly—but the building that housed it was a testament to Soviet era quality. Primitive. Modernization, decades overdue, was finally occurring, though these dark, dank rooms, had escaped even the slightest upgrade. Alexander was used to the smell, having worked here for over fifty years as a custodian of the records. Regimes had come and gone during his tenure from as far back as Khrushchev.

Today, he was on a mission for his true masters. Neither the current regime nor any previous had held his true loyalty. That was reserved for the Triarii. And today, he would fulfill his mission to protect an artifact the KGB had recovered from the Nazis after conquering Berlin. Hitler's obsession with archaeological relics had netted him one of the precious skulls. The Triarii had been unable to stop it from being stolen from the Jewish family in Warsaw, its keepers for generations. When the Soviets recovered it, they merely cataloged it and filed it away as a meaningless religious artifact. The atheist policies of the communist era meant anything with a religious connotation was of no importance.

He had recognized it immediately, however. A member of the Triarii through his father, he had obtained the job in the one agency that would know if the skull existed in the Soviet Union. It took years of work to gain the security clearances to search the records, but he had finally done it, and soon found what had been lost.

It had been decided at the time, the safest place for it was right where it was—in a forgotten box in a forgotten room. Now, however, nothing was safe. Today, for the first time since the end of World War II, the skull would leave its damp home.

The British Museum
London, England

The buzzer to the control room sounded and Laura stepped inside, the night security chief, Clive Obrock, rising from his seat to shake her hand.

"Has your friend returned?"

Laura hesitated. "No, actually I'm getting a little concerned."

"Is Professor Acton familiar with the city?"

"Who?" Reading's voice was loud enough to startle everyone in the room.

"His name is Jamison," said Laura, "and no, he's not familiar with the city. He's a visiting professor from the United States and is probably lost. I told him to hail a taxi if that happened, and to go back to the university. He's probably there now."

Reading stepped closer to Laura. "Now listen carefully, Professor. We are looking for a Mr. James Acton, a professor from the United States, in connection with *eight* deaths today. So, I'll ask you one time." He leaned in even closer. "What is your friend's name?"

Laura desperately tried not to tremble. Then her fear turned to anger. There was nothing they could do to her. She had done nothing wrong, and Acton couldn't be involved in those deaths because he had been with her almost the entire day.

She stalled, staring Reading straight in the face. "His name is Jamison."

"Very well." Reading turned to Clive. "Pull up the footage of the back entrance. I want to see this professor." Clive nodded, and his fingers flew across the keyboard. Within seconds, they were viewing footage of the conversation between Rodney and the two professors. "Pause it there." Reading pointed to the screen. "Can you blow that up?"

"Yes, sir," said Clive. A few more keystrokes followed by a drag of the mouse, and they were staring at a block of pixels. A few more keystrokes, and the software sharpened up the image so they were looking at a perfect picture of the man in question.

Chaney held the photo of Acton up to the screen. Both

he and Reading said at the same time, "Acton."

Reading stared at Laura. "Care to change your answer?"

Laura sighed. "Okay, fine. I met him today. What's he supposed to have done?"

"He's wanted for questioning in connection with the torture death of a tourist, a theft from this museum that resulted in the death of seven people, and two explosions that seriously injured several police officers."

"He only arrived in London this afternoon!" exclaimed Laura. "How's he supposed to have killed half the bloody city when he's been with me almost his entire time?"

"I didn't say he'd killed them personally, but he's connected somehow. And I'm not sure I believe you when you say nothing is missing." He turned to Clive. "Is there someone else you can call to verify the contents of that room?"

Clive stared nervously at Professor Palmer. "I, ah, yes, I mean, there should be a backup."

"Okay, call them and have them go through the storage room and let me know the result." Reading headed for the door. "Professor Palmer, I'd like you to come down to the Yard with me for questioning."

"I'll do no such thing! I've done nothing wrong!"

"Professor, if you want, I can charge you with interfering in an ongoing police investigation." Reading's tone was firm now. "Or, you can come down voluntarily for questioning."

Laura's expression conveyed how angry she was, but she acquiesced. She followed Paul out the door with Chaney and Reading bringing up the rear.

THE PROTOCOL

The C17 Globemaster III Tactical Transport Aircraft had just landed, its four Pratt and Whitney PW2040 turbofan engines, each capable of over forty thousand pounds of thrust, were still winding down. Red was already yelling at the ground crew to hustle on the unloading, knowing they would need the equipment quickly. "Get the bird set up and armed, ASAP!"

"Armed?" asked the Crew Chief. "With what?"

"What do you mean, 'with what?'"

"In case you're not aware, we have a little thing going on over in Iraq and Afghanistan," retorted the Chief. Red glared at him. "I'll see what I can scrounge up."

"You do that."

BD is going to be pissed.

He climbed into his Humvee and headed back to the temporary headquarters. Entering the rec room, he found Dawson relaxing with the team, enjoying themselves for the first time in days. Dawson sat in a reclining chair, squeezing a stress ball. He looked at Red as he entered the room and gestured for him to come over.

"That'll learn ya!" bellowed Smitty, winning his fifth straight game of pool. He took the money from the table. "Who's next?"

Red smiled at the display as he sat in a chair across from his friend. "Our gear's arrived. They're setting up the bird now, don't know about ordnance though."

"Explain."

"Apparently there's a shortage."

"Fine, we'll make do."

"We always do."

Dawson leaned closer to Red and lowered his voice. "When you were seconded to DARPA, did you ever hear of anything called Structural Amorphous Metals?"

"Yeah, the SAM project, something to do with extremely strong metals or something. Why?"

"Any chance that our sculpture could be made of it?"

Red shook his head. "Not unless the project took a U-turn. They were dealing with crystalline structures, not blocks

211

of crystal."

"Do you still have any contacts there?"

"Yeah, one or two. Want me to make some calls?"

"Discreetly, on secure lines."

Red got up and headed to the communications room.

Dawson watched Red leave and took a long drag from his bottle of water, returning his attention to his men playing pool. He found himself continually reviewing the events of the past week, his mind no longer at ease after today's mission in London. Everything that had happened before arriving here he could reconcile. A terror cell steals a DARPA project, killing American soldiers in the process. They flee to their training camp in Peru with the stolen item. These same terrorists are confirmed by Control as on the Termination List. A charismatic professor, who led these kids astray, escapes, kills and wounds his own government's soldiers in the process, taking the stolen item with him. He sends a decoy package, elicits help from other members of his cell, evades capture in London, while an accomplice is found within the White House.

This all made sense, all the actions of terrorists, no matter how young many of the perpetrators had been. If Acton were innocent, why had he run? Fleeing Peru, he could understand, but once he was back in the United States, he should have simply walked into the first police station and told his story.

It's what an innocent man would have done.

But that wasn't at all what he had done. He had sneaked across the border, sent a decoy package, elicited the help of others to get him to London, then met with an accomplice who arrived at the same time from France, an accomplice who refused to divulge any information about the terror cell, or its mastermind, proclaiming his innocence until the moment Dawson injected him with an overdose of morphine, Control indicating the man was on the Termination List.

He had his doubts, though if he assumed what Control was telling him was the truth, then those doubts should have been assuaged.

But now they had a crystal sculpture in their possession, and knew that this terrorist cell led by Acton was but a tiny cog of a bigger, international organization that Control Actual seemed to be toying with, setting off bombs outside their headquarters.

And injuring innocent police.

Control Actual had assured him that an anonymous tip would be phoned in so that the area would be evacuated, though obviously that call had never been made.

And now the injuries to those innocent British policemen were on his conscience.

And that was unacceptable.

The door to the rec room opened and Red walked over, leaning down to whisper in his ear. "I made those calls, but it'll take some time." Dawson nodded as Red rose up and raised his voice. "You've got a call in the comms center."

Dawson stood and headed to the room where they had set up their secure satellite communications equipment, grabbing a headset. "Zero-One here."

"Zero-One, Control Actual. A Professor Palmer is being held at Scotland Yard. Details are being sent now. Retrieve her, alive. She may know where the item is. If not, she can be used as bait for Professor Acton."

Dawson never had a chance to reply, never had a chance to demand to know why the phone call about the rigged trucks hadn't been made. Instead, he was left to question yet another set of orders progressively getting more outrageous.

Retrieve a prisoner from Scotland Yard? This is getting ridiculous!

Control was setting mission parameters that were putting his men at risk. Rigging the escape vehicles to explode after taking down the terrorist cell's van was one thing. But to position them on either side of the terrorists' known headquarters was ridiculous, and he had said so when the orders were given.

They'll know we're on to them!

Control hadn't cared, spewing venomous nonsense about striking the fear of God into them.

And now they were to infiltrate the equivalent of FBI Headquarters.

Somebody's going to get court-martialed, and it better not be my team.

He left the communications center and returned to the rec area as his mind raced to formulate a plan. His team stopped what they were doing and looked at their commander.

"Gear up, gentlemen, gangland cover, briefing in five."

Beijing, China

Huang stared at the text message he had received on his Chinese built Samsung phone and frowned.

One of these days, China will be designing, not just building, the products the world uses.

As a Vice-Chairperson of the Standing Committee of the National People's Congress, he was a stone's throw from leading his glorious country. He had been a general in the People's Liberation Army, then used that power and influence to become rich in the newly opened economy. This had given him even more influence, and he had been appointed to his current position. If he played his cards right, he would soon be president.

But not today.

Today, he had to fulfill his primary duty in life. Rising from his desk, he unlocked a cabinet on the far wall of his office. He entered a code on the safe inside, and it hissed open. Removing a case it contained, he closed the safe and walked down the long corridor of his office building in the Zhongnanhai complex.

As he approached the president's office, the two soldiers guarding the entrance snapped their heels in respect, one opening the door. He entered the outer office and bowed slightly to the secretary as she rose. She bowed deeply to her superior.

"I am sorry, sir, but the president is not in, he is away on business in Shanghai." She avoided eye contact, her voice meek.

"Do you not think that I am fully aware of that?" His sarcastic tone was intended to belittle her. "I have a package for him that I must personally deliver to the safety of his office."

"Of course, sir, you may leave it with me, and I will make certain that he receives it."

"Absolutely not. I am under strict orders from the Chairman himself to put this file in his office personally." With that, he walked past her, opened the door to the inner office, then closed it behind him, leaving the flabbergasted secretary wondering what to do.

Swiftly walking to a side table, he opened his case and

removed a velvet wrapped package from inside. He unwrapped it, revealing a crystal skull. Walking over to a pedestal in the corner that contained the genuine skull, his charge of many years, he switched the two, placing the real skull in his case, again carefully wrapped. He locked the case, looked about the office, and strode out, purposefully ignoring the secretary.

THE PROTOCOL

Triarii Headquarters
London, England

The Proconsul was pleased. *Very* pleased. All of the plans had been executed like clockwork. All around the world, the skulls were being moved into secret locations known to the individual members in this room, and one backup each. No one in the room knew the backup location of more than one skull except for him—he knew where the original two were.

"Now that we have protected our charge, we must now consider relocating, at least temporarily. We have a rogue element with unknown intentions that has just detonated two bombs on the streets above, who clearly knows our location, and has the capability to reach it." There were nods of assent from around the room. "Very well, we will move immediately to our Beta Site. Is there any other business that must be concluded before we adjourn?"

The British Museum member spoke up. "Sir, I have just learned that Professor Palmer has been taken into custody for questioning. As well, our operative is currently with Professor Acton. One or both of them definitely knows where the third skull is. We should try to bring them both in for their protection."

"Agreed. Make it happen." The Proconsul stood, ending the meeting, and headed toward his office with a heavy heart. He had served as Proconsul for over ten years, since the last, his uncle, had died of cancer. As he headed down the long stone corridor, he passed the offices of the other members, some of whom were already inside packing their personal items in boxes, and destroying papers. He gazed fondly at the British Museum member's office as he passed. It had been his for almost twenty years.

He entered his office and closed the door, locking it behind him. Walking over to the large bookcase on the left, he pulled open two panels in the middle, revealing an assortment of liquors and glasses. Selecting a 1968 Macallan scotch, he poured a double shot into a glass, held it up, and shrugged.

I won't be taking it with me.

He added more, then went to a large, comfortable chair sitting in the far left corner of the room.

Gentle ambient lighting gave the illusion of being above ground, making it easy to forget how isolated he was down here. He sat then put his feet up on the ottoman and closed his eyes, the drink balancing in his right hand on the arm of the chair.

Don't worry. Once this crisis is over, we'll be back. You won't lose the council's home of four hundred years on your watch.

THE PROTOCOL

Montague Place, London, England

"I can't believe that he's involved!" Acton shivered at the thought of it.

Or is it this damned alley?

"And what do you mean by former member?"

Rodney rubbed his arms, feeling the cold as well. "He was a member of the Triarii until about ten years ago. He was actually a member of our senior council. He began to push the view that mankind was ready to unite the skulls and see what their true power was. He felt technology had reached the point where they could be controlled. The council, of course, disagreed. He stole the skull he was responsible for from the Smithsonian. As with many of our members, he was already quite wealthy and powerful. He used this wealth and power to get into the position he now occupies. Since then, he's been searching for the skull that you found. He launched the operation that killed your students."

"How are you going to stop him?"

Rodney smiled. "We have our ways, but remember, he needs three skulls. As of tonight, he has two, and we're already taking steps to have the other skulls placed into safekeeping."

"What happened tonight? You said there was a robbery?"

"We had a team enter the museum and switch the real skull for a fake."

"Laura was right!"

"Yes, we did this once before, when it was going to be examined for a BBC documentary. It was unfortunate that Professor Palmer was so embarrassed by that incident, however she seems to have recovered from it, since she is now the head of the department."

"Yes, but something went wrong this time?"

"Our team was ambushed and killed. They managed to switch the skulls, but when they left, they were attacked, and the real skull was taken. I don't know more than that. I'll know more when we go in."

"You keep saying 'we,'" said Acton. "Why do you think I would go in with you? Just because you told some long, elaborate story, doesn't mean I trust you or even necessarily believe you. It all seems a bit fantastic to me."

Rodney's cellphone rang. He flipped it open and listened, then hung up and looked at Acton. "Professor Palmer has been nicked. We're going to retrieve her. It would be beneficial if you were at the Triarii headquarters to meet her upon her arrival."

"Why are you taking her?" Acton suddenly felt protective of a woman he had only met earlier that day. "Why not leave her there? Surely she's safe in a police station?"

"The men we are dealing with have all of the resources of the United States government at their disposal. And clearly no qualms about killing. Do you really believe they didn't intercept the radio call telling the station that they were bringing her in, and why?"

Acton thought for a moment. "I suppose you're right. Assuming you're telling me the truth."

God, I hope he is.

"You'll just have to trust me. Now, come with me. We'll go to the council chambers and wait for her arrival."

Acton nodded and followed Rodney out of the alley. He shivered, chilled to the bone after having spent so much time in the cold. A police car cruised by, the officers inside staring at the two men closely, then continuing on when another vehicle pulled up in front of them, Rodney opening the door.

"After you."

Acton climbed into the car, unsure if he had made the right decision.

THE PROTOCOL

New Scotland Yard
London, England

Laura sat in the interrogation room, staring at the mirror, then the acoustic tiles in the ceiling. She yawned and started to count the holes.

I hope James is okay.

She stared back at the mirror. It was one of those two-way jobs, someone probably on the other side observing her. The police constable assigned to watch her so she didn't "hurt" herself stood by the door, staring at the floor. Sipping the tea Reading had brought her earlier, she waited.

She hadn't waited long before the lights went out, emergency lighting kicking in, dimly illuminating the room. "What's going on?"

"Wait here." The constable opened the door and looked into the hallway.

Reading heard snoring on the other side of his office door. He peered through the glass and saw his two American guests who had been waiting for hours, sound asleep in their chairs. He slapped Chaney on the chest and pointed. Chaney smiled as Reading threw open the door, loudly hitting the doorstop and rattling the glass.

"Good evening, gentlemen, or rather, good morning, I should say," said Reading in an overly loud voice. Jasper and Lambert scrambled up in their chairs, jarred awake. "How can I help our American allies today? Tea?"

"Coffee if you've got it." Jasper straightened himself then checked his watch and frowned.

"Same." Lambert rubbed his eyes and Reading nodded to Chaney who left the room to find a PC to fill the order.

"So, how may I be of service?"

"We're looking for this man." Jasper leaned forward and handed a file folder to Reading. "His name is Professor James Acton. We were told you were looking for him as well."

"Yes, he's wanted in connection with several investigations." Reading opened the folder, which only contained a photo. He handed it back. "Why, may I ask, are you looking for him?"

"I'm afraid that's confidential," replied Lambert.

Jasper stared at his underling with a slightly exasperated expression. "We're looking for him in connection to an investigation we're working on—the slaughter of his entire archaeological team in Peru. He was the only survivor and has stayed in hiding."

"Professor Acton seems to be a very popular man. And busy," said Reading to Chaney as he reentered the room. "Our colleagues here are looking for him in connection to killings in Peru."

Chaney raised his eyebrows in surprise. "He certainly does get around. Is he suspected of being involved?"

Jasper shook his head. "Right now he's just a person of interest. We've been tasked to bring him back to the United States for questioning."

"Why didn't the State Department just contact our Home Office? Why the personal visit?" asked Reading.

"Our orders come from the highest authority." Jasper leaned in and lowered his voice. "Look, we nearly had him in New York, but lost him. Basically, my career is on the line here. I was told to come back with him or not come back at all."

Reading nodded. "Well, I'll certainly keep you informed if we find him. He's not suspected in any of the murders, so after questioning, we will probably be able to release him into your custody."

"That would be acceptable."

There was a knock at the door. Chaney opened it and a PC entered with a tray containing a tea service and two coffees. As he walked toward the desk, balancing the shaking tray like a waiter on his first day, the lights went out, and he lost any equilibrium he might have had. In the dark, there was a yelp and a crashing sound as scalding hot coffee and tea splattered across the floor. When the emergency lights kicked in, Lambert stood, covered in coffee and tea, trying desperately to get the hot liquid off his hands and lap.

Ooh, that'll boil the bollocks.

"Constable, show the agent to the loo so he can clean up." Reading turned to Chaney. "Find out what's going on."

Chaney nodded and left the room, dodging a bow-legged Lambert as he gingerly walked his boys toward the bathroom, a grinning Police Constable directing him from behind.

Dawson activated his comms from the SUV's passenger seat.

"Bravo Team, Zero-One. Remember, these are our allies. Keep casualties to a minimum, non-lethal force. We don't need an international incident here. Out." They waited at the side prisoner transfer entrance of New Scotland Yard, this the most direct way to the interrogation rooms where Professor Palmer was probably held. Red was at the main entrance waiting to create a diversion, and Marco was in an underground access point, ready to cut the entire power grid for New Scotland Yard and the surrounding area.

"Zero-Nine in position," signaled Marco.

"Zero-Nine, proceed on my mark in three, two, one, mark." The power went out all around them. It was the middle of the night, and it was now pitch black except for a few emergency lights on the outside of the building. "Bravo teams, proceed."

Dawson pulled the ski mask down over his face, and the rest of his team followed. A few seconds later, the alarm rang inside the building and explosions and gunfire erupted from the front entrance. Dawson's team exited the vehicle and they raced to the prisoner transfer door. Dawson tried the handle. It was locked. He pointed at it, and Niner placed a small C4 charge. They turned their heads away, and he hit the remote detonator. The small explosion made quick work of the locking mechanism. Dawson pulled the door open, and two of his men took up position on either side of the entrance as the rest of the team rushed in.

Chaos reigned.

Most of the reduced night shift staff had run to the front of the building to see what was happening. One lone desk officer was left, and when the heavily armed men entered, he ran for cover. Dawson tasered him in the leg then motioned for his team to bind him. They blew the inner door, then Dawson and Smitty entered the next corridor, leaving the final two team members to guard their escape route. As they jogged down the corridor, peering through the windows, a lone constable stuck her head out a door halfway down the hall.

"What is it?" asked Laura.

"I don't know," replied the Constable. "There seems to be—oh my God!" She fell backward into a heap on the floor, shaking from the electric shock of a Taser that had hit her. Laura leaped from her chair as two men wearing ski masks entered.

"Come with us, Professor Palmer," the bigger of the two said. She shook her head and moved toward the back of the room. He raised his weapon and pointed it directly at her. "Now, Professor."

The smaller one, who was by no means small, approached her and grabbed her by the arm. She kicked him in the groin and kneed him in the face as he doubled over. The larger one laughed.

"Should'a worn a cup!" He rounded the table, approaching her more cautiously than the first had. She snapped a kick at him and he caught her leg, his free hand swinging at her head, a weapon gripped in it. The pain was intense, but brief, as the pistol-whipping knocked her out cold.

Explosions rocked the room and Reading leaped from his desk, rushing for the door. He turned to the Americans. "Stay here!" He yanked the door open and stepped into the hallway. He grabbed a constable running away from what now sounded like automatic weapons fire. "What the bloody hell is going on?"

"We're under attack! We have to get to the weapons vault!" He continued down the hallway with Reading in pursuit. They descended a flight of stairs and rounded a corner. As they neared the vault, some of their colleagues passed them with weapons in hand as they rushed to join the fight at the front of the building. Reading and the constable arrived as Chaney was gearing up.

"Hello, guv. I was just coming to get you. Any idea what's going on?"

"No, just that the main entrance is apparently under attack."

"Sounds like a diversion to me."

"Me, too. There's only one person here that I can think of who would attract this kind of attention."

Chaney nodded. "Professor Palmer."

Reading loaded the weapon he had been given, and was

still putting on his body armor as he followed Chaney out the door and up the stairs. They rushed through the door that led to the interrogation rooms, and as they sprinted toward the one the professor was held in, they saw two men leave, one carrying what appeared to be a body over his shoulder.

"Stop!" yelled Reading.

The man without the body whipped around and opened fire, spraying bullets along the wall, the impacts approaching their position. Reading raised his weapon and shot. The man collapsed, a tiny hole in the front of his head, a much larger one in the back. The second man turned around and shifted the body to use as a shield.

It was the professor.

"Let her go!"

No response.

The man continued toward the other end of the hallway. Reading raised his weapon again and shot the man in the shoulder. He dropped the gun he was holding, then the professor. Reading and Chaney rushed him and brought him down to the floor. Chaney picked up the professor and tried to revive her.

Gunfire erupted, the ceiling above them torn apart, shredded acoustic tile and dust momentarily blinding him. Suddenly Reading felt a searing pain as he was punched in the nose by his prisoner, and he stumbled back, losing his balance.

"Let's go!" yelled Chaney, grabbing him by the shoulder and hauling him to his feet. Reading was forced to follow the voice, still partially blinded by the stinging pain radiating from his nose, and the dust in his eyes. He abandoned their prisoner, the gunfire getting nearer, but still not finding its mark.

As his eyes cleared, he spotted Chaney running toward the other end of the hallway with the professor in a fireman's hold. Reading stumbled after him, crouching and firing blindly behind him, hoping their aim would be as bad as his if they had to keep taking cover. He dove through the door at the end of the hallway as it slowly closed, then swung around, kicking it shut. Chaney again hauled him to his feet.

"Let's go!"

Reading peered through the window and saw the two newcomers continue to advance. Chaney headed toward the rear emergency exit with the professor still over his shoulder. Reading followed, then realized where they were headed.

"Where are you going?" He pointed down another hall that would lead to where there were more armed police. "This way!"

"No, sir, we have to go this way!" Chaney continued toward the exit, Reading chasing him down the hallway. As they neared the end, the door behind them burst open as the two attackers reached it. He launched himself through the exit and saw a black van with its side door open, idling. Chaney handed the professor over to two men in the back of the van, then climbed in after her. He turned around and reached out his hand. "Sir, you have to come with us!"

Reading stared at him, bewildered. "What the hell is going on?"

"There's no time, sir, you have to come with us or they'll kill you!" Reading still didn't move, and in desperation, Chaney ripped off his watch and turned his wrist inside out, showing it to Reading. "We can protect her, sir!"

Reading's jaw dropped. His underling had the same tattoo as the dead bodies in the morgue. He made a split-second decision to trust his long-time subordinate, and jumped in the van as the hostiles erupted through the door behind him. The van sped off with a hail of gunfire hitting its reinforced skin and bullet resistant glass. Chaney reached out and slid the side door closed as they rounded the corner. He sat back on the floor and looked at Reading.

"Welcome to the Triarii, sir." He took one of the guns from another man in the van and pointed it at him. "Sorry, sir." He fired before Reading could say a word.

Jasper and Lambert sat in Reading's office with only a faint light coming from the hallway as gunfire and explosions sounded in the distance.

"Screw this!" Jasper got up and headed to the door. Lambert followed his boss as they made their way toward the action. Not knowing where they were going, they tagged along with several heavily armed men who didn't seem lost. They soon found themselves in the main reception area of New Scotland Yard.

All of the windows were shattered, and the interior walls and ceilings were scarred with bullet holes. Amazingly, no one appeared injured. The few armed police officers were providing cover fire as civilians escaped deeper into the building. Bullets from the hostiles continued to spray over their heads.

"Who's attacking?" Lambert asked a nearby constable.

"I have no bloody idea!" He popped up from behind the desk he was using as cover, and fired off a few rounds. He ducked back down and looked at Lambert. "Get the hell out of here, I'll cover you!"

Lambert shook his head and squatted beside him. "I'm U.S. State Department. Do you have a spare weapon?" The man tossed him a Glock. Lambert, poking his head up, took a look. He could see several of the attackers hiding behind concrete flower boxes as they popped up and took fire. Turning to Jasper, crouched behind a half-wall nearby, he yelled over the noise. "Looks like gang-bangers, boss!"

Jasper nodded as he leaned over to take a shot from around the wall, a nearby constable having supplied him with a weapon. The high beams from the attackers' vehicle were aimed at the entrance, preventing those inside from seeing most of their enemy. Jasper fired two quick rounds, taking out the lights and plunging the room into darkness save a couple of emergency lights on a far wall.

"That's more like it!" The constable beside Lambert rose again and let loose a burst of gunfire that hit one of the attackers outside. "That'll bloody teach ya!"

Dawson retrieved his weapon and grabbed Smitty's body as his men pursued the professor. He made his way toward the exit, dragging the body of his fallen comrade and nursing a sore shoulder, his vest having caught most of it. As he cleared the inner doors, he found Spock had redeployed from the main entrance to cover both doors when he had fallen under attack.

"Take him."

Spock's eyes widened, but he grabbed Smitty's body and hoisted it over his shoulder, double-timing it back to the SUV.

Dawson covered the inner door, staring down the long hallway, when his men returned.

Empty-handed.

Shit, Control's not going to be happy.

He radioed Red. "Zero-Two, Zero-One. Abort the operation, I say again, abort." When his men reached him, they fell back to the SUV. He turned to Jimmy.

"What happened?"

"Someone else was here and evacuated the subject. They were well equipped and trained."

Dawson cursed. It had to be the terrorist cell.

We need to take them out. Once and for all.

And then it was over.

Inside the main entrance of New Scotland Yard, the gunfire stopped, replaced by the squealing of tires outside. A few tentative moments of caution, then officers inside started to emerge.

Jasper looked at Lambert to make sure he was okay. "What the hell just happened?"

Lambert shrugged. "I don't know, but I bet it's related to our professor."

THE PROTOCOL

Triarii Headquarters
London, England

Laura slowly woke to an unbelievable pain on the side of her head. She tried to sit up, but a hand on her shoulder gently pressed her down. She opened her eyes then snapped them shut again, the brightness momentarily blinding her. Blinking a few times, her vision began to clear, revealing a shape leaning over her. She blinked one last time, and the shape became Acton, gazing down at her with a smile.

"You okay?"

She reached up and hugged him with both arms as hard as she could. Her head throbbed, but she held on. For some reason, she felt tremendous relief at seeing him. He hugged her back, and she lost herself for a moment in the comfort of the embrace. She heard a knock and let go of him as the door opened.

"Hello, Professors, I was just…." Chaney ducked his head. "Sorry, I didn't mean to interrupt." He stepped forward, extending a hand. "Professor Acton, I'm DI Chaney, Scotland Yard, and a member of the Triarii." Acton shook the man's hand. "Rodney Underwood has brought me up to speed on what he's told you, and I'd like to thank you for trusting us enough to come in."

Acton grunted. "I didn't have much choice. You were going to take Laura."

Chaney bowed slightly, then smiled at her. "How are you doing?"

"Much better, thank you." Laura slowly sat up in the bed and swung her legs over the edge. "Where am I?"

"You are at the Triarii Headquarters in London," said Chaney. "I can't tell you any more except that we are currently evacuating this facility."

Acton's eyes narrowed. "Evacuating? Why?"

"It's been compromised. You both will be evacuated with us, however, we need you to tell us where you've hidden the skull you found."

Acton shook his head. "No way, that's our only piece of insurance. I'm not sure whether or not I trust you, yet."

Chaney nodded. "I see. Let me put it this way. If those who have been trying to kill you get their hands on it, they

229

will have three skulls. As Rodney explained to you, that's enough to cause significant damage."

"So you believe," interjected Acton.

"Yes, so *we* believe. But are you willing to take that chance? You know who your opponent is. He's proven that he will stop at nothing to find you and take the skull. Obviously, they've made the connection between you and Professor Palmer."

Acton turned to Laura, and she knew he was looking for guidance on what to do. She stared back at him and shook her head almost imperceptibly.

He turned back to Chaney. "Let us think about it."

"Very well. I've got to look in on my old boss. Something tells me he's going to be narked." Chaney smiled and closed the door behind him.

Acton turned to Laura. "So, what do you think? Should we give them the skull?"

Laura shook her head. "No, I don't think so, however, something tells me there's more going on here than I know about. What did that security guard tell you?"

Acton laughed. "Good thing you're sitting down, you're going to love this."

Reading lay on a bed, staring at the ceiling.

I'm alive. That's good. Now why?

His body armor had been removed and placed on a table near the door. His suit jacket hung on the back of a chair. He rubbed his leg where he had been hit, and found the tiny hole the dart had made. Chaney hadn't tried to kill him, though he had still shot him.

He was pissed.

There was a knock at the door.

"Come!"

The door opened slightly, and Chaney poked his head in, a broad smile on his face. "Is it safe for me to come in?"

Reading growled. "You better have a damned good explanation for this."

Chaney laughed. "I do, guv, and"—he pushed the door open all the way and wheeled in a cart—"I have tea!"

Reading couldn't help but laugh. They had been together for years, and his underling, whom he considered a friend, knew him all too well. Reading shook his head. "Sure, butter me up." He took the proffered cup and sipped. He hadn't had any since Heathrow.

Too long.

Chaney took a cup and sat in the chair. "Well, guv, I believe it's time you were let in on a few things."

He told Reading about the Triarii and the events of the past few days. Reading's eyes narrowed in disbelief.

Bollocks!

But then, here he was, sitting in a room, having been shot by his longtime colleague with a tranquilizer, a confessed member of some type of cult, who had seven members executed by men who later attacked New Scotland Yard.

Okay, maybe not bollocks.

"And I think that's it," finished Chaney. "Oh, and we have Professor Acton."

"Acton is here?"

"Yes, in the next room with Professor Palmer."

Reading stood and straightened his tie. He put his jacket on and turned to Chaney. "I think it's time I finally met our American guest."

USAF 48th Fighter Wing, RAF Lakenheath
Lakenheath, England

Control Actual was mad. Actually, irate would be more accurate. Dawson had informed him one of his men was dead, two were wounded, including himself, and the mission had failed.

"You're the most highly trained special ops in the world, and you couldn't take a civilian away from a bunch of unarmed police?"

"With all due respect, sir, these were police officers of our greatest ally. We couldn't just shoot them, and contrary to popular belief, many of them were heavily armed. Besides, we know who has her and where."

"Yes, we do. It's time to take them out, once and for all. Do you have the resources for an assault on their location?"

"My men can handle it."

"You better. I want these terrorists out of our way and the DARPA package retrieved. And if possible, try to capture their leadership alive for interrogation."

"Yes, sir. Zero-One, out." He sat back in his chair and stretched the arm that had taken a round. His body armor had caught most of it, so it was barely a flesh wound. It would leave a scar, but wouldn't leave him out of the fight.

Red entered. "Back to work?"

"Yeah. Any luck with your contacts?"

"The feelers are out, but nothing yet. Should hear back soon. It *is* the middle of the night."

Dawson grunted. "Some rack time would be nice." He stood and headed for the door. "Unfortunately, it's time to get ourselves in deeper."

THE PROTOCOL

Triarii Headquarters
London, England

Acton watched as Laura processed what he had told her about the 2000-year-old organization whose sole aim was to protect humanity from destroying itself by hiding dangerous objects in plain sight. It sounded crazy, yet the day's events had proven someone other than the Triarii also believed it was true.

"So, what are we going to do?" she asked.

"I don't know. So far, they've done everything they said they would. They haven't hurt us, they rescued you. They've used non-lethal force. I think we can trust them."

"I'm beginning to believe so as well."

"Besides, the only way they'll stop pursuing us is if they know we don't have the skull," said Acton. "I'm thinking we should give it to the Triarii and make it known that we've done so, then maybe we can live out our lives without being constantly afraid."

Laura nodded. "That makes sense." There was a knock at the door. "Come in!"

The door opened, bringing Chaney and another man into the room.

"Well, well, well." The man stared at Acton. "At last we finally meet."

Acton looked back at the man, leery. "And you are?"

"Detective Chief Inspector Reading, Scotland Yard. And you are Professor James Acton, St. Paul's University of Maryland, wanted for questioning in regards to the torture and death of one Serge Savard, the massacre of seven men who apparently stole nothing from the British Museum, the serious injury of six police officers who were nearly blown up trying to apprehend the killers of the apparent non-thieves, the armed assault of New Scotland Yard, and the attempted kidnapping of one Professor Palmer. You've had quite the day, Professor Acton. Enjoying England?"

Acton smiled. "Haven't seen much of it, what with all the ducking."

Reading didn't seem amused. "You know, I have two State Department Agents in my office looking for you."

"Really?" Acton flashed back to his friend Milton, who

had told him State Department agents had come to his office before he died. "Are you sure they're State Department and not part of this"—he gestured with his hands—"whole thing?"

"I had them checked out, and they seem legitimate," said Chaney. "They have no connection with us, of course, and seem to be just two agents trying to find out what happened in Peru."

A low beeping tone emanated from a loudspeaker in the room, interrupting their conversation.

"Attention all personnel, attention. Evacuation Stage One has been completed, proceed to Stage Two. I repeat, evacuation Stage One has been completed, proceed to Stage Two."

"What the hell was that?" asked Reading.

"We're evacuating. We can't risk having the council or the Oracle of Jupiter captured."

Acton's eyes widened. "It's here?"

"Yes, the Oracle of Jupiter is always kept with the council, although hidden away somewhere in this complex, and only brought out on certain occasions."

"What are Stage One and Two?" asked Laura.

"Stage One means that the Oracle has been successfully transported out of the building and is on its way to our Beta Site. Stage Two means all other artifacts such as our ancient volumes, are to be evacuated. Once that is complete, then Stage Three is to evacuate all of our personnel—people can always be replaced, but the ancient knowledge never can. There is not a person here who wouldn't die to protect that knowledge."

"Present company excluded," said Acton. "I have no intention of dying to protect the skulls."

"Me neither," agreed Laura. "If we give you the skull, do you think the others will stop pursuing us?"

Chaney nodded. "Yes, I think they would. Once we have it, we'd simply let them know, and that should clear you."

"Good, let's go get it," said Acton, Laura rising beside him.

Reading put his hand out. "Not so fast, I'm not letting you two out of my sight, not until I have some answers."

"Fine," said Acton. "As long as you realize I had nothing to do with this."

"Oh, I know you're not to blame, but I still have a few

loose ends I need tied up before I'm satisfied. Besides, you may need protection." Reading turned to Chaney. "We need weapons."

"I'll be right back." Chaney left the room and returned a few minutes later with body armor and weapons. He handed each of them a vest, and Reading a weapon. He turned to Acton, holding up a Glock. "Do you know how to use one of these?"

"National Guard."

Chaney handed it over along with several magazines, then turned to Laura. "And you?"

She took the gun out of his hand, removed the mag, inspected it, reloaded it, and aimed the weapon at the door, checking the sight. She looked back at the surprised men. "Female on five Middle-East and three African digs."

Acton laughed. "You're just full of surprises, aren't you?"

Laura grinned then tucked the gun in her belt at the back of her pants.

When they were all suited up, Chaney opened the door. "Let's go, I'll show you the way out." As they filed out the door, all of the lights went out momentarily, then came back on. A rapid beeping alarm blasted from the speakers.

"We're under attack!"

Fleet Street, London, England

Dawson's feet hit the rooftop of the four-story Triarii headquarters. He unhooked the line tethering him to the helicopter above, and directed his men into position as they landed. They immediately went to work, laying cord explosives in predetermined areas their penetrating radar had indicated were the center of the rooms below. Dawson waved off the chopper as the last man unhooked and took cover.

"Ready?" he asked Marco.

Marco, holding the detonator, gave a thumbs-up.

Dawson raised his fist in the air and counted down with his fingers from three. Marco flipped the switches, activating the remote detonators attached to the cord explosives. The explosions ripped through the night, leaving the air thick with concrete dust. Dawson and his men flipped their thermal imaging goggles down and surrounded the newly formed holes in the roof, opening fire on the unsuspecting victims below.

Dawson and Spock dropped into a room on the northeast corner of the building. The two occupants, who had both taken cover after the explosion, were shot as soon as they stood. In the other three rooms, Dawson heard sporadic gunfire, then the team leaders radioed the all-clears.

"Bravo Team, Zero-One. Prepare to proceed to Level Three on my mark, over," said Dawson.

In each of the rooms, the teams laid cord explosives again and waited for the signal.

"Execute!" Dawson took cover behind a desk as the blast showered debris across the room. They ran to the edge of the hole and peered through the smoke with their infrared goggles. Across from him, Spock's weapon discharged. Dawson hopped down to the next level, followed by Spock. The room below turned out to contain only the single occupant, already eliminated. Heavier gunfire came from the adjoining rooms.

"This is Zero-One. Begin room-by-room clearing, over." Dawson ran to the door, followed by Spock, and opened it carefully. He saw nothing in the hallway from his vantage point. He stuck his head out to look down the other end and was met with a hail of gunfire. He jerked back just in time.

Grabbing a flashbang grenade from his belt, he pulled the pin and tossed it down the hallway. The resulting explosion caused a scream of pain as he and Spock rushed their opponent's position. A man writhed on the floor, gripping his ears and squinting his eyes. Dawson raised his weapon and shot him in the head.

He stared down the stairwell the now dead man had been guarding, and saw movement below as Niner's team joined them. Dawson looked at his men, then pointed to his eyes then down the stairs. They nodded and took up covering positions on either side of the hallway, inside doorframes that provided some cover.

Down the hall, the gunfire had ceased as the other two Bravo teams finished mopping up the remaining resistance. The all-clears again came over the radio. Coming through the ceiling wouldn't work again—this time it would be a direct assault. He looked down the hallway at Bravo Teams Three and Four, giving them the thumbs-up as they set up position at the stairwell at the other end.

"Bravo Team, Zero-One. Proceed to Level Two."

The Proconsul jerked awake in his chair, the alarm blaring a rapid beeping tone, periodically interrupted with messages.

"Level Three Compromised. Reinforcements to Levels One and Two to hold until Stage Two Evacuation complete."

The calmness in the voice giving the instructions was eerie. He hit a button on his desk phone.

"Yes, Proconsul?"

"Status."

"We're under attack by unknown numbers from the upper levels. It appears they gained entry via the roof. We've lost all communications with the third and fourth levels, however they were mostly evacuated. Casualties should be at a minimum. We're reinforcing the first two levels to hold until Stage Two Evacuation is complete."

"Estimated time remaining for Stage Two?"

"Five minutes, sir."

"Very well. As soon as they announce Stage Three, you get out of here right away, no delays. I want to see you at the Beta Site."

"Yes, sir, and thank you, sir, it's been an honor."

"Likewise," said the Proconsul, cutting off the conversation.

And I hope it still will be after today.

He had only one item in his office that needed to be removed, and that was the latest volume of the Triarii Journal. He was the third Proconsul to have kept records of the Triarii business in this particular volume.

Taking the leather bound tome from the antique desk along the far wall, he carefully placed it in its fireproof container. He then walked behind his desk, reached under it, and pressed a hidden button. The bookcase swung out. Hundreds of years of paranoia were about to pay off. Opening the case wider, he stepped into the passageway behind it, then pulled the hidden doorway shut, and followed the dimly lit corridor, leaving no evidence as to where he had gone.

"What do we do?" asked Laura.

"We get the hell out of here." Acton turned to Chaney. "Which way?"

"I doubt the street entry is safe. We're on the ground floor. We'll need to go down the stairs at the end of the hallway three flights. There, we can evacuate through the sub-levels with the others."

"Okay, let's go!" Acton grabbed Laura by the arm and ran toward the stairwell. As they entered, there was a hail of gunfire from above, then a loud explosion.

The assault on both staircases began simultaneously with a series of flashbangs and sprays of gunfire. The two separate Bravo teams cautiously entered the stairwells, searching for enemy combatants using their infrared goggles. Through the eerie green haze, Dawson saw a figure enter the doorway on the next floor down and aim a weapon toward them. Dawson fired and the target collapsed. They continued down the stairwell, slowly but deliberately, until they reached the doorway.

One flight below them a door opened. He peered down and saw four figures rapidly descending the stairs. Removing his goggles, he peered through the clearing smoke and recognized their targets.

"Bravo Team, the targets have been spotted in the east

stairwell heading down," reported Dawson over his radio. "Zero-Two, take your team and continue clearing of the second floor, then proceed to the first, we'll pursue the targets, over."

With that, he rushed down the stairs after the two professors.

Nelson was still going over the charred remains of the SUV that had exploded earlier in the evening, when another series of explosions rocked the roof of the building across the street. He couldn't see any smoke or fire, but the sound that followed was unmistakable—gunfire.

"Central, this is DI Nelson," he said into his radio. "We have further explosions and gunfire at this location. Requesting immediate armed backup and a half mile radius cordoned off."

"Roger, backup is on the way, ETA fifteen minutes."

It'll be over by then!

Nelson picked up a weapon from the ground, left over from one of the wounded members of the Armed Response Unit. He confirmed it was still in working order, and started across the street. The remaining ARU members followed him and took up position on either side of the large, wooden doorway at the entrance to the building, gunfire still sounding over their heads.

Nelson reached out and tried the door. It was locked. He turned as two ARU members ran up with a battering ram. They took up position on either side of the door and swung the heavy object back and forth. On the third swing, they launched it into the center of the door. The wood splintered, but the door held. Again they swung and hit the door with full force. This time the door gave a couple of inches as the lock shattered. One more swing and the two doors flew open.

Nelson looked in and saw several armed men behind desks aiming weapons at them. He grabbed a bullhorn from one of his men.

"This is the police. Drop your weapons and come out slowly with your hands raised above your heads."

"Did you hear that?" asked Chaney.

"Yes," replied Reading. "It sounded like Nelson. Where

could that be coming from?"

"He must be at the main entrance. The four-by-four that exploded tonight was right across the street from this building."

Reading continued down the stairs. "What will your men do?"

"They'll defend this building. They have no way of knowing if those really are police officers or not. They'll assume they are hostile because of the assault from upstairs."

"We've got to warn them."

"There's no time. If we don't get the professors out of here so that they can retrieve the skull, all could be lost."

"Those are *our* men out there. Don't give me bullshit about time or skulls. Their lives are just as important as anyone's."

Chaney glared at Reading. "Don't assume for a moment I don't realize the choice I'm making. But you have to understand, there's a bigger picture here that I believe is more important, whether you choose to or not."

They paused at the next flight of stairs near a door to the first sub-level. Footsteps approached from above. "Listen, guv, go through that door all the way to the other end of the corridor. Go up the stairs one level, and you'll see the entrance where our men are. Try to get them to help us."

With that, he continued down the stairs after the two professors.

Reading opened the door and sprinted down the corridor toward the door at the far end.

As the door closed behind him, several dark figures continued down the stairs after his partner.

Dawson heard voices below them. They were taking the stairs as fast as they safely could without walking into a spray of bullets. As they reached the first sub-level, a door clicked shut. A quick glance down the stairs, however, showed his prey was still below him.

"Zero-One, Zero-Two. Second level cleared," came Red's voice over the radio. "Proceeding to Level One, over."

"Copy that," said Dawson as they continued down the stairs.

Reading ran through the door at the other end of the

corridor and climbed the stairs as fast as he could. He heard footsteps above him, and assumed they were hostile. He reached the first-level door and opened it as a hail of gunfire tore at the wall next to him. Launching through the doorway, he rolled on the floor as more bullets hammered the door.

As he got up on his knees, he looked up and saw several men had their weapons pointed at him. They opened fire. He fell back down and covered his head. "Bloody hell, I'm with Chaney! I'm a friendly!"

The bullets sprayed over his head. They were firing at the doorway, not him. He crawled toward a desk turned on its side, now used as cover. As he neared it, a powerful hand grabbed him by the back of his body armor and pulled him to safety.

"Watch the main entrance!" ordered the man firing at the doorway. "I think those blokes belong to you, don't they?"

Reading looked toward the main entrance and spotted the flashing blue lights outside the forced open doors.

"This is your final warning, come out with your hands up, or we will open fire!" yelled Nelson over a megaphone.

Reading launched toward a desk closer to the main entrance and rolled as gunfire opened up the tile floor behind him. Another Triarii member pulled him behind the desk then returned fire.

"Hello, Inspector," said the man. Reading was about to thank him when he saw who it was. It was Rodney.

The gunfire had reached the lobby.

"Okay, on my signal we go in." Nelson put down the megaphone, and the ARU members quickly double-checked their weapons, readying for the assault.

"Nelson!"

Nelson looked about to see who was calling him.

"It's coming from inside, sir," said one of the ARU members. Nelson cocked his ear toward the door.

"Nelson! It's DCI Reading, hold your fire!"

Reading?

"Sir, what the hell is going on in there?"

"Too long a story. This building is held by friendlies, but is under attack by the same men who assaulted the Yard earlier. We need your assistance."

Nelson looked at the skeptical ARU members around

him. He wasn't sure what to believe. "Sir, I'm not—"

"Provide assistance, Detective Inspector!" boomed Reading. "That's an order!"

"Yes, sir!" Nelson turned to the ARU team. "You heard the DCI! Let's get in there!"

Two members rapidly approached the doorway with large bullet resistant shields, as the rest of the team huddled behind them. They entered the building, gunfire rattling from the west stairwell. They made their way to the apparently friendly position returning fire. The occupants, who had been pointing their weapons at them, now turned their attention to the two stairwell doors at either end of the lobby, no doubt relieved they would not have to fight on another front.

"This is it." Acton kicked open the door to the second sub-level. As he came through, he was knocked down from behind, and a boot pressed into his spine.

"He's with me," said Chaney as he and Laura cleared the door. The foot lifted off then hands pulled him to his feet.

"Sorry, sir."

"They're right behind us, coming down the stairs. Shoot whatever comes through that door."

"Yes, sir!" The man moved back down the hall to take cover. Laura and Acton followed Chaney down the long corridor. Now underground, there was no natural light, and the dampness of the old walls in combination with the dim emergency lighting, was claustrophobic. The musty smell of hundreds of years of history reminded Acton of several of his digs.

Early seventeenth century?

He couldn't believe he was determining when this part of the structure had been built.

Leave it alone, Jim!

As they rounded a corner at the end of the corridor, they all turned as a brilliant flash and ear-piercing explosion erupted at the other end.

"Come on!" urged Chaney. "We're almost there!"

Dawson tossed a flashbang through the door. Two of his men exited the stairwell, hugging the walls on either side, clearing the doorway as quickly as possible. The hallway was thick with smoke, and their opponents answered the grenade with a hail of gunfire. One of his team went down, the other dove out of the way and returned fire, finding cover in a doorway. He stuck his hand out with his submachine gun and sprayed lead down the hallway, providing cover fire for those still in the stairwell.

Dawson and Niner cleared the door, crouching and firing at the same time, and managed to reach the cover of a corridor entrance. Dawson drew his Glock, and using the infrared goggles, kneeled then shifted his body into the open so he could take aim. As his men provided cover, forcing most of their opponents to fire blindly, he took careful aim, and as each enemy poked their head out to fire, he picked them off, one by one.

Nelson, Reading, the ARU members, and the Triarii were now directing heavy fire toward the stairwell the attackers were holding. Reading grabbed Rodney by the shoulder to get his attention.

"Is there any way to outflank them?"

"That's the only way in," responded Rodney, firing again.

"What about the other stairwell?"

Rodney thought for a moment while he was firing. "That's right, sir! You can go through that stairwell then up one flight of stairs. At the end of the hallway is the stairwell they're in."

Reading turned to Nelson. "You stay here. I'm going with the armed unit to that stairwell."

"Yes, sir!"

"Let's go, let's go!" Reading slapped the ARU members on their backs. The entire group, still behind shielding, backed toward the other stairwell. Once there, they continued through the door and proceeded up the stairs.

Reading opened the door slowly and peered down the hallway. He could see one man at the other end guarding the entrance to the stairwell. He appeared distracted by the gunfire below, and kept looking down the stairs while holding the door open.

Reading turned back to the ARU team. "Who's the best shot?"

"Clayton is, sir," said one of the men.

"Okay, Clayton, get up here. There's a target at the end of

the hallway that I need you to take out." Clayton, taking up the rear, maneuvered up the stairwell, around the ARU team's body shields. When he arrived at the top of the stairs, his expression was all business. Reading was shocked at how young he was until he thought back at his own life.

I was probably his age when I was in the Falklands.

"Okay, Clayton, at the end of this hallway is one of the hostiles. I need you to take him out fast and quiet. I don't want him getting a shot off to warn his mates down below."

"No problem, sir." Clayton removed his sniper rifle from its case and set it up. Less than sixty seconds later, he was ready and lying prone on the floor of the stairwell landing. He nodded to Reading. Reading slowly opened the door a couple of inches so Clayton could acquire his target. Clayton raised the butt of the rifle higher when the target spotted them and reached for his radio.

Clayton put a bullet in his head, sending him to the floor in a crumpled heap.

Reading stuck his head out the door and gave a satisfied grunt, slapping Clayton on his back as he got up off the floor. "Good work, lad." He turned to the other ARU members. "Let's go!"

They rushed from the stairwell, sprinting down the corridor.

"Stage Two Evacuation Complete, Proceed with Stage Three Evacuation, I repeat, Proceed with Stage Three Evacuation."

Acton, Laura, and Chaney reached the final evacuation staging area when the announcement came over the PA system. There was a loud cheer from the dozens of people left as they piled into vehicles and disappeared down a series of tunnels that, judging by the materials used to construct them, had been there for hundreds of years.

"Where do these tunnels lead?" asked Acton.

Chaney herded them toward an idling SUV. "Each will come out at a different part of the city," explained Chaney as he opened the passenger side door for the professors. "Multiple points of egress means a greater chance of at least some members escaping."

Acton climbed in the back seat, and Chaney ran around the vehicle to the driver's side door. "Let's get the hell out of here!"

Dawson finished eliminating the last target when the announcement was made over the PA system. He charged down the hallway toward the only corridor being protected, his men following. As they rounded the corner, they saw several guards as they headed out a door at the end of the hall.

The Bravo team sprinted down the hallway toward the door. Dawson opened it as Spock and Niner took a knee and set up opposing fields of fire. They could see the evacuation area, dozens of people getting into vehicles as those already loaded left at high speed down various tunnels.

Dawson entered and saw one of the policemen from the Scotland Yard raid about to get into a nearby SUV. He raised his weapon and fired.

Reading heard the announcement as they reached the body of the lookout. They entered the stairwell, careful not to alert their enemy below. Reading peered down and saw three men taking turns firing through the doorway. They were not looking up.

Reading turned to one of the ARU members. "Two flashbangs, down there," he whispered. The man nodded and motioned to his partner. They both removed a grenade from their belts, then pulled the pins at the same time. They mouthed silently "One, two, three," then tossed the grenades down the stairwell. Everyone turned, covering their ears and closing their eyes.

The explosion was deafening, incapacitating the enemy. One fell forward out of the doorway and was shot by the Triarii guards below. The other two fell backward into the stairwell. Reading and his team rushed down the stairs to apprehend them before they had a chance to recover.

As they approached, one of the wounded attackers raised his weapon. Reading put two bullets in his chest as another, now on his knees, spun around. On the landing above, Clayton fired, taking the man out with a shot between the eyes.

Reading slowly opened the stairwell door to let the Triarii guards know everything was now secure. "It's the police, we've secured the door!" he bellowed. There was no response. He peered out the door and saw why. The Triarii were gone. Nelson, standing in the middle of the lobby, looked at Reading and shrugged.

"As soon as the tossers heard Stage Three, they legged it out the blasted door!"

Chaney fell into the driver's seat, face down, gasping for breath. Acton spotted a hole in Chaney's vest, blood slowly seeping out.

"Leave me," Chaney wheezed.

"To hell with that!" Acton reached forward and hauled Chaney into the back seat. As soon as his feet were clear, Laura jumped into the driver's seat and put the idling vehicle into gear. As she reached out to close the door, someone grabbed her arm. She screamed at the figure of a tall man, dressed in black with body armor, guns, grenades, knives, a facemask, and some type of goggles on his forehead.

"Not so fast, Professor."

Laura tried to wrench her arm away from him but couldn't. In her panic, she popped the clutch and the vehicle lurched forward. The door swung inward and smacked the man squarely on the back, knocking the wind out of him. His grasp loosened momentarily, and Laura gave one final tug of her arm then hit the gas. The SUV launched toward one of the tunnel exits under a hail of gunfire. The armor plating and bullet resistant glass took a beating but held long enough for Laura to guide the SUV into the tunnel. She glanced in the rearview mirror at Chaney. "Is he okay?"

"I'm not sure. We better get him to a hospital."

The tunnel wasn't long, maybe a quarter mile. At the end, it ramped up, and garage doors automatically opened as they approached. They emerged in an alleyway, and were soon on a city street. Laura turned right and blended in with the thin nighttime traffic while she got her bearings.

"We'll be at the hospital in less than five minutes."

Dawson picked himself up off the ground, cursing. He couldn't believe he had failed twice in a row, both times with his target literally in his grasp. He looked around and saw several empty vehicles. By now, the rest of the complex was empty, and these were waiting for people his team had already killed.

He and his two remaining men climbed into a nearby van.

"Zero-One to Zero-Two." There was no answer.

Could be the tunnels.

His radio crackled, and a voice came through he didn't recognize. "This is DCI Reading. Your men are dead or captured. I suggest you give yourselves up before anyone else gets hurt."

Dawson clenched his teeth.

The balls on these Brit cops.

He gunned the engine and followed the same tunnel his target had used.

The White House
Washington, DC

"Sir, are you okay?" asked the surprised guard. "Do you need medical attention?"

Wheeler had let them bandage up his arm at the scene, but had refused to go to the hospital. He had taken another detective's car and driven directly to the White House, consumed with thoughts of his partner, blown to shreds, possibly by an order given from this very building. Although it was now late, he was betting Darbinger was still there. He imagined he presented quite the dilemma to security with his blackened face and clothes, and a bandaged and bleeding arm, revealed by a shirtsleeve cut open by the paramedics.

"No," replied Wheeler curtly, reining in his temper. If the guard thought he was a danger, he would never let him in. "I need to see Lesley Darbinger."

"Do you have an appointment?"

"No. I don't need one." He pulled out his badge and showed him. "Mr. Darbinger is assisting us in an investigation, and I need to speak to him immediately."

The guard picked up the phone. "I'll see what I can do."

Darbinger hung up the phone as one of his aides poked his head into his office. "Did you hear? There's been a bombing at former Speaker Guthrie's house. Wasn't that Billy's dad?"

"What? Was anyone hurt?" Darbinger reached for his remote control and turned on the television mounted on his wall. CNN came on, about the only channel he watched these days. It showed an aerial view of a large house with the smoking ruins of a car in front.

"A cop was killed. Do you think that's why Billy was killed? Maybe they're after Speaker Guthrie?"

Darbinger shook his head. "I don't know," he murmured.

As he sat watching the limited coverage, another aide entered. "Sir, a Detective Wheeler is at the front gate demanding to see you."

Darbinger sank back in his chair as a close-up played on the screen of a gurney with a body bag being loaded into an emergency vehicle.

This has gone too far.

He rose from his desk and headed out the door. "Have Mr. Wheeler meet me here. I'll be back in a few minutes." He headed toward his old friend's office.

He was announced then shown inside the Oval Office, finding Jackson sitting with his elbows on his desk and his hands clasped over his head, pulling at his thinning hair. Darbinger sat in one of the leather chairs facing the desk, watching his old friend figure a way out of the mess they were in.

"I can't believe the most highly trained special operations unit we have, failed to capture a *female* civilian professor twice in a row!"

"Neither can I, Mr. President," said Darbinger. "The police seemed to know what we were after. They didn't all fall for the diversion. And we knew the Triarii headquarters would be extremely well defended. We lost a couple of men, but managed to eliminate several dozen members."

"There are thousands of members!" Jackson lifted his head from his desk. "From all accounts, not one of the council was eliminated, and all we have is one of the skulls we didn't already have before."

"Yes, Mr. President. The Triarii enacted The Protocol before we could reach them. We have the skull from the British Museum, and, as far as we know, the newly discovered skull is still at large. If we just wait a few years for things to cool off, maybe the Triarii will let down their guard, and we can find a third skull then."

"The Triarii will never let their guard down, not so long as there is a skull missing. I'm going to end this now."

"But, Stewart—!"

"Now!" roared Jackson.

London, England

Reading and Nelson surveyed what remained of the lobby as backup arrived.

Nelson held up his ID to the armed officers. "Just *after* the nick of time, lads."

"Sweep the building, top to bottom, there may be more," said Reading. "Take these two for interrogation and the injured to the hospital. Put a guard on them."

"Yes, sir." The PC hustled the surviving men out of the building as the new arrivals fanned out for the search. Those who had been involved in the earlier action relaxed on bullet-ridden leather couches in a corner.

Reading pulled out his cellphone and called Chaney's number.

"Hello?" asked an unfamiliar voice.

"Who is this?"

"Umm, who is this?"

"This is Detective Chief Inspector Reading of Scotland Yard," said Reading in his most commanding voice. "And you are?"

"Sorry, Chief, this is Professor Acton."

"What are you doing with Chaney's mobile?"

"We're at the hospital, he's been shot."

Reading strode toward the door. "Tell me where you are." He commandeered a vehicle, and minutes later, he shoved through the doors of the waiting room and saw the two professors sitting nearby. He walked briskly toward them as they rose from their chairs.

"Hello, Chief," said Acton. "He's been in surgery for about half an hour, no word yet."

"How did it happen?"

"He was shot in the back trying to save us," said Laura.

"It hit his vest, but went right through. Some type of armored piercing round. I pulled him into the vehicle and Laura drove us here."

"What's the prognosis?"

"He lost a lot of blood, but was conscious when we arrived."

Reading frowned, finally noticing Acton was covered in blood. "Okay, I'm going to go and see if I can find out what's going on. And professors"—Reading put a hand on each of their shoulders—"thank you." He made eye contact with each of them for a moment, then headed to the nurses' station.

Dawson turned the corner and pulled the SUV to the side where they could see the entrance of the Triarii headquarters. Ambulances and other emergency personnel were still arriving. He grabbed a scope off his vest and peered through it for a better view. Spock did the same from the back.

"That's Red!"

Two attendants carried a gurney down the front steps. Dawson watched as his friend, strapped down and cuffed, was pushed into the back of a waiting ambulance. Two more men were led out and loaded into the back of a squad car.

Dawson radioed their chopper pilot, Wings, to see where he was. He had been ordered to insert the team on the roof of the Triarii HQ, then return with a vehicle for pickup.

"Just approaching your position now, Zero-One. ETA thirty seconds."

"Copy that, One-Two." Dawson watched his rearview mirror. A few seconds later, a box van turned the corner. "We're in the black SUV, tinted windows, about fifty meters in front of you. Come up beside me."

He watched as the van pulled up, then glanced back at Spock and Niner. "Spock, you go with Wings and take out that squad car. Niner and I will retrieve Red."

"Roger that." Spock jumped out of the SUV and into the van. It took off after the squad car as Dawson put the SUV into gear to follow the ambulance. He let it get far enough away from the scene so backup wouldn't be too close, then gunned the engine to overtake it.

Cutting in front, he slammed his brakes on, blocking its path. He and Niner rushed out. Niner yanked the driver out and coldcocked him before he could radio for help as Dawson ran to the back and pulled open the door. The cop and paramedic were both still picking themselves up off the floor, when he stepped up into the vehicle. He pistol-whipped the officer and pointed his gun at the paramedic.

"What's his status?"

"BP is one hundred over—"

Dawson cut him off. "Is he going to die if I move him?"

"N-no, it's just a leg wound, he'll be fine with proper treatment." Dawson breathed a sigh of relief as he undid the straps holding his friend to the gurney. He searched the officer's pockets, retrieved the cuff keys, and unlocked his friend.

"'Bout time you showed up." Red grimaced as he was helped out of the back of the ambulance.

"Good to see you, too," replied Dawson. Niner had already pulled their commandeered vehicle up to the door. Dawson helped Red into the back seat then climbed in with him. "Go! Go! Go!"

Niner floored it and headed back to their secondary rendezvous point, where they could switch vehicles without it traced back to the base.

Dawson turned to check on his friend's wound. "Looks like a through-and-through. Bleeding's under control." He stared his friend in the eyes. "You'll live."

"To fight another day." Red laughed then stopped, his face contorting in pain. "I think I'll just sit here and be quiet until you get me some drugs." Dawson smiled then pressed his earpiece when a transmission came in from Spock.

"Zero-One, Zero-Five. Engaging target now." There was silence for about two minutes as Niner drove them through the relatively empty streets of nighttime London. The wait seemed interminable until finally a burst of static sounded in the earpiece, followed by Spock's voice, "Zero-One, Zero-Five. Two targets retrieved, heading to rendezvous point Alpha, out."

"They're okay," said Dawson to Red who had had his communications gear confiscated earlier. Red smiled and closed his eyes as Niner headed out of the city.

THE PROTOCOL

Dawson read the secure communiqué that had arrived for Red. *Structural Amorphous Metals (SAM) project not capable of transparent structures. Hope that helps.* He clenched his jaw.

Control lied. What the hell is this thing all about?

The communications gear beeped, demanding his attention. He put the headset on and entered a code to unscramble the transmission. It was Control. Dawson listened to the voice over his headset.

"Zero-One, Control Actual. I want you to eliminate the two professors with extreme prejudice."

"Control Actual, Zero-One. Extreme prejudice, sir? Please clarify, over."

"I want a message sent," responded the voice. "I don't want them just killed. I want them eliminated in a public way, so that no member of this organization will ever sleep again with both eyes closed. Use one of those choppers if you have to."

Dawson tensed at the phrase, his breath held as he finally realized who Control Actual was. *"They'll never sleep again with both eyes closed."* He had heard it in enough speeches about terrorism to know who had ordered him to kill two civilians, one a foreign national, in public, on foreign soil.

The President of the United States.

"Control Actual, Zero-One, please confirm. We are on a foreign ally's soil, and these are civilian targets. A public take-down could result in other civilian casualties."

"Carry out your orders, or your identities go public."

Rage surged through Dawson's veins.

Threaten me, fine. Threaten my family, or that of my men? You die!

Yet he had to be delicate. He had to figure out a way to placate this madman so he didn't follow through on his threat.

At least not until I can kill him first.

"Sir, what is this all about? I know the SAM project has nothing to do with this."

There was silence for a moment. "I'm looking at your file. You have a sister in Connecticut, don't you? And a godchild named Bryson?"

Dawson remained silent as he pictured his sister and his niece, as well as Red's son.

"If you want to see them again, follow your orders. Control, out."

Dawson sat back in his chair and ripped off his headset, whipping it on the table.

He's lost it!

He sat for several minutes, calming his racing heart as adrenaline and fury did a number on his system. Sucking in several slow, deep breaths, he rose and made his way to the infirmary, formulating a plan.

"How ya doing?" he asked as he entered the room where Red was being looked after.

Red smiled. "Not bad. The doc said I'll be fine, hopefully operational within a few months." He eyed his friend. "What's wrong?"

"Control's lost it." He sat on the edge of the bed and leaned closer so no one else could hear. "He wants the professors eliminated publicly. *Very* publicly."

"Permission to speak freely?"

"Granted."

"BD, this sounds like an illegal order to me. You don't have to follow it."

"Yes, I do."

"Why?"

"Because I found out who Control is."

"Who?"

"The president."

Red paled slightly as his heart monitor beeped faster.

"And he threatened Bryson and my sister, all of our families, if I don't. I have no choice. I'll try to keep the civilian casualties to a minimum, but this one is going to be a Charlie Foxtrot."

Red's heart monitor beeped even faster. "He threatened our families?"

"Yes. Like I said, this is out of control. If we make it out of this, we'll talk about what we're going to do about it." Dawson watched as the heart rate increased. He placed a hand on his friend's shoulder. "Don't worry, I'll take care of things. Nobody is going to hurt Bryson or your wife. After tonight, Control won't be able to hide."

Red's eyes narrowed as he stared at his friend. "Why,

what are you going to do?"

"Don't worry about it. Like I said, everything will be fine." Dawson stood and raised his voice. "You take it easy now, and I'll see you when I get back." He strode out of the room before his friend could say anything else.

I don't know if I'll be seeing you again, my friend.

The White House
Washington, DC

Darbinger listened in horror as his friend of many years turned off the communications gear and rose to face him.

Jackson glanced at him. "What's wrong? This will end it, once and for all."

"You've gone too far! You have to let this go! These are innocent people who have done nothing wrong. You're risking an international incident with one of our greatest allies, just to settle a grudge because you're pissed you failed."

"Watch your tone with me!"

"You had Billy killed, didn't you?"

"Who the hell is Billy?"

"Guthrie's kid. He saw the file, and you had him killed."

"I couldn't risk him getting in the way of God's plan."

"God's plan? God doesn't want innocent kids killed!"

"Enough!" screamed Jackson. "We may be friends, but don't forget who got you where you are today!"

Darbinger shook his head. "You're not my friend. My friend wouldn't be doing this. My friend would realize this had to stop," he pleaded. "Please, you have to let this go!"

Jackson smiled and started toward the door. "This has only just begun. After I rid the world of that damned professor, I'm going to hunt down the Triarii until I possess all of the skulls. God put me here for a purpose, and this is it!"

He opened the door and slammed it behind him.

Darbinger stared after him in disbelief.

He's gone mad!

He remained seated in the Oval Office for several minutes, wondering what to do, when the door opened again. It was one of the Secret Service agents assigned to the room.

"I'm sorry, sir, just doing a routine sweep. I thought you had left," he said politely. When there was no reply, he closed the door behind him. "Sir, are you okay?"

Darbinger finally acknowledged him. "What's your name, son?"

"Agent Sharpe."

"No, your first name."

"Peter."

"Peter, you're sworn to protect the president with your life, correct?"

"Yes, sir."

"But you've also sworn to uphold the Constitution and protect this country, correct?"

"Yes, sir."

"What would you do if those conflicted?"

"Sir? I'm not sure I understand."

Darbinger sighed, then slowly stood. "Never mind, son. I hope you never have to make the choice." He approached the desk, and with his back to the agent, picked up the heavy statue of a bald eagle, and looked at the base of it. "I'm sorry, Peter," he murmured. He swung around and hit the young Secret Service agent on the side of the head with the statue. Sharpe fell to the floor unconscious, blood trickling out of a small wound on the side of his scalp.

Darbinger checked Sharpe's pulse to make sure he was okay, then reached under his suit and found the shoulder holster. He retrieved the gun and inspected it, checking the safety. He hid the weapon in his pants and straightened himself.

Then calmly left the office.

Palmer Residence
London, England

Stucco stood watch as Casey picked the lock to Professor Palmer's apartment. They were Mickey and Spaz' replacements, and weren't surprised to be off on their own doing side missions while the rest of the team, who had trained together for months, were involved in the main action. Within seconds, they were in the apartment. Stucco searched as Casey planted a couple of bugs. Near the doorway, Stucco found a set of car keys. "She's got a vehicle!" he called to Casey, planting the last bug in the master bedroom. "We'll need to tag it."

Casey entered the living room. "Do we know which car?"

Stucco tossed the keys to him. "Use the fob."

Casey approached the window and pressed the button to unlock the doors. On the street below, lights flashed on a car parked in front of the building. He pressed another button to lock it back up. "Got it!" He tossed the keys back to Stucco.

Within a few minutes, they had searched the apartment top to bottom, leaving no evidence they had been there, and finding nothing of interest. As they headed out, Stucco radioed in. "Zero-One, Zero-Three. Come in, over."

"Zero-Three, Zero-One. Go ahead, over," replied Dawson.

"We've swept the location, no sign of the item. We've left some ears, and are about to tag a vehicle. ETA to base, thirty minutes, over."

"Copy that, Zero-One, out."

They exited the building and Stucco looked around. "Which car is it?"

Casey pointed, and Stucco whistled in appreciation.

THE PROTOCOL

Royal London Hospital
London, England

Reading, Acton, and Laura stood by Chaney's bedside as he regained consciousness. Reading looked at him and smiled.

"Just like a junior copper to get shot in the back while running away!"

Chaney smiled. "Good to see you too, guv."

Reading laughed and turned to the professors. "He'll be okay."

"Professor Acton," whispered Chaney weakly, "you must get the third skull to the Triarii."

"Yeah, I realize that now," said Acton. "How do we find them?"

Chaney smiled then passed out.

"Great, what do we do now?"

"You'll need to leave now," said a voice from the doorway. "Mr. Chaney needs his rest. You can come back tomorrow to see him." She handed Acton a card. "Here are the visiting hours."

"Thanks." He put the card in his pocket as they filed out the door and headed for the elevator.

"What now?" asked Laura.

"Well, I guess we go get the skull from your apartment, then wait for the Triarii to contact us."

"I'll come with you," said Reading as they entered the elevator. "You may need protection. And besides, I still have a few questions for you." As they left the hospital, Reading flagged a waiting squad car—the bullet-ridden Triarii SUV they had made their escape in having already been taken away as evidence.

Minutes later, they were at Laura's apartment, and Reading watched in amazement as the two professors opened the secret compartment in the tabletop. Acton removed the package, opened it, and held it up for the inspector to see.

"It's beautiful," he whispered in awe. "Can I hold it?"

"Sure." Acton handed it to him. Reading took it and cradled it carefully in his hands. He held it up to the lamp, gasping as the skull's design collected the light and focused it through the eyes.

"Absolutely unbelievable. Incredible that something so beautiful could be the cause of so much death and destruction."

"Indeed," said Laura. "If you believe the Triarii, these things have been the cause of a lot more death than we saw today."

"I'm not sure whether I believe that stuff or not," said Acton, "but I'll tell you this. I don't want to have anything to do with it anymore. Clearly, someone believes the stories, and is willing to kill us for it. The sooner that thing is out of our hands, the better."

"Agreed," said Reading. "Now, how do we contact the Triarii to give it to them?"

Acton shrugged then sat. "I have no idea, but these guys seem to have a habit of showing up when you least expect them."

"Perhaps we should just wait?" suggested Laura.

"Something tells me the men who are after you two can find out quite easily where you live," said Reading. "I think we should leave immediately. We can go to the Yard and wait there."

Laura frowned. "That didn't help us before."

"Security there will be tight, now. There'll be no repeat of last night's incident."

Acton pulled out his cellphone and the card the nurse had given him, glancing at Reading's raised eyebrows. "Sorry, old habit I guess." Acton sheepishly typed away. "Whenever I get a business card, I put it in my phone, so I don't have my pockets cluttered up with them." He flipped the card over and a smile spread. He held it up for the others to see. "Look familiar?"

They both leaned in to look. The card had the Triarii logo embossed on one side.

"The Triarii!" exclaimed Laura. "Where did you get that?"

"The nurse in the hospital gave it to me. She said it had the hospital visiting hours on it."

"Let me see." Acton handed it over to Reading then clipped the cellphone back on his belt. Reading examined the card. "There's just a phone number on the other side then a series of three two-digit numbers under it. I wonder what those are?"

Laura lifted the cordless phone off the table. "I guess we

call and find out. Who wants the honors?"

"Allow me." Acton took the phone and the card, then dialed the number. The phone rang once, then someone picked up. There was silence on the other end. "Hello? Is anyone there?" Again silence. "Listen, if someone is there, this is Professor Acton. I have the skull. Someone gave me this card. I assumed I was supposed to call you to arrange for pickup." Again silence. Acton turned to Reading. "Nobody seems to be on the other end."

"Try keying in the numbers, maybe it's an automated system?" suggested Reading.

Acton punched in the six numbers from the card. Still nothing. "But why would they be in groups of two if you're meant to key them in? Wait a minute. Seventeen, Thirty-Four, Oh-Five."

"One moment please."

He covered the mouthpiece with his hand. "It worked! They're putting me through."

A moment later, a man's deep voice came on the line. "Hello, Professor Acton, this is the Proconsul of the Triarii."

"Ah, hello, sir. I have what you're looking for. When can we meet?"

"Do you have a vehicle available to you?"

Acton frowned, not sure if the squad car that had dropped them off was still outside. He covered the phone and whispered, "Do we have a car?" Laura nodded. "Yes," said Acton, returning to the conversation.

"Get to Coventry. You will be met at the train station." The line went dead.

"He said to go to Coventry and wait at the train station," repeated Acton as he hung up the phone.

"That's about two hours from here," said Laura.

Acton stood. "Then we better get going."

"It's probably better if I call for a car." Reading reached for his phone.

Laura shook her head, grabbing her keys. "No, we'll take my car, it'll be faster."

"Are you sure?"

She smiled. "Trust me."

USAF 48th Fighter Wing, RAF Lakenheath
Lakenheath, England

"BD!"

Dawson turned in his chair to see Niner's head poke through the door. "What?"

"We've got movement on Palmer's vehicle."

Dawson leaped up and ran to the communications room where the tracking equipment had been set up. "We have a fix on them?"

Niner sat in front of the laptop. "Yeah, the transmitter we placed on her car is working perfectly."

"Excellent. Any idea on where they're headed?"

"Yeah, the ears did their job, so we heard everything. Looks like they're heading to Coventry. Stucco and Casey aren't far from them. Should I have them follow?"

"Yes, but at a safe distance, this is going to get messy."

"Roger that." Niner turned to radio the replacements. Dawson headed to the rec room and pointed at their master of all things aerial, Wings.

"Wheels up in five."

Dawson returned to the communications room and sat in front of the satellite gear, punching in his access code. "Control, Zero-One, requesting Control Actual, over."

He waited for Control Actual to be notified, and a few minutes later the response came through. "Zero-One, Control Actual, go ahead."

"Control Actual, Zero-One. We have located the targets and are preparing to engage, over."

"Remember your orders, Zero-One. I want *spectacular*. I will be watching from here, out."

Dawson turned off the equipment and geared up.

This is going to get real messy.

He stepped out into the hallway and found Wings waiting for him. They drove in silence in the Humvee as Dawson weighed his options. It was clear to him that this mission was off the rails. With it under the personal control of the president—something unheard of—it would be completely off the books.

And now that he knew the DARPA project story was bullshit, it meant nothing had been stolen from the US government. It also meant those students and their professor were exactly what the newspapers said they were—students and their professor. No terror cell, no indoctrinated students, no stolen top-secret military project, no murdered military guards.

Innocents.

And if the professor was innocent, then so was his supposed contact he was ordered to torture. He likely was indeed a poor French tourist who had the misfortune to meet the professor by chance.

The terrorist headquarters they hit had him slightly confused. Those men were armed to the teeth, something you didn't see in England. Who were they? All the intel on them matched up. But were they a terror cell? And if they were, and they had no connection to the professor, then why not have the British deal with them? But if the professor had nothing to do with them, why had he come to London? Why was he at their headquarters?

Dawson growled in frustration.

"You okay, BD?" asked Wings.

Dawson shook his head. "It's this mission. Something's not right."

"No shit. I'm glad I'm not the only one thinking it."

Dawson pulled onto the tarmac, stopping fifty yards from the Apache they had shipped over. As he climbed out, he frowned, the ground crew apparently still prepping the gunship. "Status?"

"Just finishing up, sir," said the crew chief who walked up to greet them.

"What's loaded?"

"The cannons are fully armed, and we've got half the Hellfires loaded."

"No Hellfire IIs?"

"Sorry, sir, those are all in theater. We've got a shortage. You're lucky to get these."

Dawson cursed.

The Hellfire IIs would have made this a lot simpler.

"Okay, what kind of Hellfires?"

"Ks."

"Are you kidding me? I didn't know they even made those anymore."

"Sorry, sir, like I said, everything's in theater."

"Fine, that will have to do." Dawson opened the cockpit canopy and stowed the bag containing the skull. "Clear the area."

This mission just got a whole lot harder.

Wings was about to climb in when Dawson stopped him, having come to a decision. "I'm going on this one alone, report back to the unit." He shut the canopy, leaving a confused Wings walking back to the Humvee.

Dawson knew what was about to happen, and he didn't want his comrade associated with it.

If one of us gets blamed, it's going to be me.

THE PROTOCOL

"Not exactly designed for adults back here," grumbled Reading as he surveyed the back seat of the silver Porsche 911 Carrera S. Laura was driving, and Acton had educated him on the value of calling "shotgun" first when Americans were involved, leaving him stuck in the back.

"It was my brother's."

Acton's eyebrows rose. "I thought he was an archaeologist like you? How could he afford this?"

"Oh no, he just came on the digs with me sometimes for fun. He made a mint on the Internet before the bubble burst. He left me enough money to never have to work again, but that's just not me. It does, however, let me fund my own digs when I can't find anyone else to do it. I was going to sell the car, but he got me hooked on racing it at some of the local tracks, so I decided to keep it after he was gone."

"I'm surprised he raced Porsches. I thought you Brits liked those things?" Acton pointed down the road at a British sportscar notorious for electrical problems.

Laura laughed. "Do you want to get there, or just look good broken down on the side of the motorway?"

Reading chuckled. "So, you know how to drive this thing?"

Laura glanced back at him and smiled. They were waiting for a red light to turn when she issued a warning. "Hang on!" She turned off the traction control and lit up the tires when she floored it. The 355-horsepower engine nailed them to their seats, and the 295-pound-feet of torque ate up the road. Seconds later, they were at the next red light. She came to a stop in a hail of screeching tires. The light changed, and she hammered on the gas again, soon turning onto the main road that led to the motorway. She raced down the near empty streets.

Reading leaned forward. "Remember, just because I'm in the car, doesn't mean I won't give you a bloody ticket!"

Laura and Acton laughed as she eased off the accelerator, though it was clear she had a lead foot. Acton, who loved the adrenaline rush, leaned back to enjoy the ride, disappointed it was still too chilly to put the top down, but thankful his ordeal was almost over.

They soon sailed onto the motorway and sped toward Coventry. "We should be there in about one hour," announced Laura. There were relatively few cars on the road, though a fair amount of transport traffic. Laura kept to the right and flashed anyone who got in her way.

Reading settled back in his seat, shaking his head.

The White House
Washington, DC

Wheeler sat in Darbinger's outer office, waiting for him to return. The staff kept nervously glancing at him and whispering among themselves. He didn't care.

Yeah, that's right. Look what your boss has done.

The longer he sat, the more pissed off he became. He could stand it no longer. He stood and strode out the door.

"Sir, you have to wait here!" called the surprised secretary as she pursued him. He rounded a corner and saw Darbinger at the end of the hallway, getting on an elevator.

"Darbinger!"

Darbinger stuck his head out the door then ducked back inside as Wheeler charged toward him. He could see Darbinger mashing on the *Close* button, the doors shutting as he reached the elevator. He slammed his fist against them as the secretary screamed for security.

Darbinger pounded on the *Close* button. He didn't have time to deal with the cop right now. He had a much more important thing to take care of. The doors slowly closed as Wheeler ran toward them, and much to his relief, they shut before he got there. As the car descended, pounding rattled the doors above him.

A cold sweat broke out on his forehead as he neared his destination. He reached into his pocket for a handkerchief, and wiped the sweat off when the doors opened three levels underground. Two guards greeted him as he stepped out. After swiping his pass, he walked down the short hallway. At the end was a large set of wooden doors flanked by two Secret Service agents, who opened them for him as he approached. As he entered, he found his president and longtime friend sitting alone at the center of the conference table, watching a large video screen on the wall directly opposite. The doors closed behind him.

"Ah, there you are." His friend smiled. "You got here just in time, it's about to start."

He looked at the video feed and saw a helicopter taking off. Slowly walking around the table, he stood in front of the screen, blocking his friend's view.

"Sit down, you're in the way!" said Jackson, annoyed.

"I must ask you to stop this operation immediately."

Jackson had been leaning over to see around him, but now straightened and made eye contact. "Are we back to this?"

"We never left it." Sweat beaded again on Darbinger's forehead. "If you don't stop this operation, harm could come to the United States. You have authorized illegal military operations, without the knowledge of Congress, on the foreign soil of an ally. It must end now!"

His friend stood and placed both hands, now balled into fists, on the table in front of him. He leaned forward and scowled. "I thought you were with me on this. You and I have wanted the same thing for the past twenty years—to bring together these skulls and reveal their true meaning."

"No, I never wanted that. You were my friend long before you recruited me into the Triarii. I hadn't even heard about the skulls, but when you told me about them, it never occurred to me that you would have killed for them."

"I'm on a mission from God. These skulls were left by Him to enlighten us. Look at the Bible, my friend, it's written there. *'And he bearing his cross went forth into a place called the place of a skull, where they crucified him, and two other with him, on either side one, and Jesus in the midst.'* Don't you see, 'The Place of a Skull' is where these came from. The original skull was discovered near the place Jesus was crucified. The three skulls together unleash the power of God. Jesus was crucified with two others. There were three of them when the power of God was unleashed!"

Darbinger shook his head. "You've gone mad. Your obsession has clouded your judgment, and you must stop."

"But you hate the Triarii as much as I do! We left them together, ten years ago!"

"Stewart, I never left."

Jackson stared at his friend, dumbfounded. "What do you mean you never left?"

"I've been working for them all along, hoping that one day you would confide in me where you had hidden the Smithsonian Skull."

"But you helped me!" Jackson's voice cracked, revealing the depth of betrayal he felt at his life-long friend and confidant's admission.

"No, Stewart, I didn't. When you came to me about leaving, I informed the council immediately. They assigned me to watch you, to gain your trust by pretending to go along. But you initiated the theft before we could have the skull moved, so I was ordered to stick as close to you as possible, in hopes of one day retrieving it."

"It's been ten years!"

"Yes. Ten long years of lying to you, lying to my wife, lying to everyone. But the Triarii have been around for two thousand years. If it takes another thousand, we will eventually retrieve the skull you stole."

Jackson was defiant. "I'll never tell you. I'll go to my grave before I reveal it to anyone."

"So be it. We are if anything patient, which is why we let you continue the way we did. But now you've gone too far. You're hurting my country. You know me, Stewart. I've always been a patriot first, even as a member of the Triarii. I could never betray my country, nor can I just stand by while you destroy it."

Jackson shook his head, his shoulders slumped in disappointment. "I'm sorry you feel that way." His disappointment turned to anger, and he straightened to face his betrayer. "I intend to finish my mission. I cannot be stopped!"

"I'm sorry my friend, but you must be." Darbinger reached behind his back and drew the gun.

Jackson stepped backward and raised his hands. "What are you doing?"

"I'm ending this now, before anyone else gets hurt. Before our country gets hurt." Darbinger aimed at his friend, tears welling up in his eyes. "I'm so sorry. I never thought it would come to this."

Jackson slowly brought his hands together and twisted the face of his watch. The doors flew open, the two Secret Service agents entering as they drew their weapons.

Darbinger, startled, glanced over at the guards for a split second. They spun toward him and fired as he squeezed the trigger. Pain seared through his body as two bullets slammed into his chest and stomach. His legs gave out, and he collapsed to the floor. He caught a glimpse of his friend's face frozen with shock, but couldn't tell if he had hit his target. All he could see was a pool of his own blood rapidly expanding on the floor, draining the remaining life out of him, the voices of the guards slowly fading away as they shouted, "Mr. President!"

Two Secret Service agents watched Wheeler while he waited in Darbinger's office. He glared at the floor when several people rushed past the door. Both agents touched their earpieces at once.

"Did he say shots fired?"

"Yeah, I think so. I'll go check it out, you stay with him."

Wheeler was now looking at the remaining guard. "Has someone been shot?"

There was no reply.

He rose. "Look, I'm a cop, I can help."

The agent put out his hand, motioning for him to get back in his seat. "Sit down, sir. You have no jurisdiction here."

Someone yelled from the general office area. "He's been shot!"

Two medical personnel pushing a gurney rushed past the door and Wheeler jumped up and ran after them, the Secret Service agent's footsteps pounding behind him.

THE PROTOCOL

The morning sun had not yet broken the horizon, giving Dawson decent cover from prying eyes on the ground. Traffic would be relatively light on the freeways, keeping casualties to a minimum, though that's not what the president wanted. With the light traffic, he should be able to send the spectacular message required, while hopefully avoiding civilian deaths.

He rapidly approached the red dot on his navigation screen, barely skimming the ground to avoid being picked up on radar, London's famous Ring of Steel not extending skyward as some residents thought. Soon his target would appear on his Heads-Up Display System, then it would be the beginning of the end.

His HUDS beeped, and the three-dimensional display in front of him indicated his target had been acquired. He pushed the stick forward and accelerated, watching the transport trucks and thin civilian traffic through the infrared. Within seconds, he was about 1000 yards behind his target. He dropped to the deck, about thirty feet off the ground as he neared the vehicle.

They appeared to have no idea he was there. A lull in the traffic provided him the perfect opportunity to play with them, giving the president his lightshow without hopefully killing anyone.

You want spectacular, I'll give you spectacular.

Reading opened his mouth to once again complain about the lack of room in the back seat when he heard something behind them. He twisted around and peered through the small rear window, but couldn't see anything. Then he noticed the stars were blocked by something, and when his eyes focused, he realized what it was. Before he could say anything, flames erupted from the front of the object.

"Look out!" he warned, ducking. If the other two occupants of the vehicle hadn't known what he was yelling about, the burst of gunfire and the six-inch holes left in the pavement clued them in pretty fast. Laura slammed on the brakes and brought the car to a halt as the gunship overshot them. It turned around for another run.

"Get us out of here!" yelled Acton. Laura dropped the car into first and floored it. Within seconds, they were speeding under the helicopter as it opened fire. The bullets flew harmlessly over them but struck a large semi-trailer behind them. The driver locked up his air brakes and jackknifed the truck, blocking three lanes of the highway before coming to rest.

Reading peered out the tiny window again, trying to spot the helicopter. "Here he comes!"

Another burst of gunfire. This time Reading watched the tracers instead of ducking, knowing full well if one of those bullets hit them, they were done for anyway. He could see they were coming down on the left side of the vehicle.

"Break right!"

Laura swerved the Porsche to the right and the bullets missed by several lanes. The next volley seemed to be coming directly down at them.

"Left!" he cried.

Laura again swerved. Not only did she have to contend with the bullets, but she was also weaving in and out of the traffic that had thickened as daybreak approached.

"Jim, I need you to spot for me! I have to call for help!"

Acton squirmed in his seat. "I can't see a damned thing!"

"We need to get this top down!" yelled Reading.

Laura's eyes widened. "Are you crazy! That's the only thing between us and those bullets!"

"Professor, those bullets can penetrate the armor on a tank. This roof isn't going to do a damned thing!"

"How long does it take to go down?" asked Acton.

"About twenty seconds."

"Okay, the next big overpass, stop under it and put it down."

Laura floored the car, tumbling Reading in the back seat, leaving him cursing as he tried to regain his view out the tiny window.

"Left!" Another salvo of gunfire erupted from the attacking helicopter. Laura swung the vehicle again and saw a large six-lane overpass ahead. As they approached, she locked up the four-disc vented brakes, and they screeched to a stop, sending Reading headlong into the front seat.

Laura was already pushing the button for the roof to go down. It slowly opened and folded into the trunk in what seemed like an eternity. "Faster! Faster!" Laura pleaded as she watched it close. Reading was already dialing his cellphone as he strapped into the back seat.

Acton whipped his head around at the whooshing of blades in front of them. The chopper had passed over the ramp and banked to face them. He was about to yell to Laura when a small beep indicated the roof retraction was complete. Laura was already revving the engine at about seven thousand RPM, when she popped the clutch. The car leaped forward, directly toward the helicopter now about twenty feet off the ground and belching lead.

Laura shifted into second, and the tires squealed again as the powerful engine launched them past sixty miles per hour in under five seconds. As they surged under the chopper, gunfire tore through the air above them, this time hitting a fuel tanker as it merged onto the highway. It erupted into flames and lit the night sky. Acton looked back and saw the helicopter silhouetted by the flames as the driver leaped to safety.

Are those missiles?

Reading was on his phone, yelling at someone on the other end. "This is Detective Chief Inspector Reading of Scotland Yard, we're under attack by an armed helicopter and need assistance!" Acton watched him as he listened to someone on the other end clearly saying something Reading wasn't pleased with. "Listen, put your guvnor on now!" he roared. A moment later, he identified himself again.

"Right!" Acton cried as more gunfire erupted from the cannons on the helicopter. This time a Mini was taken out, bringing it to a shuddering halt, as Laura swerved to avoid the bullets.

"No!" Reading yelled. "A police helicopter is not going to cut it! This is a military helicopter that is attacking us and blowing the shit out of everything in sight!"

Laura was now doing over one hundred miles per hour as she tried to outrun the chopper to no avail, the pilot continuing to fire as she swerved left and right.

Acton suddenly realized he wasn't trying to hit them.

He's toying with us!

Dawson shook his head as he squeezed the trigger again and sent another volley of deadly lead to one side of the Porsche.

It swerved in the opposite direction.

Do they really think I'm trying to hit them?

The Porsche sped up the side of the highway then cut across two lanes, surging ahead of a rig.

She's a damned good driver, though!

He flipped a toggle on his stick and switched from his guns to his Hellfire missiles.

"Dammit, what do you need to hear?" yelled Reading. Then it dawned on him. "We are under attack by terrorists. Do you hear me? Terrorists! We need one of those bloody Tornado fighters that have been circling the city since nine-eleven, here now!"

There was a moment's pause before Reading continued. "We are northbound on the M1 heading toward Coventry. Just have him follow the path of burning vehicles!"

There was another pause then Reading hung up, leaning forward to be heard. "We should have help in a few minutes!"

"If we last that long." Acton's eyes widened. "Brake!"

Laura stomped on the brakes as a large plume of fire and smoke left the side of the chopper. They came to a sudden stop, the missile overshooting them and slamming into the road ahead. Laura propelled the car forward again, steering around the debris, as the chopper started to turn for another pass.

"Try to stay under him!" yelled Reading.

Laura looked up and slowed, positioning herself directly under the chopper. As its nose slowly dipped toward them, it couldn't help but have forward momentum, and she let it get ahead of them.

"Holy shit!" exclaimed Stucco. "What the hell is he doing?" He had had a hell of a time keeping up with the target, their SUV no match for her Porsche, but the couple of times he had lost her, the GPS tracker hadn't let her get far. Now he was dodging stopped cars and the torn up road caused by the Apache's bullets.

"I have no idea." Casey triggered his radio. "Bravo Command, Zero-Six. Do you know what Zero-One is doing? Over."

"Zero-Six, Bravo Command, maintain radio silence until

otherwise notified, out."

"Shit! They ordered radio silence!" Casey punched the dash as they passed a rig engulfed in flames, its driver sitting on the embankment, holding his head in shock. "Have you ever worked with this guy before?"

"No, not until today."

"Something tells me we won't be tomorrow."

"Get me the Home Office!" ordered the head dispatcher. At first, he hadn't believed what he heard on the 999 call, though when the traffic cameras showed explosions along the M1, he was quickly convinced. A moment later he was connected.

"This is London Central Dispatch. We have reports of an armed military helicopter shooting civilian vehicles on the M1. We require immediate assistance."

"An armed military helicopter? In London? Did you just get back from the pub, lad?" said the voice in disbelief.

"Listen, I've got vehicles in flames on the M1, and a DCI who says the helicopter is after him and under the control of terrorists."

The reply was dead serious. "One moment."

Niner ran into Red's hospital room. "Red, BD's gone whack!"

"What?" Red struggled to get out of his bed. "What's going on?"

"He's shootin' the shit out of everything on the highway!"

"Get me a damned wheelchair!" ordered Red as he swung his legs over the side of the bed. Niner grabbed one from the hall, helped Red in, then pushed him toward the communications center. "Faster!"

The Home Office Operator hit the keypad in front of him and was connected with the duty officer. "We have a report from central dispatch that there is terrorist activity on the northbound M1 motorway involving an armed military helicopter."

"Reliability assessment?"

"High, sir. Visual confirmation of several vehicles on fire, and a report from a DCI on the scene."

"Okay, out."

The Duty Officer called the Home Secretary's office. The line was immediately answered.

"We have confirmation of a rogue armed helicopter operating on the northbound M1, request immediate tasking of an Overlord aircraft."

"Assessment?"

"High, visual and independent non-civilian confirmation," replied the Duty Officer. "Apparently an armed military helicopter firing on civilian vehicles."

"Stand by."

By the time Red and Niner reached the communications center, the rest of the team was gathered, listening to the comms chatter and watching the visuals from the Apache's camera.

"Oh my God!" exclaimed Jimmy as they watched the cannon chew up half a lane, the Porsche dodging the bullets.

"Report!" Red ordered as Niner rolled him up to the communications gear.

"BD's gone nuts. He's shootin' up half the damned city!" explained Jimmy.

Red put the headset on. "Zero-One, Zero-Two, come in, over." There was no response. "BD, it's Red. Talk to me."

"A little busy right now."

"Listen, buddy, is this really necessary?" asked Red, trying to calm his friend down. "Think about what you're doing."

"I'm under orders from Control, you know that. You know what will happen if I don't complete this mission. Now I want radio silence!"

"Get me the Duty Fighter Controller," said the Home Office Operator.

A tired voice answered. "Wing Commander Talbot here."

"Sir, this is the Home Office Security Operator. We have dual confirmation of a terrorist attack in progress involving an armed military helicopter. It's firing on civilian vehicles northbound on the M1 motorway."

"Reliable?"

"Yes, sir, visual and independent non-civilian confirmation."

"Okay, I'll take it from here."

Talbot ran out of his office and down the hallway into the situation room. "Who's up right now?"

"Overlords One and Two have just taken over from Three and Four," was the controller's reply.

"Who's closest to the M1?"

"Two, sir," replied the Intercept Controller.

"Get him for me." Talbot grabbed a headset and plugged into the controller's communications gear.

"Overlord Two, this is London Mil, come in, over."

"London Mil, this is Overlord Two, go ahead, over."

"Overlord Two, this is Wing Commander Talbot. You have new orders, over."

"Copy that, London Mil, awaiting authentication, over."

Talbot read today's code off a key card he'd never dreamed he would have to use. "Overlord Two, your authentication is Zulu Kilo Bravo Niner Five Seven Execute. Confirm, over."

"London Mil, this is Overlord Two, confirming authentication code Zulu Kilo Bravo Niner Five Seven Execute. What are your orders, over?"

"There is an unauthorized military helicopter on the northbound M1 that is believed to be under the control of unknown hostile agents. You are to make contact if possible, and neutralize if necessary. Designate target Tango One, over."

"London Mil, this is Overlord Two, acknowledging new orders and heading to target. ETA sixty seconds, over."

The cat and mouse game his target was playing below him was pissing Dawson off. He had created the spectacular scene the president wanted. Now it was time to end this thing before any more bystanders got hurt, but he needed them out of the damned car, and no matter how close he came to hitting them, they refused to abandon their vehicle. After about a minute of aborted turns as the car tried to stay under him, he finally pulled back on the stick and banked, moving back a few hundred yards. He could see the car accelerate forward again, its little trick no longer working.

Something came in over his radio. "Overlord Two to unidentified helicopter located over the M1, identify yourself immediately, over."

Shit!

Dawson pushed the stick forward again and accelerated toward his target. He switched back to his cannons and tore up the road behind them.

"Overlord Two to unidentified helicopter, cease fire immediately or I will be forced to open fire."

Dawson glanced at his radar display to see where the aircraft was, but couldn't find it. He redirected his attention to his target and launched two Hellfire missiles at the road ahead of them. He didn't have much time left. At that exact moment, the Tornado fighter flew directly over him, missing the helicopter by less than ten feet, the backwash from the engines shoving him toward the ground and backward, leaving Dawson struggling to regain control.

"Right!"

Laura dutifully swerved the car again. Acton was about to say a silent prayer when the helicopter lost control and the missiles collapsed into the pavement. The resultant explosion sent a rush of hot air over their heads. They all ducked.

"What the hell was that?" cried Laura.

"That, Professor, was a damned Tornado fighter!" cheered Reading. "I never thought I'd be so happy to see a flyboy!" They all stared up as the plane banked sharply to make another pass. Gunfire erupted behind them and Laura swerved, but this time too late. Half a dozen rounds tore through the rear of the car, penetrating the engine compartment and puncturing the rear right tire. Laura fought to control the vehicle as gunfire sprayed around them. She brought them to a stop as the helicopter flew past them and banked.

Reading leaped out of the back seat and hauled open Laura's door, yanking her from the cramped cockpit as Acton scrambled out the other side. The three of them ran toward the guardrail as the helicopter launched two more missiles at the now empty car. It erupted in a huge ball of fire, the resulting shockwave throwing them off their feet.

"Overlord Two to London Mil, preparing to engage Tango One, over," said the pilot of the Tornado as he completed his turn and reacquired his target.

"Copy that, Overlord Two, over."

His Heads Up Display reacquired the target, and he waited for tone. "Overlord Two to London Mil, I have a lock, over."

"London Mil to Overlord Two, you are cleared to fire, over."

"Roger, London Mil, Foxfire One away!" He selected the air-to-air missile, then launched it. The aircraft rocked slightly as the missile dropped off the wing and fired its liquid propellant, hurtling at the target less than a mile away.

Through his infrared display, Dawson saw the three figures who had escaped the now-destroyed vehicle, lying on the ground. They rose and cowered behind a guardrail. He took aim with his cannons, knowing the armored piercing rounds would slice through the metal of the guardrail and shred anything unfortunate enough to be hiding behind it, yet held off. If Control was watching, he'd see the HUD showing a lock, but he was seconds away from having an excuse to fail the mission.

His threat alarm went off, confirming his hopes, his display indicating a radar lock from the north.

Dawson reactivated the comms. "Red, are you still there?"

"Yes, BD, I'm here."

"Goodbye, my friend."

He glanced over his shoulder and saw the flame from the missile rapidly coming toward him. He jerked up and over on the stick to evade it, knowing it was a futile move, as he reached for the canopy jettison handle.

Acton, Laura, and Reading lay as flat as they could behind the guardrail, watching the helicopter through the periodic holes in the metal. Acton held Laura tight as they silently said their goodbyes to loved ones they would never see again.

Then the helicopter banked away from them.

They rose to their knees in shock, and watched as a missile streaked by and slammed into the chopper.

"Get down!" yelled Reading. They all hit the ground and covered their heads as the helicopter ripped apart, its ordnance exploding. The rotors split off from the main assembly, slicing directly toward them through the air like giant knives. As the remains of the helicopter collapsed onto the road, the Tornado blasted past, the wash from the jet warming the entire area. The rotors spun over their heads and dug into the ground a few hundred feet beyond in a farmer's field, the earth shuddering from the impact.

Laura stared at the burning vehicle. "Oh my God, the skull!"

Acton tapped her on the shoulder. She looked at him as he held the bag up, grinning. "You didn't think I'd leave our friend in there, did you?"

The three of them rolled onto their backs and stared up at the sky as the morning sun broke over the horizon. The Tornado made several slow passes overhead as sirens approached from a distance.

"So, how far are we from Coventry?" asked Acton. Reading groaned, and Laura hit Acton on the chest. He laughed. "You're right. I think I'll just lie here for a while and hurt."

Stucco and Casey pulled up to the crash site and jumped out of their vehicle, surveying the wreckage. "No one survived that," said Stucco. They spun toward laughter behind them and drew their weapons. Following the sound, they approached the guardrail and found their targets lying on the ground. The laughing stopped as soon as they raised their weapons. One reached for a gun.

Casey cocked his weapon. "We'll have none of that, now."

"Bravo Command, Zero-Three. We have the targets, awaiting instructions, over." There was silence. "Bravo Command, Zero-Three. Should we eliminate the targets, over?"

Again silence. Then a burst of static. "Zero-Three, Zero-Two. Abort, I say again, abort, over."

"Roger that, Zero-Three, out." He turned to Casey. "Let's go." They both walked away, still covering the three as they climbed in their vehicle.

Acton slowly rose to watch the SUV race away. "What just happened?"

"I don't know, but I'm glad it did," replied Laura.

Reading stood to see if he could get a tag number, but it was still too dark. "I think we just got a reprieve."

Acton surveyed the warzone surrounding them. "Yeah, but for how long?"

Coventry, England

Reading turned the unmarked police car into the parking lot of the train station in Coventry. He had refused to let Laura drive again after experiencing her 100-plus mile-per-hour driving. It wasn't much of a refusal, since she said she didn't want to drive again for at least a year.

Acton didn't even offer. "You Brits are crazy, driving on the wrong side of the road!"

Reading found a spot and parked. They were hours late. The chaos on the M1 had ended long ago, but the extensive questioning had taken time. They had all agreed there would be no mention of the skull or the Triarii. Reading had lied to his fellow officers for the first time in his career. The pit in his stomach told him he was still a good cop. If he hadn't felt guilty, he would have handed in his warrant card.

Half an hour passed and they had all nodded off when there was a tap on the driver's side window. Reading rolled it down.

"Hellooo, I'm from the Coventry Tourist Authority, welcome to our city!" The old lady held out a pamphlet to Reading, who took it. "While you're here, you should visit the ruins of the old cathedral. It's fifteenth-century, you know. It was destroyed during the war. The new cathedral was built beside it, and opened to the public in 1962. Its spires—"

Reading cut off the speech. "Thank you, ma'am, we will if we have time." He rolled up the window and waved to the old lady who slowly made her way around the front of the car. "You should visit the new church too, it has some beautiful relics inside." Reading smiled and waved again as she moved to the next occupied car and repeated her speech. He tossed the pamphlet into the back seat where Laura was dozing on Acton's shoulder.

I'll bet those two will be bumpin' uglies before this day is through.

Reading laughed aloud, and the two backseat passengers woke out of their stupor.

"What?" asked Acton. "What's so funny?"

"Nothing, sorry. Just a mental image."

Laura spotted the flyer that had landed beside her on the seat. "What's this?"

"Oh, just some old lady handing out tourist flyers."

"Did you look at it?"

"No, I...." Reading reached back and grabbed it from Laura's hands. He opened it up and saw a map showing various places of worship, with one circled and a handwritten note.

First confessional. Noon.

Reading checked his watch.

Five minutes from now.

"Shit!"

He put the car in reverse then squealed out of the parking lot, gunning the engine toward the Catholic church indicated on the map. The motor whined for a moment before it finally took off.

Definitely not a Porsche.

"What's going on?" asked Acton.

"Just trying to keep an appointment." Reading guided the car through traffic, and three minutes later was at the church. They all jumped out and ran inside. Reading raced down the center aisle, trying to remember the order of the sign he was supposed to do, as it had been at least ten years since he had set foot in a church.

Spectacles, testicles, wallet, watch!

Elated, he ran up to the altar, did a quick sign, then ran toward the confessional indicated in the note. Acton and Laura followed behind him, still confused. When they reached the confessional, Reading glanced at his watch, catching his breath. "We're on time. Okay, Professor, this is your show." He opened the door to the confessional and waved Acton in.

Acton was still confused, though when Reading pushed him, he realized this must be where the Triarii wanted to meet them. Reading closed the door behind him. Acton looked around and kneeled. The window separating the two halves of the confessional opened, revealing a screen. He could barely make out who was on the other side.

"Blessed are those who confess their sins," said the deep voice. "Confess your sins to God and all shall be forgiven."

Acton shifted awkwardly, not sure if he was in the right place. "Umm, sorry, Father, but I'm not Catholic, so I've never done this before."

283

"If you are not Catholic, my son, then I cannot pardon your sins, however I can listen."

Acton was at a loss as to what to say. Finally, he decided to hell with it.

Well, maybe not hell.

"Are you from the Triarii?"

"And what if I were?"

"Then I have something for you."

"Then leave it for me, and I will take it."

"I'll need proof before I leave it."

"Very well." Acton heard shuffling on the other side as the priest held a wrist up to the screen to show him the Triarii tattoo. "Is this enough proof for you, my son?"

"Yes, it is. Tell me one more thing though, before I leave."

"Of course."

"Are you really a priest?"

"Of course I am. It would be sacrilege to pretend to be a priest in the house of God."

"But I thought you guys believed in the ancient Roman gods?"

There was a deep chuckle on the other side of the partition. "We all have to believe in something, but we do not all have to believe in the same thing." With that, the screen closed. Acton placed the bag in the corner and opened the door to the confessional. He stepped out and walked toward Reading and Laura, waiting a few paces away.

"What happened?" asked Laura.

"The priest was Triarii. He told me to leave the skull there, so I did."

"You just left it there?" Reading was clearly not pleased. He walked to the confessional and opened the door. The bag was gone. He shook his head. "How can we be sure it was the Triarii?"

"He showed me his tattoo. And besides, there was something in his voice that just made me believe him." Acton flinched as his phone vibrated. Smiling sheepishly at the others, he answered it.

"Hello?"

"Thank you for returning the item."

Acton beckoned the others to move closer as he put it on speaker. "You're welcome. How can we be sure this is over?"

"Have you not listened to the news this morning?"

"No, we haven't had time. Why, what happened?"

"Your president is dead. You will have no one else after you."

"The president is dead?" Acton was stunned. "How?"

"We had an agent on the inside that followed his orders, even though it resulted in his own death. Thank you, Professor Acton, the Triarii are in your debt." The line went dead.

Acton stared at the others for a moment in shocked silence. "It's over," he said quietly, still not sure whether to believe it.

Laura hopped up and down, excitement on her face. "It's over!" She hugged and kissed Reading on the cheek, then grabbed Acton and held him tight, her head pressed into his shoulder.

A smile spread across Acton's face as reality set in. "It's finally over!" he shouted at the ceiling, the immense pressure of the past week lifting off his shoulders. He gazed down at Laura, still in his arms. Their eyes met, and he leaned in slowly, still uncertain. When her eyes closed, he bent down and kissed her. All of the day's events melted away as they lost themselves in each other's embrace. His heart pounded with excitement, instead of the near constant fear he had felt for days.

Laura's knees almost gave out as she enjoyed the thrill of a first kiss. She hadn't felt this way since she was a schoolgirl. The butterflies in her stomach made her both nervous and excited at once.

And she hoped the feeling would never end.

Reading watched the two of them for a moment then looked around. "Ah, kids, we're in a church." There was no response. "I'll be in the car." Reading walked away shaking his head and smiling. His phone vibrated with a text message:

State Department agents still waiting in your office.

He laughed.

Later That Day

Several members of the Crime Scene Unit sifted through the wreckage of the helicopter, searching for the body of the pilot, when one of them came across a charred metal box. Reaching down, he carefully opened it. Inside was a crystal skull.

He shivered.

He closed the box, then casually took it to his vehicle. Another man approached him, and they both climbed in the back. Inside, the man opened the case and carefully handed the skull to the other, who placed it into a bag and exited the vehicle. The investigator closed the case and returned to where he had found it. As he bent over to put it back on the ground, his watch slipped down his wrist, revealing the Triarii tattoo.

In Paris, Henri swept the hallway in front of the storage room, then swiped his pass and backed in, pulling his cart inside. Reaching under the cart, he pulled out a package, then casually strolled to the last row of shelves. Opening it, he carefully unwrapped its contents. He switched the fake skull with the real one from his cart, and resealed the box, placing it on the shelf. Then, wrapping up the fake, he put it under his cart, leaving the room, and continued to push his way down the hallway, whistling.

Chen pushed open the large doors of the temple and entered the main hallway. He quietly approached his master and kneeled beside him.

"You have returned, my son."

"Yes, Father."

"And your destiny?"

"It has been fulfilled."

"Very good. Let us pray."

A sense of peace and serenity swept over his body at the completion of his task.

Madely and Johnson knocked on the door of the cute Victorian style house. Rustling inside preceded footsteps as the occupant crossed the hardwood floors to the door. The locks unlatched, and the door opened.

"Ahh, my shadows!" the old lady said. "Please, come in." She beckoned for them to enter, then closed the door behind them.

"Ma'am." Madely held out a carefully wrapped package. "It is with great pleasure that I return this to you."

"Everything is fine now?"

"Yes, ma'am, everything is fine."

"That's good. Now, you must join me for tea."

Madely smiled. "Of course, ma'am."

And in the desert of Saudi Arabia, Faisal awoke to find the skull back on its shelf, and praised Allah. In Moscow, Alexander returned the skull to its cold, dark hiding place, while in Beijing, Huang again switched the skulls in his president's office.

And in the desert of southern New Mexico, Leroy awoke to find his safe opened yet again, but with his precious skull returned. And he fell to his knees, thanking the Crystal Gods.

EPILOGUE

It had been six months since Acton had fled the camp. As he surveyed it now, he could hardly believe what he saw. It was a bustle of activity as new students continued the work of his previous class. His cabin still stood where it had always been, and new tents created a circle around the center of the camp. The gridlines had been laid out again, and excavation continued, this time with twice as many people.

Laura squeezed his hand. He looked at her and smiled, then leaned in to kiss her. He had her to thank for this, as she was the one funding the new excavation. At first, when she suggested it as a way of finding closure, he had thought she was crazy, but after mulling it over for several weeks, he had taken her up on her offer, on the condition she accompany him. "That was always my intention, dear," she had said.

Now, with students from both his university and hers, they were continuing the work cut off months before. A cross stood at the site where the previous students had been massacred, and although he didn't know who did it, each morning, fresh flowers were placed there in remembrance. He occasionally still wept over the losses suffered, though since he had arrived here a couple of days earlier, his spirits had lifted. This was what his students would have wanted.

The chaos that had ensued after the death of the president, and the resulting congressional investigation that had linked him to the murders and the events in London, had caused an international uproar. The official story was that his Chief of Staff, Lesley Darbinger, had been to blame. Acton knew that was a cover story to take the heat off the government.

The investigation had also meant the press hounded him and Laura. They had refused all interviews, though had to testify in both Washington and London. Neither made any mention of the skull or the Triarii. They simply denied any knowledge of why they had been targeted by a madman.

Of course, conspiracy theories had abounded, and websites around the world speculated on what truly happened, but eventually, the press tired of it and moved on to their romantic relationship. This was another reason they had decided returning to the Andes might be a good idea.

And the Triarii? They hadn't heard a word from them since.

And they were happy to keep it that way.

Too bad the Triarii had other plans.

THE END

AFTERWORD

When this book was originally published by LBF Books, it did not include this afterword. Over the years, this series has garnered thousands of reviews, sold over one million copies, and as of this printing, through sequels and spin-offs, spans over 40 books.

However, despite this tremendous success, I felt it was necessary to address issues raised by some readers either to me personally, or through reviews.

The biggest misconception I want to dispel is that this book is anti-military, and by extension, so am I. I am an Air Force brat, and a huge supporter of our troops. Anyone who has read the sequels can attest to that. This novel shows what can happen when soldiers are provided false intel. Dawson protects his men as best he can from the horrors of what they have been ordered to do, right from the beginning when he executed the students (who he was told were terrorists), under orders, to the final climactic sequence in London where he lets our heroes live.

Some have argued that soldiers would never execute the orders given in this story. As was revealed by the Washington Post, the Termination List referred to in this novel is very much real, and has been used to target many, including American citizens on foreign soil. These types of orders are given on a regular basis, and quite often are carried out by our Special Forces. Bravo Team receiving orders such as this would not be out of the ordinary, and the intel provided indicated they were terrorists preparing for an attack on American soil.

It is critical to recognize the concept of Point of View in this novel. What you as a reader know to be the truth, is not the truth known to Bravo Team. They have every reason to believe they are following lawful orders, and are dealing with terrorists. Our Special Forces kill terrorists under Executive Orders on a regular basis, and this is no different. In Bravo Team's mind, the students aren't students at all—they are domestic terrorists, have murdered four American servicemen, are training in Peru for attacks on the United States, and have been ordered killed by the president. Their ages, as proven by 9/11, are irrelevant. Billy, in their minds, was a terrorist who had infiltrated the White House, working only feet from the president. The Triarii were the terror cell, according to their intel, and appeared to prove their guilt by being extremely well-armed in a country where it is illegal to own a gun.

Again, it is all a matter of Point of View, of perspective. If you were to read only the chapters written from a Bravo Team character's perspective, you would think they were battling terrorists, and with the possible exception of the helicopter scene at the end, could understand their actions. In the final sequence, Dawson is trying to figure out, as he goes, how to deal with the threat to their families, leaving Wings behind to protect him. He finally realizes sacrificing himself is the only way to save their loved ones, but must make certain it doesn't look that way, which is why he waits for the fighter to launch its missiles, despite having time to kill Acton and the others.

The Bravo Team features prominently in most of my novels, and you will see they are a phenomenal group of courageous, patriotic men, who do their country proud.

Subsequent titles in this series have James Acton and Laura Palmer dealing with everything from lost tombs of Cleopatra, the kidnapping of the Pope, a discovery Marco Polo made, a Chinese coup, the Titanic, and much more. The Special Agent Dylan Kane Thrillers spin-off series deals with a former student of Acton's, and his exploits as a spy, with occasional help from Bravo Team. The Delta Force Unleashed Thrillers give Bravo Team their own series, with occasional appearances from Acton and Kane.

This series has been a tremendous success, selling over one million copies, has allowed me to become a full-time writer, and has made the USA Today Bestsellers list on multiple occasions. As you continue through the series, you will find a rich set of action-packed thrillers where Acton, Laura, and the Bravo Team, shine when dealing with humanity's worst.

Thank you for reading, and I hope you stick around.

It should be fun!

CPSIA information can be obtained
at www.ICGtesting.com
Printed in the USA
BVHW041654070323
659898BV00027B/569

9 781990 418327